LOVE
starts with
Z

Tera Shanley

OMNIFIC PUBLISHING
LOS ANGELES

Omnific Publishing
1901 Avenue of the Stars, 2nd floor
Los Angeles, CA 90067
www.omnificpublishing.com

First Omnific eBook edition, February 2015
First Omnific trade paperback edition, February 2015

Library of Congress Cataloguing-in-Publication Data

Shanley, Tera.
  Love Starts with Z / Tera Shanley – 1st ed.
  ISBN: 978-1-623421-64-9
  1. Contemporary Romance — Fiction. 2. Zombies — Fiction.
  3. Apocalypse — Fiction. 4. Urban Fantasy — Fiction. I. Title

10 9 8 7 6 5 4 3 2 1

Cover Design by Micha Stone and Amy Brokaw
Interior Book Design by Coreen Montagna

Printed in the United States of America

*My mom has always supported me
with all of my crazy (I pitched them as creative) ideas,
and my dad has always encouraged me
to be the strongest woman I can be.
He taught me weaponry and safety the second I showed interest,
and gave me the tools I needed to write a book like this.
It didn't matter what I was interested in,
they were always up for the adventure.*

This one is for my parents, Paul and Paula Muller.

Prologue

Colten McTavish was as good as dead.

He slowed his breathing just enough to hiss, "Kaegan, do you copy?" into his handheld radio. "Kaegan, if you can hear me, I need backup."

The hum of static was his only answer. He cursed softly, dropping the radio dexterously back into its sling on his hip and pulling his Glock in one fluid motion. After confirming his lack of ammunition he looked from one gruesome, decaying, fleshy face to another. If he didn't thoroughly believe Deads were brainless monsters, he would've sworn they had been hunting him like a pack. They had successfully cut him off from his team and cornered him in an area littered with only the oldest and most unclimbable pine trees in all of the Rocky Mountain range.

This was the first time Kaegan hadn't been there to pull him out of trouble. His loyal-to-a-fault best friend must be dead or turned. It was the only explanation.

"Well, brother," he growled, "I'll see you there soon enough." Colt whipped the cold metal of the handgun against his temple and took three quick, steadying breaths. He'd feed the monsters, but he'd be damned if he was going to be alive for the show.

Just as his finger brushed against the trigger, the storm clouds that hid the heavens opened up just enough to let a single ray of sunlight escape. It blanketed a tree a short distance away. One lone branch hung low enough for him to be able to reach if he got a running start. Sign enough. He sprinted and fired on the running Deads closest to him. One shot, drop, one shot, drop, arc the gun, *click. Click.*

The hollow sound was a fighter's worst nightmare. It was the sound of an echoing, empty chamber. It was the sound of impending doom. One monstrous Dead blocked his path to salvation, and lacking another option, Colt flung the gun at his age softened skull. It wasn't a kill shot by any means, but it had the desired effect just the same. The creature's mouth had been eaten away, and a row of dirty, jagged teeth jutted out of the hanging flesh of its face. The Dead roared an inhuman bellow as he was knocked backward just long enough for Colt to blow past him. Colt leaped through the air and huffed out a triumphant laugh as his fingers found purchase.

His muscles strained with the effort to hoist himself upward into the sanctuary of the branches above. Deads couldn't climb — a byproduct of decayed muscles and lackluster motor skills. He'd be safe up there where the tip of the tree touched the cloud speckled sky. Just a couple more branches.

An unwavering hand clenched onto his calf. The chill of long-dead flesh seeped through the thickness of his cargo pants, and the pull and strength of that grip was a weight Colten's slipping hands would lose to.

A scream he didn't recognize burst from his chest as the Dead ripped into the flesh of his leg.

Chapter One

Soren Mitchell felt sorry for Deads. Zombies really didn't have much going for them on the pro list, while the cons stretched on for eternity. Take the one shuffling slowly through the woods in front of her, for example. From the length of her matted, auburn hair, and the once likely attractive sundress that hung in tatters against her gray, putridly rotting flesh, she had probably been an attractive woman before. Back when the world made sense. Soren guessed at boyfriends she'd had and parties and schools the Dead attended. The only pro she could see from her vantage point as she sketched the walking corpse furiously before she disappeared, was that Deads seemed to find solace in traveling in groups. Pro—at least they probably weren't lonely?

Soren rubbed her back distractedly against the base of the giant pine she leaned against and scanned the woods. This one was definitely alone, and a wave of pity washed over her again.

The Dead swiveled her head toward Soren's small movement. She waved but the creature only stared back with yellowed, vacant eyes. Her blue-tinged lip curled slightly as she flared her nostrils toward Soren and switched directions. The pine needles that blanketed the forest floor made a muffled sound under the Dead's bare feet as it shuffled closer.

Soren's heart hammered, as it did every time she found herself in such a situation, but she didn't move. Instead she cocked her head and waited to feel a connection with the red-headed creature. The Dead stopped just a few yards in front of her and tilted her chin up, scenting the air again. It took a long drag of mountain air and dropped its head. Grunting as if disappointed, it meandered off in the direction it came from.

Soren didn't smell like food. Yet another reminder that she wasn't human.

Hybrid. That's what Dr. Mackey, the Dead Run River colony doctor, proudly called her. Twenty years of testing and experimenting and researching, and still they had never been able to track down another living creature—or unliving?—like her on the entirety of the ravaged planet.

One of a kind. Yippy-freaking-wee.

Even though the sky was covered with clouds, and she couldn't really see the sunrise, her internal clock said it was time to get going. The colony might take her for a complete and utter freak, but she was a punctual freak. She shoved her sketchbook and pencils into a leather satchel that had molded to fit across her shoulders perfectly through the years, and headed up the mountain to Dead Run River.

Andrew Dennison stood watch at the colony gates with an older guard. He was easily the hottest of the guards with loose brown waves framing smoldering eyes only a shade or two darker. Eyes that basically dared a woman not to give him everything he could want. He was only a few years older with an easy smile for all of the girls who tripped over their own feet to swoon for him. Except with her, when his smile looked more like the grimace that prefaced a gag. Good with the boys, she was not.

Now, it could've been that he had a prejudice because both of his parents had been turned by Deads when he was a child and he had been an unfortunate witness to the traumatic events, or it could've been that she didn't look all that human and her eating habits were a little off-putting. In her defense, she tried her best to hide her preference for raw meat, but the rumor mill spun out of control when it came to her. This week she was apparently eating baby soup for breakfast.

She stifled a smile at Andrew's withering look at her approach. So she wasn't his Juliet. Accepted. But he was a barrel of monkeys to mess with on a slow day.

She pulled her shirt over her head before she even reached the gate, and his eyes narrowed. The older guard, Bear everyone called him, chuckled and shook his head. She started to unfasten her bra but Andrew furiously held up his hand in a halting motion. Oh, she could imagine what he saw. Pale skin the color of alabaster, hip length, wavy hair so blond it was almost white, and eyes that would terrify even the bravest of children. They were the color of the moon — so pale they couldn't pass for human on even her best day. She wasn't albino, but she was pretty damn close.

"Stop it, Z! You know good and well we don't do bite checks like that anymore!"

The nickname stung. Z. Zombie. "Just wanted to be thorough," she said with an empty smile.

"Just go!" he yelled, waving his hand impatiently for her to pass through the opening gates. "You can't even be turned, so just keep your clothes on next time. And put your muzzle on, or I'm calling it in to Mel!"

She gave a two fingered salute to a smiling Bear, gave Andrew the finger over her shoulder, and slid her shirt back over her head without breaking stride.

"Douche-wagon," she muttered under her breath as she pulled the muzzle around her face and fastened it in the back. Her heart always grew a little heavier at the sound of it clicking closed. Straps to hold it in place, mismatched pieces of leather sewn together, a metal grill over her mouth, and now she looked like the Hannibal Lecter of the apocalypse.

Dead Run River was a huge colony, completely fenced in by the tallest of toppled pines and safe from roving undead looking for an easy meal. The air was crisp and clean, and worn trails snaked all through the colony, capped by the mess hall, an antique sawmill, an exit to the gardens where organics sustained hungry stomachs, and last but not least, houses. Log cabins to be exact. Some stood alone, old and sturdy looking, while newer construction models consisted of rows of attached log units that housed various families. Farther up the mountain were rows of RVs that had been painstakingly dragged in and lined up years before, and beyond that, at the highest peak, was Mel's sprawling home. She was the long-time leader of Dead Run River and arguably the most successful. If one didn't count the Denver colony, which she did. It was Mel who had put the muzzle rule in place when she'd walked through those gates two years ago, but she couldn't blame her. It was Mel's job to keep everyone safe, and after what had happened...Well, the muzzle was obnoxious and degrading, but it was a small price to pay for the safety of the human race.

Soren kept her head down as she walked the trails to Dr. Mackey's office. She slid her sunglasses over her inhuman eyes and tried her best not to scare the others who passed. There were a lot of new families in Dead Run River, and they weren't used to a zombie trying to strike up a conversation about the weather just yet.

The door to Dr. Mackey's office creaked open. If she wasn't muzzled she would've given a greeting, but as it stood, she hated the muffled slur her words adopted behind the mask. Instead she plucked paperwork from her box and scanned it distractedly while she ambled to the back room. The hurriedly scribbled paper said a different variation on the same thing she read every day she came to work.

No cure yet.

A woman screamed, shrill and terrified. "Get her away from me! Get her away from my baby!"

Soren froze in the midst of the chaos around her. A woman she'd never seen before cried hysterically with a finger jabbed in her direction. Soren turned to look behind her and pointed to her chest in question. The woman grew even more frantic and clutched her newborn baby tighter as Dr. Mackey rushed in and tried to calm her. At a loss, Soren backed up until she hit a wall near the front entry.

Dr. Mackey rushed from the room and shut the door firmly behind him. He was an older gentleman who wore a worn Yankees baseball cap to cover the hairless dome of his head. His thick glasses covered intelligent eyes that missed nothing. He gave her an apologetic, lopsided grin.

Soren nodded slowly. "Got it. When should I come back?"

"I'm moving them to a cabin nearby this afternoon. Come back to work after then."

She headed for the door.

"Oh and, Soren?"

"Hmm?"

"How long did you sleep last night?"

"About an hour."

"And how do you feel?"

"Fine."

He scribbled furiously on a notepad and hummed to himself. "Great, we'll see you this afternoon then."

She stood there longer than necessary after he disappeared back into the room with his newborn patient. Sometimes she wished he would just ask her a question because he cared about the answer, not because she was a lab rat. He would add the notes to the thirty other pounds of charts he had been writing up since the day of her birth, and she would keep answering him with the secret hope that he would one day ask her questions as a person and not a scientist.

The birds outside chirped their song like they hadn't heard the screeching new mother inside, and Soren tilted her chin up to the sky before taking a deep breath. She'd give her left femur bone to be a bird. Or a newt, or a millipede, or a pterodactyl, or basically anything other than a whatever-she-was. Her senses tingled like the thin web of a spider vibrating under the small weight of a struggling fly. "You're late again," she said.

Seamus grinned shamelessly and stepped around the brush he had been using to shield his body. "One of these days, Soren."

She snorted. "Please. Your stalking skills are horrendous."

"Well, excuse me if I didn't have the infamous Laney Landry as my mother and trainer."

"Well, you have Aaron Guist as your dad, so you really have no excuse for all of the noise you make in the woods. You're worse than a Dead."

Seamus shrugged and pushed his glasses farther up his nose. His gray eyes twinkled under sandy brown hair that threw hints of red in direct sunlight. "You calling in sick today or what?"

Soren headed down the stairs. "One too many baby humans in there. I eat baby soup now, or haven't you heard?"

He chuckled warmly. "I did hear that one. Well, forget you then. I'll find the cure and you'll be green with envy that you skipped out today when I save the world without you."

Seamus really did want to find the cure almost as much as she did. Growing up together and just a few months apart in age, they had dreamed of becoming famous scientists who saved the human race with their discoveries. Their childhood fantasies had turned into a full-blown obsession as they got older, but Seamus had very different reasons for wanting it than she did.

His friendship really was a miracle in and of itself. She frowned at his back as he disappeared into Dr. Mackey's office. Despite having seen the monster that lurked just below the surface, he had stayed loyal and unprejudiced and bestowed one of the only unwavering friendships she had ever sustained. Seamus was slight, and opinionated, always had his head in literature, and was convinced that books were the real weapons that would save the planet. In return for his friendship, she'd happily kept the bullies at bay. A sparkless and symbiotic relationship.

She hopped off the worn path and blazed her own trail through the woods. Home sweet home was well away from the other cabins to give the distant neighbors peace of mind that she wouldn't storm their tiny castles and eat them in their sleep.

The spring breeze wound through the pines as she walked the well-worn dirt path up the mountain. Lodgepole pines and alder branches groaned at the caress of the wind. Nature's song, if one had time to listen. And these days, everyone had time to listen. Nature won the right to serenade mankind twenty-four years before when she took the earth back. Now the great civilizations of men, skyscrapers and technology…all of it was dust.

She'd never actually seen any of the good old days, because she'd been born after the end of the world, but she'd heard stories. Old timers talked about the pre-apocalypse world like it was Valhalla come to earth, but she didn't know. Most of it sounded kind of sad. People so immersed in technology they lost the ability to connect with other humans; the shocking rate they trashed the earth with their oil spills and pollution; the way countries warred for anything, or so it seemed. Now man battled against one thing—turning into something like her.

"Z!" an obnoxious voice trilled through the quiet of the forest. Marie.

Soren barely avoided a groan. There was a wary family traveling the trail in the opposite direction, and whenever she moaned in complaint, people tended to run for the hills or go for a brain shot.

"Let me guess," she said as Marie approached with a plate of what smelled suspiciously like burned meat. "You're my handler again this week."

"Lucky me." Marie shoved the plate in her hands into Soren's chest and commanded, "Eat."

Soren lifted the edge of the cloth rag covering her breakfast and had to work hard to swallow the gag that clawed its way up her throat. A fully cooked steak sat still warm and slathered in some of Chef's homemade barbecue sauce. The meat was firm to the touch when she poked it.

"Chef said you didn't eat this morning. Again." Marie's dark eyes narrowed with her obvious disdain, and her perfectly arched eyebrows drew down as she dropped her gaze from Soren's sunglasses to her muzzle. "Mel said you have to eat at your regularly scheduled meals or you don't have a place here anymore. You know the rules. Mind them or leave. It hasn't changed in all the time you've been here. You're contagious, Z."

"Don't call me that," Soren muttered.

"It's what you are."

Soren clenched her jaw until the muscles there ached. "I can't eat this."

"You can and will. It will do you good to eat more like the other people around here. Maybe if you didn't eat raw flesh, people would be more comfortable around you."

"I don't eat raw flesh, Marie. Just raw meat, and that's not my choice. It's all my body will digest. This," she said, shoving the plate back into Marie's hands, "will make me sick. I'll start eating at regular intervals if you and Chef will stop cooking my food into hunks of charcoal."

Marie twitched her head and pursed her lips. "Mel wants to talk to you." The corner of her lip turned up in a smile like she'd won.

If ever Soren decided to start eating people, she would begin with Marie.

"Fine, bye." Turning, she lengthened her stride until her heels dug into the soft soil of the path.

Marie didn't take the hint of dismissal. That or she wanted to watch her get reamed by Mel again, which was the more likely culprit, and she followed directly, loud, like a drunken giant in the woods.

"You're not allowed to talk to me like that, Z. I'm your handler. You do what I say, when I say it, no back talk. Also in the rules."

She'd like to see where these magic rules were written, because she was pretty sure Marie just made them up as she went along. Her other handlers, Jake and Margaret, weren't as overbearing as the tiny titan that stomped after her now. Oh, they hated her, but they were quieter about their distaste for all things Dead. And they didn't try to force feed her human fare. Theirs was more of a somber acceptance.

Dead Run River housed a monster, and it was their duty to protect the colony from her when they were assigned to do so. They followed at a distance, brought her food, and at least seemed to control the disgusted looks on their faces as they watched to make sure she ate everything on her plate. As a reward to Jake and Margaret, for not being Marie, she at least made an effort to eat on Mel's rigorous dining schedule at mess hall so she could spare them collecting the food and tracking her down.

As if she could read her charitable thoughts, Marie said, "Margaret quit."

"What?" Soren said, spinning. "Why?"

Marie's laugh echoed through the quiet forest, and a bird above them took flight at the noise. One of her eyebrows arched until three deep wrinkles etched into her forehead. "Because she hates you," she whispered.

Closing her eyes against the unexpected pain the words caused, Soren turned and strode up the path again. Marie was just trying to get to her.

"I'd quit too, but we're already going to have a hard time filling Margaret's position. Nobody wants to watch you eat like an animal and stare at lab equipment all day." A put upon sigh sounded from behind her. "Mel needs me."

Marie wouldn't ever give up power over her. If she quit, she'd be just another colonist—one who didn't control the house Dead. She liked the attention too much to ever resign. Most of the rumors probably started directly from the conniving woman's mouth.

She could just imagine Marie's conversations with her friends. *And then I made her eat cooked food, because it's important that she adjust her body to fit in. I only try to help her, but monsters are instinctively ungrateful...*

Soren clenched and unclenched her hands until she didn't feel like strangling her handler anymore.

Mel's cabin topped Dead Run River. It stood proudly, looking over the paradise its leader had created. Mel had been the head of this place since before Soren had been born. It seemed she had only grown tougher over the years under the strain of keeping her people alive, and the woman had very little patience for threats like her.

"Come in," the leader called when Soren rapped her knuckles against the door.

The door creaked as she opened it, and the smell of peach pie enveloped her as soon as she stepped over the threshold. It smelled divine—tart, juicy, with underlying currents of sugar, which she imagined to be heavenly from the looks on people's faces when they ate rare delicacies in the mess hall. Too bad she couldn't eat a slice without retching.

"In here," Mel called from the office.

The entryway led to a sizable kitchen, with a dining area visible from the front door. A living area with plush, dark furniture sat to her right, and to her left was Mel's office. The back wall was covered in corkboard, and pinned to it were handwritten letters, requests, pictures of missing men, women, and children who they'd lost to the apocalypse. Every colony had one. Somewhere to put all of your hope into finding lost loved ones. Only a few had ever been answered, if rumors were true, but people sent out pleas for information anyway. Such a deep, resonating sadness washed over her when she saw the somber faces drawn on the wall. How could Mel stand to be in a room with so many ghosts?

Mel gestured for her to take a seat and the doorframe creaked as Marie leaned against it with a smug look on her face.

"Have you eaten today?" the colony leader asked.

Soren took a long, steadying breath and opened her mouth to defend herself.

"I brought her food, and she flat out refused it," Marie said from behind.

"Cooked food," Soren said through gritted teeth. "I can't eat what she brought me."

Mel studied her for a long moment. "Have you tried?"

"Do I need a doctor's note? I'm sure Doc would be happy to oblige. He has medical journals that stretch for miles about my immune system, my reproductive system, my respiratory system, and most importantly, or so it seems to every person who lives in the colony, my digestive system. I can't eat the food cooked. I'm not like you, or you." Thank God. "It's like trying to feed a Dead a burned carcass. They might force themselves to eat it, but they'll pay for it later."

Mel had gone green, but so what? She'd been living there for two years and still, she was a pariah.

"Do I need to remind you what happened when you were ten, Soren?"

A wave of ice hurtled over her insides and she froze. Her hands were the only part of her she had feeling in, and she gripped the arms of the chair until it whined under her palms. Of course she didn't need to be reminded. No one would let her live a day without bringing it up. "Of course you don't."

"Now, I respect your parents. Laney and Mitchell have helped Dead Run River in more ways than we can ever repay. But they stole away in the night with you in your infancy for a reason. This place isn't the right fit for you."

"But my research is here. They don't have more than a makeshift doctor's shack in the Denver colony. Doctor Mackey has everything we need to find a cure. The vaccine isn't enough. We need to be able to reverse the effects of decay on the newly turned. I can't go anywhere else."

"Which is exactly the pitch I took from your parents. You can *infect* people, Soren. And still, I allow you to live inside the gates. I put the people who live in Dead Run River at risk every day just by allowing you to stay here. And I do that for your parents. That's it. They are the thin thread between your home here and woods full of your own kind." She pulled a small stack of papers from a desk drawer and slid them in front of her. "I've had six complaints this week from colonists."

"About me?"

"Yes. Sometimes it's more, sometimes less, but we rarely go a week without having to douse the fires you start. I didn't tell you before because I know it has to be hard enough on you, being different. But this?" She curled rigid fingers around the papers and held them in the air. "This has been going on for too long, and people are getting more and more upset about your behaviors. Eat in private from now on. Eat plenty and on time. That's not a friendly suggestion."

Marie snickered behind her, and Mel stabbed her with a sharp look.

"Listen to your handlers, because I've instructed them to report any inconsistencies in your routine to me. I had to lay down those orders to soothe the colonists you've pissed off."

Unable to take her eyes from the fluttering, damning handmade paper clutched in Mel's hand, Soren slowly nodded her understanding. She couldn't lose the lab. She couldn't just go back to the Denver colony with her tail between her legs and wait for others to find a cure. "Is that all you wanted to talk to me about?"

"I assume you've heard Margaret quit her handler position." At Soren's slight nod, she said, "She forced our hand. Said she'd leave the colony if we made her watch you anymore. As you probably know, her entire family was taken by your kind, and it became too much. We'll assign you a new one as soon as we're able, but until then, give Jake and Marie a break with the rule bending, okay?"

"Okay." She'd sell her pride to keep the lab. She'd do anything it took to ensure her future.

As she stood to leave, Mel tossed the complaints to the edge of the giant desk she sat behind. The handwriting on the top page blurred as she hesitated to touch it. The curving ink etched into the fragile paper fibers would only cause pain.

The paper crinkled against her palm, and she fought the urge to drop them into the wastebasket by the door as she left.

"Oh and, Soren?"

She turned slowly. "Yes?"

"I don't want you leaving the front gates to spend time with the Deads in the woods anymore."

That was her time to be herself, unmuzzled, out in the open and unconcerned with people staring or being frightened of her. Mel was asking too much.

"But I go out there to draw. It's what keeps me sane."

"You'll draw inside the gates and remain sane. You communing with Deads makes people here uncomfortable."

She didn't even know anyone had noticed until this very moment. "People? Or just you?"

The hard look in Mel's vibrant green eyes said it didn't matter. The rule was set and wouldn't be taken back.

Chapter Two

A three-man team was pushing it, but two? If Kaegan Langford lived to the end of the day, it would be a miracle. Colten groaned again, and Kaegan adjusted his weight across his shoulders.

He couldn't keep this pace for much longer. Already, his legs burned like he'd stepped into a campfire, and a hollow numbness crept up his calves, making each carefully placed footstep treacherous.

Bit. Colten had a chunk taken out of his leg the exact size of that giant Dead's jaw. He'd come up on his friend right as the monster clamped his teeth on him. Damn it. He'd never get that scream of pain out of his head as long as he lived. And really, he should be used to it by now. He'd heard it a hundred times. Still, it was different with Colten. He'd known him since he was a boy.

They'd lost the rest of the team in the fight, got separated, but he knew their outcomes. He'd put Trevor and Mike down when they came after him with their vacant eyes and gnashing teeth. They hadn't been fighting together long, but it was a loss that echoed through him. Every human life lost counted. Every friend he lost left a scar on his soul.

He'd twisted an ankle tripping over a root when one of the Deads he fought landed on top of him, and now he tried and failed to focus on placing one foot in front of the other without grimacing. Acknowledging the pain would only make it worse.

Colten was vaccinated, so he would at least stay human. The problem lay with the raging fever he'd been incubating for two days. The bite looked grotesque, and every so often, Colten whispered incoherent mutterings about family and friends who were long dead. He spoke to them as if they were walking beside them through the woods. Honestly, it was unhinging Kaegan more than a little, and the chills that brushed his spine in waves didn't help the feeling they were being hunted — or haunted.

He knelt with a grunt and set Colten down as gently as his exhausted arms could manage. He had to rest, but more importantly, he needed to check the map again. If he'd managed to stay on track, he should be nearing a colony called Dead Run River. Some said it was paradise. Some said it was full of Dead sympathizers who let them in their gates. Whatever demons it housed, he was going to find out, if he was lucky enough.

Pouring over the map, he checked his compass twice and measured the distance thoroughly to make sure he wasn't mistaken. He was so close. There was a Denver colony not terribly far away, but he wouldn't make it that far. Not with Colten as bad off as he was. He needed help and shelter. A sanctuary where he could rest his ankle, trade for a good meal, and make sure Colten survived the infection that was burning him from the inside out. Dead Run River was their best shot.

Only then would he be able to deal with the startling information he'd gathered at the last colony they'd stayed in. Right now, there was only room for survival mode in his head. If he didn't live through the journey, the information would die with him, and then every risky decision he'd made over the last few weeks would've been for nothing.

A twig snapped in the brush to the right. He froze and stared at the shaking brush with a sense of dread so heavy, he found it difficult to move his arms. *Snap!* Another branch broke behind him.

His heart tripped to a galloping pace, and he shoved the map in his pack and shouldered Colten with the aid of the adrenaline that pounded through him.

"They're coming," Colten rasped.

No crap they were coming. Deads were always coming for them like they were two limping cheese cubes trying to escape a hungry pack of Dobermans.

More crackling leaves sounded to his left. They were closing in, and he gritted his teeth against the pain in his ankle. If he set

Colten down to fight, they'd be all over him. The best shot at both of them making it out alive was to run. They were so close, groans and hitched breaths filled the forest. A steep embankment jutted out of the earth, funneling him into a ravine. Oh God, if a Dead came from the other direction, he was trapped.

Gripping Colten's legs harder, he pushed until sweat ran in streams down his face. His breathing was ragged and loud against his eardrums, and Colten spoke a steady stream of gibberish that told the Deads exactly where they were. It was useless to try to get him to shut up. Colten hadn't understood a word he'd said in over twelve hours. Lungs burning, he escaped the ravine just as he saw the first onslaught of Deads out of the corner of his eye. There were so many, ten at least, and he was only one man, carrying the dead weight of a friend he wouldn't drop to save his own hide.

There. An ancient spruce with a jagged and painful looking split down its middle, likely from being struck by lightning, stretched up toward the heavens. He could almost feel the Deads breathing on his neck now. Any moment, a clawed hand would grab his shirt and pull him back. His body screamed to rest, or slow down at the very least, but he couldn't. Not yet.

Ducking, he shoved Colten into the opening of the injured tree and turned just as the first flesh eater was on him. Sunken eyes and blood stained clothes. Lips curled in hunger away from yellow teeth. Sagging, cold looking flesh clung to jutting bones, and one of its arms was missing completely. The foot long bowie knife slid out of its sheath in one fluid motion, and he arched it into the temple of the monster.

This was it. His last stand.

"Come on!" he screamed as a roiling rage wracked his body. After everything, he was going to die here in the woods. He and Colten. After every skirmish they'd outlived, every time they'd been treed and weaponless, every time they'd survived a bite. And now here they were, at the end of their lives. Kaegan was angry at the world. At the necessity of situations like the one he was in. At the mindless Deads who lived to hurt him and the ones he loved. He kicked one back and put the blade into another's head. Stabbing uselessly at their torsos wouldn't prolong his life. They didn't feel. The creatures would just keep coming. It was a kill shot to their head or death by being eaten alive. He'd only lived this long because he was much more efficient at killing than the horde.

He wouldn't go down gently. It wasn't his style to sag to his knees and accept his fate. Oh, he knew what was coming for him, but he wasn't going down without taking out every single moaner that he could while he stood on this earth. Bellowing his fury, he slashed again and again until the number of bodies at his feet became a blur. He shoved limp Deads away from him as they cluttered the forest floor at his feet, soaking the earth with their putrid blood. And always the searching eyes, silver with death — empty, soulless.

He hoped they ate all of him so he wouldn't come back a monster.

He stood, staggered and hunched with fatigue as the last Dead fell away from his knife. Every muscle shook and red streamed down his face until it dripped from the tip of his nose and from his hair. The break was temporary. More were coming through the woods toward them, and this was his chance. He hadn't the energy to do more than throw Colten's arm over his shoulder and drag him through the blanket of leaves. He walked forever like that, arms howling their exhaustion, and stumbling from the numbness in his legs. He was just fast enough to stay in front of the seven Deads who tracked him. He was fading, and they'd have a meal soon enough, but not until he had nothing in his body left to give. The breakdown was coming.

And just as he'd decided it was enough — that he'd given all of himself to save his friend, that all he wanted to do was drop to his knees and wait for the monsters in the shadows to take him screaming to his death, a looming fence appeared through the trees.

Dead Run River.

"Open the gates!" he yelled as he rounded the curve.

Two guards stood ready.

"Please," he breathed. "Open the gates."

The Deads were catching up as his pace slowed, and he bit his lip and pressed on, sure they'd catch him in an instant.

The creaking of wood resonated through the clearing, and the doors opened slowly. He slipped through behind the guards, and two Deads followed them right in. Both were knifed before they took two steps beyond the gate.

Kaegan fell, unable to support his weight or Colten's for another second. He'd never catch his breath again, and his lungs ached as he tried to drag air into them. It was as if they didn't recognize oxygen anymore and passed it off as a gaseous poison instead. In desperation, he crawled aimlessly on hands and knees. Rocks dug into his hands, and he stared at the filth covered knife he still clutched.

"Breathe, man," one of the guards said quietly. "You're alive." He lifted up the sleeve of Kaegan's shirt. "You aren't vaccinated? We'll have to do a bite search. You can't get through the second gate until we've cleared you."

"Okay," he wheezed.

Another guard, taller than the first, pulled up the sleeve of Colten's shirt to reveal a deep, gray, pock mark scar that said he'd been vaccinated long ago. As his wind slowly returned, he kicked out of his pants and lifted his shirt for the guard checking him and waited until he gave the go ahead. Another set of gates stretched up before him and as he pulled his shirt back over his head, the giant wooden barriers opened slowly to admit them.

The guard beside him, a young man no older than twenty-two, spoke into his radio. "Advise Dr. Mackey we have someone headed his way. Bite wound, vaccinated, fever and infection from the looks of it."

"Yep," came the clipped answer from the other end before the radio dipped into static.

The guard squatted by Colten, hoisted his slight frame over his shoulder, and led the way up a narrow dirt path through the pine forest. Steadying his breath, Kaegan stood on shaking legs and stumbled after him.

The adrenaline crash that followed a near death experience was harsh. His muscles twitched so badly it was difficult to walk straight, and the pace the guard carrying Colten kept was almost too much. He jogged to keep up, but the air seemed thinner, harder to breathe. That or he was worse off than he thought after the fight with the Deads and his run for survival.

Every colony was different, but this one took the cake. The leader, whoever he or she was, allowed giant pines, alders, and spruce to take over the land. Maybe the colony needed it for wind and snow protection. He'd never been this far north before, so that seemed likely. Not many used wooden gates anymore, but Dead Run River seemed to be holding up just fine with them. Quaint wooden cabins dotted the mountainside. People sat on porches, talking in small groups, and some offered a friendly wave as they passed. He nodded greetings, unable to find his voice quite yet, and ducked out of the way as a trio of laughing kids ran down the trail. The rumors about paradise seemed to be holding true.

A sizable cabin appeared through the woods to the left, and a hand carved sign assured him they'd found the medical building. Colten was speaking gibberish against the back of the guard, and when he looked up, his eyes were wild and empty. A sick feeling slithered into the pit of Kaegan's stomach. After all of the effort to get him here, Colten might still die.

He hopped the porch stairs and threw open the door for the guard. Inside, organized chaos reigned. An older man in scrubs and a baseball cap barked orders while two younger men prepared a room.

The guard, Andrew, one of the orderlies called him, slid Colten from his shoulder and tried to steady him on his feet. The door to a back room creaked open, and time slowed. A creature entered the room, so exotic and dangerous, Kaegan was helpless to draw his gaze away. She looked down at a clipboard in her hands. Her hair was wild, but not unkempt — like a feral Viking from ages ago. It was long, brushing her hips, and the color of milk. Three small braids arched from her hairline to the tips on one side and had been tied with thick leather bands. Feathers had been attached sporadically to a few of the waves. Her long neck dipped gracefully into a green sleeveless cotton shirt that tucked into tight, tree bark colored cargo pants. Her arms were thin but taut with un-flexed muscle that belied her strength. Layers of beaded, feathered necklaces adorned her neck, and a thick leather strap encircled her left wrist.

It wasn't her hair or clothes that gave her an air of danger, though. No, that came from her face. Pale as moonlight, her skin was nearly translucent. And as she lifted her chin, the sunlight filtering through the window glinted off metal covering her mouth. The bottom half of her face was covered in some contraption that belonged on rabid animals, and when she drew her gaze to his, his heart stuttered. Those eyes. Inhuman, startling, haunting. Almost white irises froze him further — her pupils pinpointed on him and dared him to look away.

She was a witch. Magic lived within a creature such as she.

Colten bolted for her, shaking Kaegan out of his trance. A battle cry screeched from Colten's throat as he threw himself into her.

"Dead," Colten screamed.

And it clicked. She wasn't a witch. She was a Dead. Or at least mostly Dead. A cold, clammy wave washed up Kaegan's skin until it touched his neck and lifted his hair. Rumors about Dead Run River housing monsters weren't rumors at all.

Colten had landed hard against her, splaying the creature against a desk, and she stretched her neck toward his face as an inhuman snarl came from her. The tendons in her neck flexed as she gnashed her teeth from behind the muzzle, and her eyes filled with such hate, it rocked Kaegan back on his heels.

The doctor was the first to reach Colten, and he pleaded for help as he tried to pry him off the thing. Kaegan rushed forward and wrapped his arms around his friend's waist before pulling back. The knife Colten had pulled from his belt slid from the belly of the monster with a sickening sound and dripped red.

"Oh God," Kaegan whispered as she dropped her gaze to the growing red stain on her shirt.

The creature brought stunned eyes back to his. "God had nothing to do with me." Her voice was soft, melodious, and sad. Unexpected from such a terrifying being.

Colten fought like an animal, and Kaegan gripped his wrist until he dropped the weapon. The doctor slammed a first aid kit into the Dead's chest.

"Take care of it outside," he barked before turning to help another orderly wrestle Colten into a room.

If he were able to take his eyes away from her, he would've missed the sadness that washed over her features for a moment before she turned her back and left the building.

"Who was that?" he asked the attendant in scrubs who stood beside him.

"Not who…what. That," he said with a sigh, "is Soren."

"She's hurt."

"Not bad enough to kill her. Don't waste your concern on the undead," he said with a friendly pat on Kaegan's back. He turned and said over his shoulder, "They'll kill you the minute you do."

Undead.

But, she talked. She looked hurt when the doctor dismissed her. She'd been stabbed and didn't kill her abuser. How could something with human traits, feelings, be undead? And how had she come to be?

Colten thrashed against the medical bed the doctor had managed to press him into, and the older man in the ball cap slid a needle into his shoulder. Seconds passed before his sick friend went limp. His mumbling quieted, and the staff wasted no time in cutting the leg of his pants to expose the injury that had caused the fever.

Kaegan turned back to the door and narrowed his eyes at it. He'd been in this situation at least ten times before. There was nothing to do for Colten but wait for the doctors to do all they could for him. With one last glance at the team working feverishly on Colten's leg, he strode through the door and into the sunlight.

He wasn't sure which direction she went, but a mother clutched a child to her legs, and they both looked up the trail. The woman's expression screamed disgust, while the boy of no more than ten exuded curiosity from the safety of the woman's protective arms.

He lengthened his stride and jogged to catch up. The reactions of the colonists were all similar, leading him deeper and deeper into the heart of Dead Run River. Maybe it wasn't willingly housing the Dead after all. The mysteries surrounding the girl mounted by the minute. Finally, he came to a point on the trail where it thinned, as if people didn't use it as much. No one offered clues as to where she'd gone, and the deeper he traveled into the woods, the louder the song of the birds. Sunlight permeated through the canopy of thick branches and leaves, leaving the forest floor speckled with yellow light. The grass grew higher the farther he walked, as if no one lived near there. As if no one took care of this corner of the community. On and on he walked, not sure if he was headed in the right direction.

And then he saw it. An archaic tree stood stoically against the backdrop of woods and fence. In its branches, someone had built a home of sorts. It had three walls and a partial roof, and the fourth wall was open, overlooking the woods on the other side of the fence. A hammock swung in the breeze inside the tree house, and a handmade ladder leaned against the trunk. In the branches, Soren crouched with her back to him.

A slick sound came from her as her arms moved with some unseen work. *Pit, pat, pit, pat.* Red ran in a steady river from her seat on the branch to the forest floor below.

"You're not vaccinated," she said in a low voice.

He jumped at the sound of her voice. "How do you know?"

"I can smell it." She slid him a loaded glance and then turned her attention inward again.

She hadn't gone the way of the ladder, and he pulled himself into the tree, careful of his aching ankle as he climbed higher and higher until he sat on the limb where she was perched.

"Don't come any closer," she warned. Her hands were red with her own blood, and her shirt was lifted until it covered only her chest. Her stomach was flat and taut as she pulled thread tight to close the wound Colten had made. A row of raised, angry looking scars stretched low over her left hipbone.

He swallowed so his curiosity would stay lodged in his throat, and it sounded very loud in the quiet that stretched between them. "You shouldn't be doing that on yourself. Here, let me."

Her voice was muffled behind the muzzle. "You aren't vaccinated," she repeated.

"Are you contagious?"

She gave a curt nod and pulled another loop through her flesh.

"Are you airborne contagious?"

Settling her inhuman eyes upon him, she stared for a long moment. "No. The virus hasn't mutated like that. At least not yet. I'm contagious from my mouth, just like all the other Deads."

Kaegan made a show of looking up and down his red splattered arms. It wasn't his blood or Colten's that bathed him in crimson. It was that of the Deads he'd fought. "Your blood won't hurt me then, so I'll take my chances. Please, it's the least I can do after my friend did that to you."

Her eyes narrowed like she was suspicious he'd push her from the branch if she got too close. Something about it made him so sad. It must be an awful life to live as a monster.

"Fine," she muttered. Her voice was muffled, and an irrational piece of him wished he could talk to her without the muzzle. If it was there, it was put on her for a reason though, so he left it alone.

She stepped lightly over him and leaned against the trunk of the tree, stretching her back so he could reach the skin of her stomach better. Hesitating, his fingertips hovered just above the pale skin near her ribs. It felt dangerous to touch her. Not fatal, but dangerous in some way he couldn't understand. Like if he touched her, he wouldn't be the same afterward. Maybe she was a witch after all.

He plucked the dangling needle from the air and straddled the branch. Her skin was soft, warm…alive. Not what he'd expected and his vision of the monster wavered. Her ribs showed when she breathed, and though it was common to be underfed in these times, still, it made him sorry for her hunger.

"Does it hurt?"

"No. Not like it would hurt you. I don't feel things like you do. Pain is just a small discomfort for me."

"Are you immortal?"

Hurt washed over her face, and she looked away and shook her head slightly. "No and I'm glad for it." She turned serious, unsettling eyes to him. "Who would want to live more than one lifetime like this?"

Her words were an ember in his gut, igniting as it settled in, burning through him until a dull ache formed at her sad question. Who would indeed? He'd seen how people here looked at her in just the short time he'd been here. One lifetime would be more than enough if he were in her shoes.

Four more stitches did the trick. They weren't straight, and they'd likely leave tiny scars, but it was only the third set he'd given in his twenty-six years. The others had winced in pain, but she breathed steadily, chest rising and falling as she looked expressionlessly out over the gates to the woods beyond. When he turned to see what she was looking at, three Deads shuffled slowly through the trees beyond the safety of Dead Run River. Where he looked at them with disdain, she looked at them with a wistful look in her oddly colored eyes.

She was probably the most frightening creature he'd ever encountered. Why then was he tenderly cleaning her skin with a cloth like she was a friend instead of the enemy? He'd lost his damned mind, that's why.

The people here looked at her warily for a reason. He knew nothing about her, really, and he'd treed himself with a Dead with little thought to his own safety. She'd been right when she'd accused him of not being vaccinated. One nip from her, and he'd turn within minutes. And it wasn't just his own safety that was at risk. If he turned, the entire colony could go down within hours.

She frowned and dropped her gaze to his chest. Could she hear his erratic heartbeat? "Thanks. It's been years since someone helped me with my stitches." She was giving him an out. Dismissing him so he could go on his merry way and survive her.

He made for the branch below him but stopped as the same hurt he'd seen earlier took her eyes.

"You get stabbed often?" he asked.

"You'd be surprised. Tell your friend to go for the brain next time."

"Oh, she's got zombie jokes," he said with a surprised chuckle.

Her eyes crinkled like she was smiling beneath the muzzle, and his fingers itched to unlatch the damned thing and throw it to the forest floor. Her smile might be terrifying, but what if it wasn't?

"Get away from her!" a shrill scream echoed through the woods. A petite woman with dark hair and eyes and a furious countenance raced toward them. "Get away from that Dead!"

He'd been on his way down but stopped. Stubbornness at being ordered away by a stranger made him straddle the branch below Soren.

"Who are you?" he asked, cocking his head.

The woman panted as she skidded to a stop beneath them. "Who am I? I'm Z's handler. Who are you?"

"Z?" He lifted his face in question to Soren, but she was looking away. She drew her knees to her chest and wrapped her arms around them like she was shutting down.

When she wouldn't look at him, he shook his head. He was in way over his pay grade. He didn't understand the dynamic here, didn't understand why Soren was here or how she had even come to be. His head swam and he stepped to the next branch below him. When he hopped to the forest floor, the tiny woman sank her claws into his arm, and he yanked away.

"What do you think you're—"

"Don't," he said. His anger was sharp and hot, and he didn't have to answer to anyone, especially some woman bent on belittling the creature in the tree. Soren was different and dangerous, but surely she didn't deserve to be treated like this. Z. Oh, he could guess what Z meant. They called her Zombie.

For the first time in his life, he pitied a Dead, but something in him said she didn't need him to be her champion.

"Bye, Soren," he said.

"Bye," she said quickly, swinging a startled gaze to him.

He looked back twice as he walked the trail back to civilization. Both times, despite her handler shrieking at her from below, her eyes stayed riveted on his retreat.

Chapter Three

Soren leaned against a branch that jutted through her canopy house. Her legs dangled from the edge of the open wall and slowly, she drew one knee to her chest. A clear, gray dawn was just peeking over the horizon. Above her, stars twinkled in the still dark sky—winking, as if they knew something about her destiny that she didn't.

She didn't sleep much, and when she did, she never dreamed. Dreams were reserved for humans, she supposed. Seamus had always told her about his dreams growing up, and she'd been enamored by them. He said they were like a movie playing in his head, and since she'd never actually watched a movie, it sounded magical and mysterious. She'd give a finger, maybe two, to have a dream.

The breeze picked up, and the weapons tied to the wall behind the hammock clanked against each other. A warrior's wind chimes. She inhaled the crisp, clean air and tried to imagine the world before the apocalypse. The old timers described it well, and she'd listened as a child. Her old journals were full of drawings of what she imagined the world looked like before Deads trolled the land.

Her newest drawing was of Kaegan.

It was a charcoal sketch of the first time she'd seen him. He'd stood in the middle of Dr. Mackey's waiting room staring at her with surprised gray eyes the color of a dove's breast. His hair was longer and had been tied into a leather band at his nape at some point, but in his skirmish to get through the gates safely, some of it had fallen forward into his face. She hadn't a guess at the color of his skin because it was drenched in the pungent blood of Deads. His dark eyebrows matched the color of his unruly tresses, and they lifted in pity when he pulled his friend's knife from her belly.

He was a fighter. It wasn't the scars on his skin or the limp in his gait that told her so. It wasn't the thick beard he'd grown between colonies. It was his size. He was massive. A behemoth. Giants of modern times must have birthed a son as gargantuan as their lineage, because his shoulders were wide enough that he would have to step sideways through a door. He was tall enough that he'd have to duck any standard entrance, and muscle, thick and intimidating, pressed against the blood-moist fabric of his shirt when he drew his ragged breaths.

He could kill her or anyone else he pleased with no weapons and little effort.

The most irking thing about the man was his apparent lack of intelligence when it came to the vaccine. Did he have a death wish? Some people did. Or maybe he was one of those fighters who thought themselves invincible. No need for a vaccine if they were going to live forever, right?

She shook her head and tossed the leaf she'd been shredding to the ground below.

"Ca-caaaw," Seamus screeched from the woods. He got worse at bird calls with age. "Don't shank me, Mitchell. I come bearing gifts."

He was the only one on the planet allowed to call her by her last name, and he was only awarded that privilege because he'd called her that since age three. He knew exactly where she came from — understood the community and their tendency to use surnames.

"Well, if you bring me gifts, I suppose I'll cut back on my pre-dawn shankings, Guist." She said his last name with a smile. How many times had their fathers called each other the same when they were growing up?

He scaled the ladder and dropped a plastic sack beside her with a smile that begged praise. It smelled of blood, and her stomach rumbled. She'd be embarrassed if it weren't Seamus who stood beside her.

"I thought so. You haven't been eating again."

"Gah, why is everyone so interested in my diet?"

"Hey, I'm on your side. I just want to know what's going on with you."

"Marie keeps making me eat cooked food. It's making me sick. Not being dramatic. I mean, I'm really getting sick."

Seamus cursed under his breath and took a seat beside her. "I'll talk to her. You can't eat food that doesn't agree with your digestive system."

"You're preaching to the choir." Pulling the opening of the bag away, she smiled at the skinned bunny inside. "Where did you find this? I know you didn't hunt it down yourself."

"Mikey Walen does snares outside the gates now and sells his catch behind Ricky's." Game meat and moonshine, the black market of Dead Run River.

She'd never partaken in the liquor Ricky made behind his bar, but Seamus had on his eighteenth birthday with some of his buddies. He hadn't had a drink since as far as she knew. She would've paid good money to see him drunk, though.

"You can eat it now if you want. I won't gag, I swear."

Tempting if she didn't know how much it really bothered him. He liked his steak well done, and she was pretty sure that was because he'd grown up sitting with her at mess hall. The Denver colony was more accepting about her diet than the people here. It was a requirement after all. To settle in the legendary Sean Daniel's colony, colonists had to accept her presence. It was part of the rule sheet Sean and Vanessa gave all newcomers when she had lived there. If new colonists bucked against living in a place with a Dead hybrid, they were moved to Dead Run River.

Thinking of home made her ache so badly, she had to wait a moment to speak. "I'll eat breakfast when you leave. Right now I want all of the juicy gossip."

"Soren," Seamus groaned. "I'm a dude. I don't keep up with that stuff, and you know it."

"Give me anything. I'm wilting here. I've been banished from Dr. Mackey's office for three days and hanging out here is becoming seventeen shades of monotonous."

"Fine, okay, fine. No cure yet, and we're not any closer than we were months ago. Which you probably already guessed. We're at a standstill with it. Dr. Mackey needs more tissue from you, so he told me to tell you to come in tomorrow for a sample day."

"What about the tissue I gave him last week?"

"We blew through it. We followed up on a lead that did nothing but waste what you'd given us. But we still had to try."

"Did the man live? The one who attacked me?"

"Yes, he's recovering. Doc said by tomorrow morning, he'll move him into temporary housing with that big guy, Kaegan. That's when he wants you to come in so your paths don't cross. Let me see the injury."

"It's fine."

"Soren." He quirked an eyebrow and waited.

With a put upon sigh, she lifted her shirt and waited while he studied it under a pocket flashlight.

"No infection," he muttered. "Did he nick anything inside?"

"Nothing that I could find, and I was thorough when I searched. I got lucky he used a small knife. It also didn't suck that he was weak and his aim was off. It'll be nothing but a memory in a few days. Dead powers aren't as awesome as superpowers, but at least they're good for something."

"Yeah, well with the number of times you've been injured, superior healing is definitely a win. You aren't invincible though, Soren. If he'd cut an organ, we'd be having a very different conversation right now. You have to be careful."

How on earth was she supposed to know she'd be a victim of a stabbing one random day at work? Seamus was just worried though, so she nodded.

"The big guy—"

"Kaegan?" she asked, jerking her head to Seamus.

His lips set in a grim line, and he pressed his glasses farther up his nose. "Yeah, Kaegan. He asked Dr. Mackey about you. He wanted to know why you're here."

"And what did Dr. Mackey say?"

"He said you're here for observation. And that if Kaegan values his life, he needs to get vaccinated or stay away from you completely. He chose staying away."

"Well," she said, stomaching the hurt, "why wouldn't he choose that over a needle prick? He doesn't even know me." The gray had lightened to pink on the horizon, and she sighed.

Seamus stared at her for a long time, then said, "It won't be like this forever. We'll find the cure, and then your life will be different. Easier."

"And if the cure doesn't work on me?"

He turned to the breaking morning light. "We can't think like that. It'll work."

Kaegan hefted another bundle of lumber over his shoulder, and when it was balanced, walked it over to the proper pile and came back for more. He'd been at it all morning, but his shoulders barely complained. He was too lost in his own thoughts to pay much mind to the ache of fatigue. At least pain meant he was alive, and that was more than anyone could say for Trevor and Mike. The loss ate at him. Over and over, he imagined what he could have done differently, but every time was the same. He couldn't save them. He'd barely been able to get Colten to safety.

The noise of the antique sawmill was the perfect soundtrack to his internal struggle. Blades against wood, the hollow clunk of lumber as it was stacked, the shouted orders from the foreman, and laughter from a trio of workers taking a lunch break. It was all so…normal.

He threw down another bundle and turned, almost running into a woman with auburn hair that had gone gray at the temples. Her bright green eyes studied him for a moment before she offered him a smile. It seemed genuine enough, but failed to reach her eyes.

"Mr. Langford?" she asked.

He pulled a work glove from his hand and offered it. "You can call me Kaegan."

She frowned at the rough palm of his hand but shook it. "Mel. I'm the leader here at Dead Run River. I'd like to talk to you for a couple of minutes if you can spare the time."

"Uh." He hesitated and looked at Gary, the foreman. The man was a badger of a boss who didn't like workers taking breaks unless it was for lunch.

"Gary," Mel called. "I need Kaegan for a while. I'll send him back when we're done."

"You got it," he called with a smile.

Wow. He hadn't seen Gary smile in the three days he'd worked at the sawmill. He looked at Mel with more interest.

She led him down a less worn path that pointed toward the back of the colony. "How do you like it here so far?"

"I like it fine, ma'am. You're running one of the nicest colonies I've ever set foot in." It wasn't flattery but the truth.

"And how long do you plan to stay?"

"Well, I was going to come see you here in the next couple of days. Colten and I won't bother you for too long because there is somewhere we need to be. The reason we left our last colony was to join up."

She stopped and waited for him to take a place beside her. Pulling a leaf from a low hanging tree branch, she asked, "Join up for what?"

"The war, ma'am."

"Kaegan, if you call me ma'am again, I'm going to fillet you."

"Sorry."

"What war are you talking about?"

"At the last colony Colten and I lived in, a group of fighters came in late one night. They only stayed for a few days, but they said the Deads were migrating. Gathering little by little at the coast near Empalme. Mexico, you know. Migration has been happening for a few years, and this time around, people are starting to talk about killing them off. Taking back the cities when they get the population low enough. That's just what I've heard, but Colten and I, and our team, we wanted to see if there was any truth to the rumor. Have you seen as many Deads around these parts this season?"

Mel pursed her lips. Instead of answering, she asked, "Do you know where Dead Run River got its name?"

"No." He fought the urge to say ma'am. She seemed nice enough, but her threat sounded pretty sincere.

"When we settled here, the Deads had gathered by the river. Hundreds of them, maybe thousands, and for what we couldn't ever figure out. They seem to steer clear of water, so why would they all stand there, staring into the rapids?"

Kaegan inhaled and shook his head. "I don't know."

"I don't want you riling up the people here. We have a good life and taking innocents on some crusade because of hearsay is irresponsible and dangerous."

"Oh, I'm not planning on recruiting. Just laying over until Colten is better and my ankle can hold my weight again. You've got nothin' to worry about from me."

Her vibrant eyes narrowed. "I make it a point to know everything about everything that happens in my colony. You've been asking around about Soren."

Now it was his turn to clamp his mouth shut. Eyeing the path as they walked, he shoved his hands into his pockets and shrugged. "So?"

"So, it's natural to be curious about her. Most newcomers are, but that is where it has to stop."

"I heard you need a new handler for her."

The silence was filled with birdsong from the branches above. Finally, she said, "You aren't vaccinated, so why would you ask about the handler position?"

"I'll keep my distance from her, report everything she does." Even he could hear the tinge of pathetic desperation in his voice.

"What was your trade before you came here?"

"Fence builder and welder. My size determined it early."

"Well, that's why you've been assigned to the sawmill. Your talents are best used there."

"But—"

"No buts," she said. Spinning, she stopped in front of him. "You are new and don't know much about Soren, but if you value your life, you'll stay away."

Surprise caused him to lean closer. "Are you threatening me?"

A smile curled across only one side of her mouth. "It's not a threat, Kaegan. It's a friendly warning from one survivor to another. Have you ever heard of Laney and Derek Mitchell?"

"Of course. Everyone's heard of them. They're legends."

"Living legends, Mr. Langford. Laney and Derek are Soren's parents. She was raised by them and trained by Finn, Aaron Guist, and Sean and Vanessa Daniels. I assume you've heard of them too?" At his nod, she continued. "She has more weapons in her arsenal than you have coherent thoughts."

"She didn't use them on Colten when he stabbed her." His voice was hard and flat.

"That's because of the muzzle and likely the surprise of the attack. Your first mistake was forgetting what she is."

"And what is that?" Surely the woman could see she was more than a monster.

"A Dead. I can tell by the look you're giving me that you remain unconvinced, and so I will share information with you that most of this colony is not privy to, and I'll trust you to keep it quiet. Soren has killed people. Living, breathing people, and a lot of them. Seven to be exact, four of whom were children."

His mouth went dry as cotton, and his stomach sank to his knees. Closing his eyes against the sick feeling building in his center, he leaned against a tree behind him like he'd suffered a blow. Children. She'd killed children. She was a monster after all. Everyone had known it, seen her for what she was, but he, the damned idiot he was, had been searching for something more. And why? Why did it matter? Because he didn't like the way a girl was treated in a colony? Life was hard these days. Everyone died in awful ways. At least she had a colony who accepted her presence, no matter how ungraciously. She didn't need his saving.

"Can you understand my concern now with you, an unvaccinated civilian, getting too curious about her?"

Unable to speak around the nausea that clawed his middle, he nodded.

"This is the one and only warning I'll give you, Kaegan. And it's not your safety I'm concerned about as much as that of my colony. Get too close, she'll kill you. She seems like a nice person, and I owe her parents a great deal, which is why she is allowed to live here and work on the cure. But the moment you forget what she is, that is the moment you'll take your last human breath. I don't want you anywhere near her. The rules are the same for everyone. It's why we have handlers watching her at all times. Their job is to protect the colony, and their training is extensive. Break my rules, and I'll throw you out of the front gates so fast you'll think I'm magic. Have I made myself clear?"

He dragged a hard gaze back to her cold eyes. "Yes, ma'am."

Chapter Four

S ample day. Good times.

Soren rubbed a fingertip over the row of scars across her hip. Mom had gone through the same when she was giving tissue to help Dr. Mackey create the Dead outbreak vaccine. And now, twenty years later, she was doing the same for the cure. Hooray for genetics.

The dickhole who'd stabbed her should be long gone from the medical building by now, but just to make sure, she stalled, walking slowly and dillydallying near any shrub that caught her attention. Every bird that squawked in the trees earned a long look from her, and when a squirrel went chattering through the branches above, she stopped and watched for at least three minutes.

The work day had begun, and she'd showered in the middle of the night when the humans were snoring away in their warm beds. The upside to chronic insomnia—she used every drop of hot water in the dark and didn't have an ounce of guilt for it. It would heat up again by the time the early risers needed a shampoo. The showers, heated by water power leached off the snow-melted rivers in the mountains above, were quite the commodity. The look on settlers' faces when they moved here and figured out there was hot running water was a treat to watch. Mouths often gaped open, just before a brilliant smile. No matter how plain one looked, a smile instantly added fairness.

The muzzle itched like a tiny swarm of horseflies were eating her jaw, and she reached up under it and scratched.

"Soren," Marie warned from behind.

"Heifer," Soren muttered as she ceased the scratch.

Davey and Sara Mathis played in the woods, digging and laughing and Soren smiled at their antics. She'd had the best childhood home. Hours and hours had been spent playing with Seamus and Adrianna, just like these two. Davey started to arch his gaze toward her, and she turned away before she could see the fear that would pool in his eyes, a little trick she'd picked up over her two years at Dead Run River.

Had it only been two years? It felt like so much longer. Homesickness had been her constant companion, but she had work to do that couldn't be done from the Denver colony.

The look on Mom's face when she'd left home with Seamus still pulled at her heart. Everyone in the world knew Laney Landry. How tough she was and how brave. How lethal she was in a fight. They knew she was the origin of the vaccine and of her sacrifices to get it to the masses. But no one knew her like Soren. Mom was tender and caring. Loyal to her family and friends. Soren and Dad were Mom's whole world. Everything else revolved around them like secondary stars. She'd say, *hang the end of the world. We're the lucky ones because we have each other.* It had been all that had mattered for a while.

Mom and Dad had both understood her need to help with the cure and had never begged her to stay. More proof of their love for her. They'd let her go and held back their tears until they waved her off.

If Mom saw her now, muzzled like an animal and cowed by the stringent rules of this place, she'd burn the whole world down. It was just how Mom was. Shame heated her cheeks. God, what was she doing here?

"I swear, man," someone said through the trees. "An actual, honest to goodness sponge bath. I thought I'd died after all, but then I realized if I had, I'd be surrounded by more flames, and less hot nurses."

Kaegan's massive shoulders showed through a gap in the trees, and she froze. Shit. Wide-eyed, she looked for a hidey hole and came up with nothing.

"Move." Marie's voice was saturated in impatience.

When Soren stood locked in place, Marie shoved her hard in the back, and she flew forward, landing on her hands and knees in the dirt. A snarl rippled through her before she could stop it. Gripping handfuls of rich soil, she panted, desperate to control the red rage that filled her veins.

"What are you doing?" Kaegan's voice held steel and something more. Anger?

"None of your fucking business, civilian," Marie replied. "Move on."

"Dude," the other man with Kaegan said. "Is that the chick I stabbed?"

Soren lifted her face to the man. He was shorter than Kaegan, but still tall. Lanky where Kaegan was layered in muscle. His light brown hair was swept fashionably up and to the side like he'd found the time to hand mix homemade hair gel. His eyes were bright blue and a frown tugged the corners of his mouth. Stubble brushed his jaw. His face was all angles, and attractive ones at that.

"I don't think I regret it," he murmured, cocking his head as he studied her. "She's a Dead. Right?"

"Exactly!" Marie grabbed her shirt and pulled her upward, eliciting a loud ripping sound from the fabric in her clenched fist.

Kaegan just watched with an unfathomable expression in his soft, gray eyes. Unable to bear the embarrassment, she cast her eyes down and to the left. Anywhere but at him.

"Come on," he said quietly. Brush rustled as he led Stabby-Mcstabby-Hands off the trail and through the woods.

She clenched and unclenched her hands and took a long, shaking breath. All she wanted to do, the only thing in the world that felt right in that moment, was pinning Marie to the nearest tree and scaring the piss out of her.

But — she closed her eyes — though this place didn't need a half-Dead inhabitant, Dead Run River was vital to her.

Someone had talked to him. Why else would he look at her like that? Kaegan had been kind enough to stitch her up just days before, and now, he couldn't get away from her fast enough. She threw a longing glance at his back as he disappeared through the trees. It would've been nice to pretend for a little while longer that she could make another friend.

Dusting off the knees of her jeans, she strode deliberately down the trail. Maybe it was better someone enlightened him about the dangers of being a Dead sympathizer. Sympathizers were cannon fodder for the Deads. A vision of Kaegan, eyes open and vacant, bent across a marsh soaked in his own blood flashed across her mind, and she shook her head to rid herself of such black thoughts.

He was better off this way.

She stepped right on the squeaky step of the medical building's front porch out of spite and pulled the door. Dr. Mackey looked up from his desk where he sat pouring over a notepad and removed his glasses.

"How is the stomach?"

"Are you asking because you care or for medical observation?" She felt especially volatile after the past five minutes.

Dr. Mackey cocked his head and gave her a withering look that was answer enough. "I care that you live, but I wasn't ever worried about an injury like that to you. Hop up on the exam table and let me see it."

Lifting her shirt, she waited while he poked it with the tip of his glasses. "Good," was all he said before he scribbled across his notepad. "And what did you eat this morning?"

She slid Marie an emotionless smile as she said, "Raw bunny."

The woman's face went positively green, and Soren allowed herself a wider grin.

A frown lowered Dr. Mackey's bushy gray brows. "Where did you get a rabbit, Soren? I thought Mel told you to stay in the colony gates from now on."

Soren shrugged, not about to out Seamus or the game meat black market behind Ricky's. "A zombie's gotta eat."

A hideous noise came from Marie, and she left and slammed the door so hard, it rocked the cabin. Soren sighed. She'd bet her best knife Mel would feel the need to have a private discussion with her before the day was done.

"You shouldn't bait her," Dr. Mackey murmured.

She reached up to remove the itchy muzzle but Doc shook his head. "Until the unvaccinated civilian is gone, you're to keep the muzzle on twenty-four hours a day."

"You can't be serious. What about when I sleep?"

"Even when you sleep. There is fear of you sleepwalking."

"But I've never sleepwalked in my life. Why would I start now?"

"Because we are trying to add cooked food to your diet. Changes like that can upset your body and cause changes like sleepwalking."

"Wait, you're in on it? You know it makes me sick, Doc! My entire digestive system shuts down. It's like trying to feed a T. rex a Caesar salad. You of all people should understand how I work."

"It's just an experiment." He held his hands up like he was compromising, but he wasn't. No one compromised with her on anything.

"The muzzle is rubbing me raw."

"Soren, you knew the gig coming here. The rules weren't ever going to get easier the longer you stayed here, child. You are still just as dangerous as the day you walked in here."

Lowering her voice, she said, "I don't feel more dangerous."

"Which convinces me further that you are. You obviously don't see what the rest of the colony sees. Your refusal to mind the rules set in place to keep them safe scares people."

"What are you talking about? I wear a damned muzzle. I eat without the comfort of other people. I keep my distance from everyone and live by myself. What rules am I breaking? If anything, you and Mel sequestering me makes everyone fear me more."

"No, Soren." He snatched a hand held mirror from his desk and shoved it in her face. "That scares them."

Cold colored eyes, pale skin, a muzzle made of leather and metal, feral hair. She looked away from the glass. "Can you take my sample so I can go? Please." Tears burned the back of her eyes, but she'd be hanged before she'd shed a single one in front of someone who didn't deserve them.

Without a word, Dr. Mackey pulled a scalpel from a jar and deftly cut a chunk of flesh from her stomach.

"I'll do it myself." She snatched the gauze out of his hands and left the building. The chart sat unchecked by the front door. For the first time in months, she didn't obsess over checking whether they'd magically found the cure overnight. They hadn't. Maybe they never would.

Seamus ran out of the building after her, his tennis shoes stabbing clumsily at the earth as he ran to catch up. "He shouldn't have taken his frustration out on you." He pulled her elbow, and she slowed. "Doc's just pissed they are at a standstill with the cure. He's sick. Hey," he said gently, turning her. "He's sick. He told us yesterday. His only goal since the outbreak was to cure it, and it looks like he'll die before he gets to do it."

"We're all dying, Seamus. Nothing is promised us in this life but death. The only thing in our control is our character while we pick our way through the muck."

She was sorry to hear Doc was sick. It made her limbs heavy with sadness, but it didn't excuse unkind behavior. She should be in there. Turning, she frowned at the cabin. The Dead vaccine had been created there. It'd been added onto through the years, and giant labs could be found through a back hallway, but the main building had remained the same. It had been the place she'd worked and studied for two years. It had been the place she'd dreamed of working for much longer. What would happen to her place at Dead Run River if Dr. Mackey wasn't there anymore?

"Let's cut work and get something to eat. I skipped breakfast."

Yeah, well she could guess why. He'd brought her the gift of a raw bunny at the expense of his appetite. Seamus was a rock star in the friendship department. She usually steered wide and clear of the mess hall, but she owed him.

Throwing an arm around his shoulders, she squeezed his neck and rested her head on his shoulder. "Let's get you fed."

Despite his unfortunate taste in friends, according to the colony, Seamus seemed to be well liked. He had an easy personality and was friendly to everyone. He was so laid back he was nearly comatose and had an easy wit that seemed to make people want to talk to him.

She had none of his talents for socialization. Shyness crept through her, spreading through her arms, hands, and fingers until her throat closed over the polite *hellos* she wished she could give anyone who didn't shoot poisoned darts with their glares. Kindly, he led them to the back door of the mess hall near the Dumpsters. With a genteel bow, he opened the door and waited for her to pass.

"Why, thank you, my liege," she slurred through the muzzle.

"The pleasure is all mine, milady."

Soren snorted. She'd never be anyone's lady.

The cook's name was Brennan, but everyone called him Chef. And if anyone deserved that distinguished title, it was him. He could create food out of meager rations with very little complaint on taste from the colonists. Sometimes his dishes even looked appetizing enough for her to wish she ate normal human chow.

"You!" Chef said with a crooked pointer jabbed in her direction. "I have something for you." He pulled a raw steak from a refrigerator unit and set it on the stainless steel counter. "Hurry up and eat this before Marie stinks up my kitchen trying to cook the thing."

She pursed her lips and shot Seamus a baleful glance. "Sorry, partner."

A wicked smile took his face. "A zombie's gotta eat, right?" he said, using her earlier words.

Huffing a surprised laugh, she snatched the steak and waited for Seamus to grab a late breakfast from the serving line. Pickings were slim, as he'd missed the rush. Still, the biscuits were perfectly browned, and he managed to secure himself some scrambled eggs to go with them. Gesturing for him to eat first, she slid onto the bench seat across from him and plucked at a string that edged the frayed napkin he'd grabbed. Seamus had picked a spot in the corner, and there weren't many people left. Just guards newly off duty and people with a day off work.

She relaxed when a table full of men around her age seemed not to notice her presence. Self-consciously, she ducked her head and unclipped her muzzle. She was allowed to take it off to eat, but sometimes people still grumbled about the little bend in the rules.

"Do I have something on my face?" Seamus asked. Eggs hung halfway out of his mouth, and he lifted his eyebrows in innocent question.

"You're such a child," she said, stifling a giggle as she wiped his mouth with the napkin.

"And you're a mother hen," he accused.

Cocking her head, she waited for the punchline. She'd never been called that before. "What do you mean?"

Seamus gulped the bite and took a long draw of water. "When we were young, Adrianna tried to keep us out of trouble, you remember? But as you got older, it was you who took on that role. Remember the time we found that wasp nest right inside the gates back home? You were so worried about Ade and me disturbing it."

A mixture of nostalgia and sadness filled her at his mention of Adrianna. She missed her more than she'd ever admit out loud. To do so would be admitting her greatest weakness. Dead though she may be, she'd die ten times over for Seamus and Adrianna. A couple of humans held her heart.

"Well someone had to watch out for you." She dropped her gaze to the plate of steak beside her and movement drew her attention. Across the cafeteria, Kaegan stared openly at her. His friend sat across the table with his back to her, deep in conversation from the looks of it, but Kaegan's attention was on her. A tingling sensation zinged down her spine.

He'd shaved. Bearded he'd been glorious, masculine, as tall as a mountain with shoulders as wide as a river. Now his jaw was smooth, eliciting a longing to touch it with the tip of her finger. His cheekbones were sharp, and his gray eyes slanted slightly like a predator. He wasn't classically handsome like his friend. His hair brushed his jaw, and he leaned forward on his elbows. Dark, animated eyebrows sat low, like he was thinking painful thoughts.

"Hello," Andrew Dennison said from right beside her. He waved his hand in her face and she flinched away from his nearness.

"What do you want?" she asked suspiciously.

"I asked you if we could sit here. Three times."

She looked to Seamus for help, but he looked as stunned as she felt. "Why would you want to sit with me?"

With a sigh, he looked downright contrite as he hung his head lower to hers. "I wanted to apologize for how I talked to you the other day. I thought maybe we could start over." Three of his friends nodded behind him like they agreed with his mission.

"It's okay. Don't worry about it."

"So you forgive me then?" He slipped into the seat on her other side and offered a charming smile that probably got him invited to a lot of naked parties. Twitching his head, his wavy hair left his face for just a moment before it fell back into place.

She tried to keep the skepticism from her voice. "Why would you need forgiveness from me? You never cared about it before."

She shot Seamus a glance, but he was just staring at Andrew with a look that said he was as leery as her.

Andrew's dark eyes lifted above her shoulder for a beat and a villainous smile crooked his lips. "You're right, Z. I wouldn't ever ask the forgiveness of a baby killer."

Soren started at the sound of laughter behind her, then turned. The steak she'd been about to eat sat swaddled in a cloth napkin and looked like a tiny, bloody baby. A hiss came from her throat as she shot upward so fast, the bench seat crashed behind her. Scrambling backward, she almost tripped over the upended furniture. The vision they'd created with her food made her ill.

A gargantuan hand landed on Andrew's shoulder as he wheezed with laughter, and as he turned, his head rocked back with the force of Kaegan's fist. The crack of a nose breaking was a very distinctive sound. Satisfying also when it echoed through Andrew.

Her back pressed against the wall, all she could do was absorb the black fury that dwelled in Kaegan's grim expression.

Seamus grabbed her hand and pulled her toward the exit to escape the scuffle as two of Andrew's cronies flung themselves at Kaegan. His friend was already pummeling the third, but his face said he'd rather do anything than get involved.

Huh. At least the prick was loyal.

A cool breeze brushed her face as she hit sunlight, and Seamus looked around like he was searching for a hole for them to dive into.

"My place," she breathed, shock warring with her ability to think straight. Kaegan had jumped in to defend her. If she hadn't witnessed it herself, she would've never thought a man besides Seamus was capable of it. "Why did he do that?"

He kept a pace that rivaled flight but answered her through panting breath. "Because he's a megadick."

"No, not Andrew. Kaegan."

He didn't answer. Instead, he seemed to throw every ounce of energy into fleeing.

His panic was understandable. There was a strict no fighting rule in Dead Run River. Peace if you could, and if you had to duke it out with someone, you did it outside the gates. There were too many kids around to witness violence, and Mel seemed determined to make her colony the most civilized. But she hadn't started the fight.

"You won't get in trouble," she promised.

Seamus slowed as they approached her treehouse. "Damn it, Soren, I'm not worried about me. You'll get thrown out of here if anyone catches wind of it."

"Why me? I didn't do anything."

Seamus cursed softly and rested his hands on his hips, then stared out over the woods. "There's been talk that you've overstayed your welcome. People are looking for excuses to cut you out. You were hissing like a Dead in there. And I know you don't mean to, I know! But you can guess how Andrew will spin it."

Her chest heaved as the weight of the situation fell over her. She hadn't realized it was so bad. Where would she go if she was tossed out? How would she survive with no kinsmen, no friends? No one like Seamus to have her back? "I'll talk to Mel before she hears whatever tale they come up with," she said.

"No, you won't. I will. You arguing your innocence will only make it worse. Mel will listen to me better than you. Stay here." He reached his hands out in a placating gesture like she was some startled horse, and he spun and jogged off for the main path up the mountain.

There, alone in the quiet of the woods, it became very clear she had no control over her fate.

Chapter Five

At a rustle in the woods below, Soren peeked over the edge of her house and waited. Seamus had come back quicker than she'd expected.

Except it wasn't him at all, but Kaegan walking the trail to her tree. And if ever she'd seen a man at war with himself, surely this one was. Every few yards he stopped and turned like he'd go back the other way. She leaned her chin against the raw wood and nibbled on the corner of her lip behind the muzzle. Time and time again he turned, only to come back toward her. When finally he approached her tree, he just stood beneath it for a long time, looking back in the direction he'd come from.

"I know you're up there." His voice was deep and gravelly. Blood ran down the side of his face, his hair wet with it. His lips were set in a heavy line, but his obvious internal battle only made him more alluring. No one would ever accuse him of being a soft looking man.

"What do you want?"

"I'm coming up." And he did. Scaled her ladder like he'd done it a hundred times and scrutinized her home down to the very nails that held the boards.

She tried to imagine it through his eyes. Splintered boards bashed by the weather, a ratty mattress in the corner with the single quilt.

The row of blades, big and small, that knocked gently against the wall in the breeze. A wooden chair shadowed the corner, the seat littered with dead leaves from the branches above.

"Where do you sleep when it rains?"

The bold way in which he spoke to her, almost angrily, made her search for an escape.

"Where?" he demanded.

"I don't sleep much."

Surprised gray eyes shot to her and then away. "I brought you this." He handed her the steak she'd left behind in her haste, wrapped tightly into the knotted napkin.

Her hand shook as she reached for it, and hesitating, he searched the tiny space and settled slowly into the chair. The leaves crunched under him.

"I'll wait," he said.

"You—you want me to eat this? Now?"

A curt nod. "It's what you eat, right? Raw meat?"

Heat fanned her cheeks, and she dropped her gaze. "Yes."

"Then eat it, and when you're finished, I'll say what I've come here to say."

Sitting with her back to the unnerving man and her feet dangling off the ledge of her home, she ate slowly. Finished, she wiped her mouth with a napkin and then her hands.

"You aren't a baby killer," he said, a statement not a question. "I saw your face when you saw what they'd done to the meat. You were horrified by it. You aren't a baby killer," he repeated.

"No, not a baby killer. Just a killer."

His elbows slid to his knees, and he clasped his hands together until his knuckles were white. "Will you hurt me?"

She shook her head, afraid of the tremble in her voice if she spoke.

"I'm about to get kicked out of the colony. Colten is packing our things right now."

Heart sinking, she leaned against the wall and closed her eyes. He'd go and never think about her again, while she'd always wonder if he would've been half the friend she thought he could be.

"You don't want me to go?" he asked, searching her face.

Her answer was muffled by the contraption on her face. "No."

"Then come with me." Staring at him, sure she'd misheard, he plowed forward. "Colten and I were on our way out of here anyway, headed to Mexico. The Deads are migrating there, gathering at the coast, and there is going to be a battle if they stay like that for long. Colonies are shipping entire stashes of ammunition and weapons to annihilate as much of the Dead population as possible."

"How do you know they'll still be there?"

"I don't, but I want to help if there's a need. This could turn the tide either way. It feels…big." His eyes lifted to hers. "*You* feel big, Soren. Important. Your destiny isn't here where you're caged. You're different for a reason, and it's not to take shit from some asshole humans who take pleasure in putting you down because they're losing a war they don't understand. The world is bigger than this place."

"You don't understand."

"Make me understand then. You want the cure to cure yourself, right? It's the easiest thing to see in the world, but maybe you don't need to be cured, Soren. Did you ever think about that? Maybe you're better than all of us, a superior species, and curing yourself would only be a step back. It would make you just like every other Tom, Dick, and Harry out here."

Her parents had said variations of the same thing, but it had never really touched her. She wanted companionship though, and no one wanted to spend time with a Dead. Her kind had killed their families, loved ones, and friends. No one would ever get over that until she looked differently, ate differently, acted differently. So Kaegan picked up on her need to find a way out. So what? He still knew next to nothing about her.

"My place is here. I'm sorry to see you go, but Dead Run River is my home. Good luck with your crusade."

A fearsome expression came over his face and he didn't move for a long time. Pointing to the weapons that decorated her wall, he said, "Do you practice still?"

"No need to here."

"You'll wither if you stay. If you're a killer like you say, make it count for something. This colony has been trying to manufacture a cure since day one of the outbreak twenty-four years ago, and they still don't have it. Who knows if they ever will? It could be too big for us, like AIDS or cancer. You're fighting the wrong battle, Soren. You could be part of what saves us all."

Her heart was ripping in two. Deny it all she wanted, but everything he said made her burn for a cause that required action. But if she left, she'd never be human. Not entirely. She'd always be Other. Swallowing the sob that threatened to escape, she looked away. "Please leave."

The floorboards creaked as he stood and strode across her home. Only when he'd descended down the ladder and disappeared into the woods did she allow herself the tears that had been so heavy lately.

What he said was true. She'd atrophy until she was nothing. A fat, tamed bear who lived for food and a comfortable place to lay, begging for compliments from handlers who couldn't ever really love her.

Life had been so simple before Kaegan came along. She lived day to day, kept her head down, but then he showed up, challenged her to take more pride in herself at the risk of losing her home. Damn him. She shrieked and threw the chair, still warm from his body, onto the ground below. It shattered into a million splinters, just like she had.

"Soren?" Seamus asked from the first rung of the ladder. "Are you okay?"

Hastily, she wiped her eyes with the back of her hand. "I'm fine."

"I just passed Kaegan. What did he want?"

"For me to go away with him to fight some imaginary war against the Deads."

He wore a frown as he hopped onto the entryway of her house. "In Mexico?"

"Yeah, did he try to convince you to go join his cause too?"

"No. A messenger was in Mel's office when I went to talk to her. It was all he talked about." He looked slowly from the ground to her face and breathed, "Maybe you should go."

"Ha ha, Seamus. Very funny." She plopped onto her mattress and stared at the swaying branches above.

"What is keeping you here? The cure? It's a pipe dream with Doc fading."

"I can't leave you, Seamus. You're my only friend."

"That's not true." His voice was careful, calculating. "I can't go with you. Battling Deads was never my thing. But you and Adrianna?"

He sat cross legged on her floor and peered at the longest of her battle knives. "It's in your blood."

"Be serious. I'm not going to just leave with a total stranger. And both of them have gimp legs. They shouldn't even be out there in the condition they're in. It's a disaster waiting to happen."

"Not if you were there. You have hidden yourself from everyone here, but you can't hide what you really are from me. I've known you all my life, remember? Pretend all you want that you are harmless to the people here and the Deads out there," he said, pointing beyond the gates. "I know the truth. Don't make a decision based on me, Sor. I've had to watch you suffer here, and it rips my guts out. You are the daughter of Laney Landry and Derek Mitchell, and you're wearing a fucking muzzle. Who says in here is any better than what you'll face out there?"

"Please stop," she pleaded. She couldn't take it. The decision was too big. Go fight alongside a man she barely knew, or stay here for a chance at normalcy. Couldn't they see the choice was clear?

Seamus stood and brushed the seat of his pants to dislodge the leaves and dust. "Go live. I'm tired of watching you die here."

Overwhelmed, she drew him into a tight embrace, squeezing him as she rested her muzzled chin on his shoulder. Hesitant hands went around her waist, and he sighed. "Send word you're safe from time to time, will you?"

Silence stretched on forever between them before she finally whispered, "I promise."

Chapter Six

The sun was sinking lower and shadows stretched across the forest floor, like gnarled hands reaching for her. *Turn back*, they seemed to say. Even if Soren could, she was too far in it now. The excitement of freedom was too tempting a lure to be burdened by logic.

The cold hard fact, though, was that she'd gone half-cocked into the Dead-filled woods following two complete strangers who'd had two hours head start. They hadn't had loose ends to tie up in Dead Run River — the benefit of being strangers. She, however, had been there two years, and even if most looked relieved at her revelation that she was leaving, she still felt the need to say good-byes to anyone who'd showed her a kindness over the duration of her stay. Z she might be, but she was a Z with manners.

It should have been a lot more difficult to track Kaegan and Colten. For a human it would've been a real challenge, but she'd been trailing them for hours, just far enough back they didn't notice her. In fact, Kaegan didn't seem to notice much of anything, to the seemingly everlasting irritation of his friend, Colten. He stared in silence, taking long strides that hitched with the limp of a twisted ankle. It was Colten who she'd tracked. He was louder than anything else in the woods with his running commentary, and his leg was seeping. It smelled delicious. His bandage was pungent enough that she'd followed on scent alone for a while, and she wasn't the only one he'd attracted. A Dead shuffled beside her, badly injured and slow, but still intent on catching up to the two humans in front of her.

That idiot, Colten, was going to get them all killed.

She frowned at Kaegan's tense back through the trees. Something about Colten's carelessness made her angry. She didn't want Kaegan to die. Didn't want to see his face reanimated on a Dead. Perhaps Colten could be loud and bold because the vaccine gave him some sort of invincibility complex. He'd survived the bite on his leg after all, but Kaegan didn't have the benefit of immunity, and that put him at higher risk.

"What do you think?" she asked the Dead to her right. "Which one would you eat first?"

He was a skinny thing, and his leg had been broken in half at some point in his jaunt around the mountains looking for human snacks. His blue tinted flesh was sunken around the curves of his bones, and shoulders and ribs showed through the tattered mechanic shirt that still clung to his withered body. *Bob*, the name patch on his stained pocket read. She cocked her head and tried to imagine what he looked like before most of his face had rotted off. Maybe he'd looked like a Bob once.

He was slow and little danger to the men in front of them at this distance. They'd attracted him around the same time she'd found him, and it had been three hours and counting that they hadn't noticed they were being hunted. At this point, it was just sad.

Limping badly, the Dead stayed focused ahead, not even a groan for an answer to her question, and she shrugged. Corpses weren't the best conversationalists.

"Are you going to tell me what's going on with you or is this how it's going to be all the way to the coast?" Colten asked. "You haven't said two words since we left. I get it. You're the stoic type and all. That's why we work well together. You are the big loner who gets shit handled, and I'm the social one who gets us invited into colonies. This sucks though, man." Colten stared at him while they walked. "At the very least, you owe me an explanation on why you got us kicked out of Dead Run River over a fucking zombie."

"Don't say that," Kaegan growled.

"Fine. A *freaking* zombie."

Warning hummed in the tension of Kaegan's shoulders.

"Please don't tell me you were crushing on her, man. She'd eat you in your sleep and pick her teeth with your bone splinters. We're better off getting out of there if that's the case. That place was messed up, wasn't it? Deads inside the gates. I mean, damn, how stupid could they be? She should've been banished or caged, or I don't know, something."

A numb feeling crept over Soren as she listened. This was probably what everyone said about her when she wasn't around. She didn't want it said to Kaegan, though. If he hadn't already thought of all of it, Colten was just going to fill his head with reasons to hate her. Maybe this had been a bad idea.

Kaegan paused and turned slowly to Colten, saying something much too low for her to hear at this distance.

"Aw, crap," she muttered. "Sorry, Bob. I can't have you gnawing on my team, so this is the end of the line for you, buddy. Sorry," she whispered as she stood in front of him and slid a battle knife through his temple. Other than the rustle of leaves, he dropped without a sound.

Staring at his crumpled body, she sighed. He'd been somebody once. The only thing Bob had done to earn an empty life was get himself bitten.

"We'll make camp here for the night. The grove behind us will act as a natural barrier," Kaegan said. "You want to take care of the moaner that's been following us or you want me to?"

"I'll do it. You go take the two coming at us from over there." He gestured toward an embankment.

Soren tilted her ear in that direction. Huh. Sure enough, a pair of distant moans sounded over whispering leaves. So they'd known about Bob the entire time; they just didn't feel threatened enough to pick up the pace or fight him earlier. Maybe they weren't as incapable as she had begun to think over the past few hours.

Slipping behind a tree, she held her breath as Colten searched for Bob. He froze, likely listening for the movement typical of Deads, but when only the quiet rustling of branches sounded, he pulled a hatchet from his back. The blade whispered against its sheath, and Colten turned with a suspicious glower. "Where are you?" he muttered.

The *you* he spoke of was about fifteen yards to his left, half hidden by trees and leaves, staring vacantly in his direction and definitely dead as a doornail. Colten just wasn't looking low enough. The rough tree bark she leaned against was steady against the slight tremble that shook her limbs.

He stepped closer and Soren held her breath. Now he stood just on the other side of the large oak she hid behind.

Another step closer.

"Colten? What's taking so long?" Kaegan called.

"Nothing. I think we lost the Dead." He lowered his voice and muttered, "That or you bored him to death with the dullness of your silence."

Footsteps retreated, and when they were far enough away, she dared a peek from her hiding tree. Kaegan wiped the blade of a long machete on a tuft of grass, turning it red.

"Do we have anything to eat?" Kaegan asked.

"No. You left us zero time to gather supplies before you got us in a fight with a bunch of off duty guards and got us booted, remember?"

Unable to shake the feeling their hunger was her fault somehow, she turned and searched the ground for small rocks the perfect shape for the leather strip she'd use as a sling shot.

Kaegan had been a raging idiot. Without thinking it through, he'd jumped up to defend someone who didn't need it. Soren could've lobbed off that prick's head if she wanted. She'd been defending herself for God knew how long before he stumbled into her life. If ever there was a woman who needed a man like she needed a bullet hole, Soren was that woman. He'd heard Mel loud and clear when she said Soren was a murderer, and he didn't doubt it. She was the fiercest creature he'd ever seen. No innocent looked like that.

But when that jackhole, Andrew, taunted her in front of his friends, something inside of him had snapped. Beating his sneering face settled something scary inside of him. Watching the way people treated her around the colony made him feel nauseous. It was over now, and he wouldn't see her again, so it didn't do him any good to overanalyze what it was about the creature that made him want to protect her.

Still, it was impossible not to think about the tragedy of her cage. She was a tiger on a jeweled leash. Train her all they wanted, but someday the wild would reclaim her. And a piece of him wished he could be there to watch her rise to her potential — like a damned phoenix — instead of cowering behind that contraption on her face.

With a growl, he snapped the twig he'd been stripping in two and chucked it into the darkening woods. Colten was right. It was a good thing they got out of there when they did.

When he glanced in the direction the sticks had flown, there she crouched. Animal hide traveling pants clung to the tensed muscles of her legs, and an earth colored vest hugged her torso like a second skin, exposing shoulders, neck, and alluring collar bones that stood out against her pale skin. The muzzle sat stubbornly across the bottom half of her face. In her hands was the twig he'd just snapped.

"What are you thinking about?" she asked.

Such a personal question should've unsettled him. At the very least, her unexpected presence here should've had his heart racing. It was weird that he felt so calm. She canted her head as she waited, like his answer mattered. "You," he breathed.

The sound of Colten's knife sliding from its sheath was loud against the breezeless evening.

"What are you doing here, Dead?" Colten asked, taking a defensive stance beside him.

"I asked her to come." Kaegan followed her graceful movement as she stood.

The lift to her chin was brave, rebellious, and he followed her to stand.

"Why would you do that?" Colten asked, never taking his eyes from Soren. Venom and shock permeated his words.

The answer stayed lodged in his throat. He hadn't the power to explain why he'd wanted her to come. Her fate was bigger than that place she was trying to call home, but was it with them? He didn't know anything anymore. Since seeing her, learning of her existence, everything had gone upside down and stayed that way.

"No response at all? Really? She's isn't even human, Kaegan. Look at her!"

Soren pulled sunglasses over her eyes. "There. Better?"

Colten shook his head and stared at him like he should be as offended as he was. "No, it's not better! Now you look like a Dead wearing sunglasses!"

If he hurt her feelings, Soren didn't show it. Instead, she shrugged her shoulders like she'd tried, then tossed a trio of small, foxlike animals to the forest floor beside Colten's planted boots.

"What is this?" he asked.

"They're called American martens. Cooked, they're edible for you. A good source of protein too."

Kaegan picked up one of the small animals, the size of a large jackrabbit and turned the limp game in his hand. How had she known they needed food? He looked up slowly. "How long were you following us?"

"Since you picked up the Dead to your rear."

"And what happened to the Dead? He wasn't there when I went to find him." Colten still held his knife, which looked like a pushpin compared to the battle sword that hung from Soren's back. His weapon wouldn't be their saving grace if ever Soren decided to end them.

"Bob is dead," came the muffled reply. "Really dead."

"Bob?"

"That's what his name tag said."

"Oh, that's just fantastic. Fantastic, Kaegan. She's naming the monsters. You invited a Dead to travel with us like we're an actual team, and she's a freaking sympathizer on top of it all. Not only will we have to sleep with one eye open to keep her from eating us alive, she's going to invite all of her little undead friends to join in the buffet the second we let our guard down. This is a terrible idea."

"She killed the Dead. And besides, what is your other option? You want to walk back to Dead Run River in the dark and see if they'll take you back? We won't survive long as a two man team, surely you know that. It's too few fighters. With three we stand a better chance." He tossed one of the martens to Soren, and she caught it easily. "She stays. Her place is with us now."

"So you just make all of the decisions now? Dick, it's been me and you since we were three feet tall. We've always made these decisions together."

"I'll take first watch," Soren said quietly, before melting into the trees with the animal hanging limply from her hand.

"You're right," Kaegan said, squatting near his pack to find the fire starter. "We should discuss this. It isn't fair for me to invite people into the team without talking to you about it. Tell me your concerns, and we'll try to figure out the best solution."

"Okay," he said, holding up his marten. "How do we know she didn't inject these with the Dead contagion? Hmm? She has easy access to it obviously."

"She can smell that you're vaccinated, so that wouldn't even affect you, and if she wanted to turn me, why did she kill Bob?"

"Don't." He gritted his teeth and shook his head. "Don't call the Deads by name. They're Deads, zombies, skin eaters, risers, moaners, devourers of blood and bone, reanimators. Don't give them human qualities. They aren't anything like us anymore."

"My point is — why wouldn't she just let him continue hunting us if she wanted me turned? Or hell, why not just bite us in our sleep back in the colony? She's quiet enough. I didn't hear her tracking us, did you? And why is she still wearing the muzzle? It has to be uncomfortable, and she doesn't have anyone here telling her she has to keep it on."

"Okay, that's my rule then. If she's going to tag along, the muzzle stays on."

"Come on, Colten —"

"No, Kaegan. If she stays, we're going to be safe about it." His voice hissed to a whisper. "That entire colony was scared of her. They treated her like they did for reasons we know nothing about. If the mask keeps us even a little safer from your colossally bad decision, she's wearing it. And if I agree to this, she's on serious probation. First colony we come to, I get a say in whether she continues to travel with us or not."

Kaegan bit back his frustration. He'd never seen Colten wary like this, and maybe his friend was right to be careful. "Deal."

Colten slid his knife against the pelt of the marten. "If we survive a day, it'll be a miracle."

Funny, that's what he'd thought when he'd dragged Colten's unconscious body to Dead Run River.

Chapter Seven

Soren had heard all of Colten's concerns, late into the night in fact. His imagination was quiet creative on ways she'd find to kill them. Some made her queasy, some inflamed her insecurities, and some just made her giggle with their absurdity. She was fairly sure she wasn't going to drape their intestines around her neck like a feather boa and dance through the woods singing about her cunning anytime soon.

Kaegan's eyes drifted in her direction often, but she tried to stay out of range. The moon was only half full and bathed everything in deep blue, so it wasn't too hard to avoid him. The risk of his smoldering gaze on her felt dangerous and left chill bumps on her forearms.

"I'll spell you when you get tired," he called to Colten, before lying under a blue tarp draped over a line of rope and held down with stones. Minutes ticked by, then the steady rhythm of his breathing indicated he had no trouble sleeping in the woods.

The tree branches would be much safer for him. She didn't give a guano about Colten, but Kaegan would be well served by having a tree harness.

The smaller man sat ramrod straight against the base of the tree Kaegan slept near like he was prepared to defend his friend's sleeping body from her uncontrolled appetite. What they didn't know about her could fill an ocean. Turning from his death glare, she pushed away from the coarse trunk she'd leaned against and started another perimeter search.

Leaves and dry branches whispered beneath her careful step, and as the wind shifted, she froze. They were coming. A sensitivity to the smell of Deads was something she'd inherited from her mom. The difference was Mom had known what it was like to have a sniffer just like everyone else before she'd been bitten the first time. The smell of rot was something Soren had learned to deal with from a young age. It didn't even bother her now. She used to gag and lose her appetite when she was a little girl, but the smell had become a part of her life that she'd accepted. It was that or live in misery. Deads were everywhere. The world stank of them.

The odor of decay became stronger the closer the Deads came. The scent was laced with woodsy smells of vegetation, soil, and animals. And underneath it all was exactly what was bringing them in like sharks to chum.

Colten was bleeding again.

Pulling a roll of gauze from her pack, she approached him like she would a rabid badger. When she stood ten feet away, she tossed him the bandages. "You're bringing the Deads to us."

"What are you talking about? I don't hear anything. Stop being paranoid and go back over there somewhere."

His knife shone in the moonlight. She hadn't a clue when he'd pulled it, but perhaps he'd never sheathed it in the first place.

They'd definitely started on the wrong foot, what with the stabbing and all. "I'm Soren."

"I don't care."

She bit her lip against the curse that rattled in her chest and shifted her weight. How was she supposed to talk to someone who'd damned her with their judgment before they even knew her? "You're bleeding, and it'll bring in more Deads than we can handle alone. Please."

"You can smell blood?" His lip curled up in apparent disgust.

"And Deads. Trust me when I say they're coming. Hand me the bloody gauze, and I'll try to lead them in another direction."

"Screw you. I'm not giving you my used bandages so you can go suck on them in some dark corner of the woods. Don't involve me in your weird plans."

The rough tent flapped lazily in the breeze. Kaegan would be more receptive to what they had to do, but he'd only had a few hours of sleep, and she needed him rested if they were going to make it to the next colony. "Okay," she said then turned.

Moron. Less-than-useless, boneheaded dimwit. Was his pride so big that he couldn't believe she wasn't trying to lure them to their death? Now she was going to have to do something that turned her stomach. She thought of Kaegan, breathing softly against his arm in the tent and suddenly she was scared of the depths she'd go to keep him safe. He'd been kind when he had no reason to be. Offered her escape at great risk to himself. She may not deserve to exist, but he did. Good people still lived, and she'd make her life mean something by keeping his intact.

The wind caressed the trees as she strained her eyes in the dark. Closing them, she drew air into her lungs and sought a direction. She spun slowly until the smell became stronger from the west, and quietly, she drew a dagger from its sheath on her thigh.

The first Dead was three hundred yards from camp, zeroed in and headed straight for the resting men behind her. Spinning the hilt in her hand, she ran, chest heaving as she jammed the blade into his face, then moved to the next. The grouping wasn't tight and she had trouble tracking each down in the dark. At least with all the racket the moaning Deads were making around her, none would likely go after the men at camp. There was enough disturbance right here to hold their attention. This close to the stench, it was hard to tell where it came from. The air was saturated with death. One by one, they came, and she lost count after twelve. She shook and gritted her teeth against the unsavory job. Lucky number thirteen overwhelmed her. She missed with her dagger, miscalculating how tall he was in the dark, and his hand clamped on her upper arm in a painful grip. She tried to pull away, but he pushed her backward and snapped his yellow teeth at her face. Grunting, she scanned the woods for an escape. The commotion drew the other Deads to them, and four gruesome faces appeared out of the shadows. Hands stretched, bones gnarled into claws, they came for her.

Panic flared in her chest. She'd been stupid going out alone. Her skills were rusty after being long stifled by safety. Dead Run River hadn't protected her at all. It had made her weak. Blinking, she tried desperately to remember all Finn, Guist, her parents, Vanessa, and Sean had taught her.

The Dead's grip was unbreakable as she stretched away from him, but she ducked and barreled into his stomach, overextending her arm. He bent at the waist, and his gnashing teeth came for her back. His groaning breath came so close, it lifted the hair on her neck, and she stifled the scream that clawed its way up the back of her throat. Kicking his legs from beneath him, she pulled her battle sword as she landed on him. It wasn't graceful, but the blade made a long arc before his head was severed. Her right arm wasn't working anymore, and her left wasn't dominant, but out of options, she lurched upward, shoving the blade as she rose. A sick noise sounded as she made contact with a Dead woman with scraggly hair and blood on her mouth like she'd just eaten. Kicking her stomach, she tried to dislodge the sword from it, but with only one arm, she failed.

Next weapon, Finn's voice whispered on the wind.

Pulling a curved blade from a loop at her back, she hacked the next two and fell to her knees with the effort. Surrounded by bodies, she swallowed a gag that surged through her. Nothing stirred but the dry pine needles in the path of a stiff breeze.

Her time at Dead Run River had turned her soft, and that had to change if she was going to be of any use to anyone.

The crackle of leaves underfoot gave her a sense of relief. Kaegan had come to check on her, or maybe Colten. Any living face was better than what she'd just seen and done. The smile fell from her lips as she realized there was a lot of movement in the woods. Too much for just two men.

A tiny hole in the tarp made the perfect path for a single sunray to bean Kaegan in the sleeping eyeball. Like a fungus escaping light, he flinched backward and directly into a bigger pool of dawn's proof.

Dawn.

He shot up and shoved the blue tarp flap out of the way. The stones that had pinned the edges flew this way and that, and he looked wildly around for Colten.

His friend snored soundly against the tree to his left. What the hell? Maybe Soren really didn't get how this team thing worked. Searching the immediate area turned up no sign of the woman. It wasn't okay to refuse to wake them, then fall asleep somewhere. He kicked Colten's boot and searched the canopy. Where was she?

Colten groaned and stretched his stiff neck. Served him right for sleeping upright against a tree.

"Have you seen Soren?"

Colten shot him an irritable look and rubbed his nape. "You mean the Dead who's traveling with us against both of our better judgment? Not since the middle of the night. I drifted off. Obviously."

Piss mood grump was always Colten's favorite persona in the mornings.

"Soren?" he called.

"Shhhut up," Colten hissed. "You're going to bring every Dead within a mile to us. She probably went back to the colony. Camping rough doesn't suit many women, Kaegan. You were never going to impress Dead girl with this lifestyle—hate to break it to you."

Kaegan rested his hands on his waist and glared at the empty woods. "What was the last thing she said to you?"

"Some bullshit about how I was bleeding, and she needed all of my bandages for a midnight snack."

His patience was about as thin as rice paper, and Colten was asking for a fat lip. "Did she give you those?" he asked, pointing to a clean roll of gauze that had been tossed haphazardly to the side.

"Maybe."

"Let me see your leg."

"Why?"

"Geez, you f—" Bending down, he yanked Colten's pant leg up to his knee and shook his head at the moist, red bandages. "That's just great. She wanted you to change your bandages for a reason. Soren!"

He took off aimlessly through the woods. What if something had happened? Or what if she had decided to go back to colony? Or what if she hadn't, and they eventually left her hurt somewhere without knowing it? A separated team was a fighter's worst nightmare. Trevor and Mike attested to that. They were roaming these woods now as the monsters they'd spent a lifetime killing.

Heart pounding against his chest, he ran through the trees, but nothing stirred save the morning birds singing from the branches above. Taking a left, he slowed to a jog and called her name again.

"Kaegan!" Colten called. "We can't get split up, you dunce."

Around a thick grove, in a small clearing, Soren panted and shoveled dirt over a wide hole like she raced time to get it filled. Kaegan skidded to a stop, relief and confusion warring within him. She used her left hand, and her right arm hung limply at her side. Perspiration poured down her face, and she blinked hard as it dripped into her eyes.

When she saw him, she struggled to her feet, chest heaving.

"What the hell is she doing?" Colten asked from beside him.

Kaegan took a slow step toward her and then another. The hole wasn't deep, but considering the small shovel, it had taken extreme effort. Inside the damp earth, filth-covered faces of Deads stared vacantly at the sky, arms and legs tangled in their final resting place. She'd dug a mass grave. Unable to keep the shock from his expression, he dragged his gaze to hers, but she looked only at the carnage at her feet.

"What happened to them all?" he asked.

She shot Colten a fiery look he didn't understand and swung around to him. "Me," she answered.

He searched her face to see if she was joking, but she just stared and sucked breath like she'd never catch it again. Ticking off bodies, he tried to count heads, but couldn't because of the layers. Two layers deep. Twenty-six at least.

"Why are you burying Deads, Z?" Colten asked. Disgust soaked every word.

"Don't call me that."

"It's what everyone at that colony called you. I heard them. Why?"

"Because they deserve a proper burial. I can't do it for all of them, but I could do it for this group."

"They aren't people!" Colten barked. "They've done horrible things. They aren't starved. The remains of living, breathing people are in their bellies, and you held a funeral for them?"

"Yes! And I'd hold a funeral for you too, Colten, if you were turned. Why? Because the shit you do when you're a Dead isn't on you. It's the disease's instinct to spread to healthy hosts that is responsible for the awful, awful things they do."

Her arm looked painful, hanging listlessly from her torso, and Kaegan gestured to it. "What happened?"

"I don't know. One of the Deads turned out to be a lot stronger than I expected and yanked it."

"Colten, can you pack up camp and grab my bag?"

"Gladly," he muttered before stomping off.

"He's a tough sell," Kaegan said apologetically.

"Isn't everyone?" she asked. Her otherworldly eyes searched his, steady and curious.

He imagined that before the apocalypse, the answer had been no, but the world was different now. Harder. Drawing up beside her, he felt for a broken bone, but the shoulder was just dislocated. "I'm going to have to pop this back in."

"Will it work again?"

"Yeah, but it'll be real sore for a few days. Oh." He frowned at the soft curve of her collar bone. "I mean, it would be if you felt that kind of stuff."

Unsettling pale eyes rested on him for a moment before she nodded. The top of her shoulder was bruised like something had crushed the skin there, but she did little more than grimace as he rotated the arm into place.

Palpating the arm to make sure the bone was in the socket once again, he asked, "So you feel some of it then? You winced."

"It's a dull ache, not pain." She seemed to withdraw from him and then twitched her head to the side like she was embarrassed. "When I was little, I broke my arm. It was the first time I felt the ache, but I didn't know what it meant. It was winter, and I'd fallen off this playground set my parents and their friends had put together for us. No one was around, and I didn't want to bother anyone. And besides, I had a sweater on and didn't take a good look at the injury. So for two days, the dull throbbing was constant and finally my mom asked why I was favoring my arm." She held out her forearm and a long jagged scar showed silver against her milky skin. "The bone was sticking through, and it was the first time we realized my lack of nerve reaction was another symptom of whatever I am."

Sitting on a fallen trunk, he picked a blade of grass and tore it into strips. "Whatever you are? Aren't you a Dead and a human?"

"It's not that simple. My mom didn't boink a Dead. My parents are both human, but my mother has first generation immunity. I'm second generation, but she carried the virus after being bitten. It's in her blood, and when I was in her stomach, something happened to me. The virus warred with my genetic immunity, and I was born —" she flexed her injured hand and lifted her shoulders to her ears "—like this."

So she wasn't a Dead? Or she was but not genetically? Or maybe she was only a carrier and that's what caused her to look different? His head swam, and he opened his mouth to ask more.

"Let's go," Colten bit out as he tossed Kaegan's backpack onto the ground beside him.

Soren stared blankly at the unfinished grave, and he took the shovel from her good hand. "Let me. It'll go faster."

Despite Colten's grumbling, he didn't seem to mind burying the bodies anymore. The practice was executed for practical purposes around colonies to stop the spread of the disease. And sure, Soren was obviously doing it for sentimental reasons, but looking at her, it was easy to understand why she felt a connection with the Deads. It was wrong, but still understandable.

"We need to go west," she said as he pulled his backpack over his shoulders.

"No," Colten drawled. "We need to go south. To the coast."

"We won't make it there with what we have. We need supplies, better weapons, food. Possibly even a few more members for our team who we can trust."

"Where do you suggest we go to find all of this?" Kaegan asked.

"The Denver Colony."

"Wait, wait, wait." Colten's face morphed into a disbelieving smile. "Sean Daniel's colony?"

"The one and only." She turned and set out at a fast clip.

Colten's mouth hung open, and Kaegan smirked as he followed Soren.

"Wait, so we're just — we're just going to go visit Sean Daniels? Just roll up and be like, hey, let's do brunch?"

"He's a fan," Kaegan explained when Soren turned around with a suspicious frown.

"No, no, Kaegan, don't make it weird," Colten muttered. God, his friend was blushing like an idiot. There was a hundred percent chance he was going to freak out if he ever got to meet his idol.

"I'm not making it weird. You are." Turning to Soren, he grinned. "We used to play like we were leaders of the greatest colony in America when we were growing up, and Colten always played Sean Daniels."

A tinkling giggle trilled from behind the muzzle, and Kaegan got an uncanny urge to rip the thing off so he could see the smile behind it.

"And who did you play?"

"Myself, naturally."

"Oh, so you had big plans to run a colony someday?"

"You laugh, but that's what I wanted to do when I grew up."

"And instead you became a gym rat."

He huffed a surprised laugh. Never in his life had he been to a gym. "If you're talking about my size, it comes from my occupation."

"Which is a Paul Bunyan impersonator?" she asked over her shoulder.

The stretch of the smile over his face felt good. "A fence builder. A welder. Hauling metal is strenuous work."

"And Colten was a toothpick whittler. Or a cook? Chicken chaser?"

"I just got dissed by a Dead," Colten muttered from behind. "And for the record, I was a welder too. I just didn't, you know, haul the materials as much as Hulk Smash over here."

"Is there a big demand for your work?"

"Yeah, surprisingly. Most gates and fences are made of metal these days. In fact, Dead Run River was the first one I've seen with wood in a few years. We've spent the last six years traveling from colony to colony. The new ones always need a lot of labor to build."

"Isn't it dangerous to build the colonies?" Soren asked. "I mean, Deads are probably attracted to the commotion, right?"

"That's where it comes in handy to be able to fight," he said grimly.

"How much farther?" Colten asked.

Soren squinted at the rising sun. "About a day and a half walk from here."

"In the wrong direction," he muttered.

"It's the right direction if it ensures we get to the coast safely," Soren sang.

Her blond hair, braided and feathered like some fierce warrior, lifted in the breeze, and the leather leggings she wore hugged her curves. Bladed weapons clanked against her back with every step, and from time to time, she'd look to the side and gift him with a perfect muzzled profile.

A day and a half walking behind Soren?

That, he could do.

Chapter Eight

"What?" Soren asked suspiciously. Kaegan had shot her so many furtive glances over the past few hours, she was becoming breathless under the scrutiny.

"Nothing."

Colten trailed them, basically stomping through the woods in a fair rendition of an adult tantrum.

Gray flashed again as he snuck another look.

"Just ask," she bit out impatiently.

"Why do you wear the muzzle still? We aren't in Dead Run River anymore." He looked around. "No one is making you wear it."

Clamping her mouth closed, she regretted telling him to ask questions. Yeah, she wasn't in Dead Run River, so she didn't have to answer to anyone anymore. But he watched her, limping badly, his dark hair loose and whipping around in the breeze. He was big and scary, yet he was looking at her like her answer mattered.

Sighing, she said, "I wear it for your safety."

Long moments passed before he quietly said, "Mel told me things about you."

Her muscles seized, her blood chilled, and it became impossible to swallow. She stared at the dark clouds coming in from the east.

Sunlight still bathed her face, but it wouldn't for long. She'd hold on to his good opinion for as long as she could. Forever, if he'd let her get away with it.

"Did you hear me?" he asked.

"Look, I don't know you and you don't know me. I don't have to tell you about everything I've done or seen, and I won't ask it of you. Lay off it, okay?"

"She wears it so she doesn't snack on our livers, Kaegan," Colten said. "I vote she keeps the damned thing on. If she's concerned, we should be concerned."

"Thank you," she said with a curt nod. She wasn't thankful at all to the little twit, but at least in his ramblings, he sometimes became the voice of reason to his less careful companion.

The air smelled of moisture the deeper into the woods they traveled and she shot another suspicious glance at the impending storm brewing. Lightning slashed across the sky. Bad weather was moving closer at a furious pace. She'd always had to fight the instinct to avoid water. It was something ingrained in her since birth. Just another similarity to the Deads, and now a little alarm in her head screamed to run from the coming downpour.

And if her instincts were screaming…

"Guys," she said, slowing.

"Don't be a wuss, Z," Colten said as he clomped by with an empty smile. "It's just a little rain."

"Guys," she repeated, stopping in her tracks as the first droplet hit her arm.

"Soren," Kaegan said, slowing enough to look back at her. "We travel in rain or shine. We can't afford to waste time camping out in a shelter over a little rain. If it gets bad enough, I promise, we'll stop."

"You don't understand. Deads avoid water." Her hand hovered over the hilt of the knife tied to her thigh, body humming with readiness caused by fear that sat right above her senses.

"Great. Then we'll be nice and safe in the storm."

A twig snapped to the east and the brush shook with movement that made her draw the blade.

"Unless," Kaegan murmured, eyes on the shuddering woods around them. "Unless the Deads are running from the storm."

"Bingo," she said, forcing herself into a jog. "Run."

Colten stared at the brush as the first groan reached her ears. "Run!" she yelled again, shoving him in the back.

He stumbled, but righted himself just as the first wave of Deads stepped through the trees. Four, all soaking wet and on the run. Shirts were plastered to their emaciated frames, and their mouths hung open. Gray, vacant eyes swung to their movement, and they switched directions, hunger apparently overriding any deep-seated instinct to avoid the rain that would decay their bodies faster.

In a tight line, they fled. She gasped for breath after the first mile and cursed Dead Run River for her lack of stamina. Kaegan wasn't even breathing hard. Daring a glance behind her, she did a quick body count.

"How many," Kaegan said with a hard look.

"Fourteen."

The rain poured over them, dousing the sound of the groans behind them with a pureness only Mother Nature could offer. He jerked his head toward a pine, the only one they'd seen with branches drooping low enough for any of them to climb. It was too small for his weight though, and Kaegan gave her a significant look.

"Up you go," she said to Colten and pointed to the tree with her knife.

"We can't all fit on that," he argued.

"No, but you can," Kaegan said. "Hurry up and we'll draw them away. Stay here tonight, and if we're able, we'll come back. If we aren't back by dawn, follow the river west of us to the Denver Colony."

"Splitting up is a bad idea," he panted.

"You can't go much longer on that leg." Kaegan was almost yelling to be heard over the downpour. "We have a better shot if we take to the trees where we can. This is your stop."

Colten cursed ungraciously and tore away from their trio. Kaegan's eyes followed his friend as his limp deepened beside her. His loyalty, though it made her care about him more, was going to get him killed. Her too, because she wouldn't leave him to the insatiable hunger that drew ever closer behind them.

She cut toward the river, determined to save him. "You swim, right?"

"Not well," he answered.

"Better than a Dead?"

A smile curved the corner of his mouth. "Better than a Dead."

That was good enough for her. They raced for hours, or so it seemed, because every painful step he took tore at her innards. She'd never felt pain before, but she'd gladly take his, no matter how badly it burned. The Deads stumbled as they did, in the mud and the muck, but inch by inch, they gained on them. Soaked to the bone, pain etched on his face and determination lightening his eyes, Kaegan was beautiful. Even with a limp, he was lithe and graceful. He didn't groan in pain or give up and when she stumbled over a branch hidden in the mire, he reached out and yanked her upright before she fell face first to the ground. His hand stayed firmly on her arm as they ran, like he didn't want to risk a chance of separating, and she stared at his large fist closed over her skin. He didn't even flinch away.

Hands clawed at her back, and she pushed herself harder, faster until her legs burned with the effort. "There!" she yelled over the rumble of thunder.

A bank dropped off, and the other side stretched four hundred yards away. But where she thought it had been a shallow bank, when they drew up alongside it, the river raged far beneath them, and a rocky ledge separated them from the churning, black waters beneath. Who knew how deep it was? Surely not deep enough to sustain a fall from this height. If they dove, they could break their necks.

Gasping, the woods ahead of them came to life as six more Deads stumbled toward them.

Trapped.

Kaegan's glance didn't offer fear or hesitation. Pulling her behind him, he set their backs to the ledge of the river below. He drew a wicked looking *kukri* machete, the black blade repelling the rain droplets that assaulted it. The tip was sharp, and it curved into a thick weapon for hacking, only to flow to a thinner base that disappeared into the hilt.

Of course he'd have a weapon like this Bringer of Destruction he held ready in his hands. She peered around the breadth of his shoulders at the horde coming for them and smiled at his thoughtfulness. She could go on a good deed. Stepping beside him, she pulled the blades from her back, the battle sword and the smaller dagger with matching metal and shape. Sure, she could walk away without a single bite. Deads didn't want to eat her after all. She didn't smell like food. But something fundamental had changed inside her the day Kaegan had walked into Doc's office. That single sympathetic look as he'd pulled Colten's knife from her stomach had changed her makeup. He was hers, and he'd never even know it.

This right here, in the rain and mud, with their backs to an impossible escape, was their stand, and they'd make it together.

She screamed a battle cry as Kaegan yelled his and pulled her sword down on the first Dead. The snick of Kaegan's machete came close as he fought, but he'd done battle with a team before and worry over being cut came second to the growing number of moaners that pushed them closer to the ledge. As she pulled the sword from another, she spun and flipped the hilt of the smaller blade in the air, catching it just she brought it to the temple of a woman not long turned. Grunting, she pulled both blades free and kicked the next Dead in the chest. Raindrops flung from the fingertips of his outstretched hands as he reached for her before launching backward. She swung the blades once more and lodged them into a pair of monsters headed for Kaegan. From the corner of her vision, Kaegan fought like some graceful, feral thing. He never stopped moving, and the arch of his blade was mesmerizing. He was magnificent.

Distracted, she stumbled backward as a Dead gripped her shirt, and she pressed the blade into his temple, gritting her teeth. That moment of hesitation was all they needed, and a surge of undead pushed them to the edge of the cliff. Mud and rocks slid from the ledge, limiting their footing and splashing in the waters below. Kaegan was losing ground too, and she screamed his name. If she was going to die here, that crucial word would be the last on her lips.

He turned, and for the first time, she saw fear in the gray depths of his gaze. It wasn't for himself, but for her and her breath caught as he grabbed her hand. Water poured from the ends of his hair, and his dark eyebrows drew down with the seriousness of his request. Voice void of emotion, he said, "Jump," and pulled her over the cliff with him.

The fall stole her breath as they plummeted to the ebony waves beneath. Kaegan held her hand until they hit the water, and she was ripped away from him in the fury of the current. Silt laden water choked her and she clawed at the inky waves, desperate to find air. She swam and swam, but couldn't tell which way was up. Her body was thrashed against downed trees and boulders, and panic spurred her efforts. She was drowning. What a horrible way to go.

And just as she thought she'd die, her head broke the surface, and she filled her lungs with vital oxygen. Her body snagged on debris, and she pulled herself to shore, choking and coughing.

"Kaegan," she rasped. "Kaegan!"

Standing, she scanned the thin beach and waves but couldn't see him. Movement drew her eye. A hand broke the water up the river, and she bolted as fast as her legs could carry her. Why wasn't he coming up for air? His hand just reached out as if he were hailing her, and then it disappeared beneath the water. Unthinking, she dove in and swam for where she thought he'd been. The current carried her quickly, and a log under the water stopped her progress. Opening her eyes under water, she pressed against the log as the water pushed her toward it. A hand latched onto her leg, and as she screamed, a bubble of air burst from her.

Kaegan must be stuck on something. She pulled herself down, feeling his body until she came to his ankle, wedged in between a rock and the log. Oh God. He was drowning. He was tall, just not tall enough to break the surface of the water and breathe! Her lungs burned as she pulled and clawed at the log. No good.

Pulling the knife from its sheath, she wedged the blade between the surfaces and pried to no avail. Kaegan's hands had been scrabbling at his ankle but floated away as his body jerked and went limp. *No, no, no!*

Bracing her feet against the boulder, she pulled up with all of her strength, and the log gave a little. Her body screamed for oxygen. Readjusting, she pulled again, releasing the last of her air as she screamed her anger at the unfairness of the world.

The log moved, and Soren yanked his ankle free. Pushing against the rocky bottom, she clung to his body as her lips found air. The raging rapids pushed them farther and farther downstream, and she struggled and kicked to bring them closer to the shore. Kaegan still hadn't shown a single sign of life, and adrenaline laced her veins as she pushed him against the shore's shallow craggy bottom. Shaking, she pulled him safe of the current and pressed her ear against his chest. She couldn't hear anything over the rain and sat up, pushing her balled fists against his chest rhythmically. She looked around helplessly. She couldn't give him mouth to mouth without turning him. He wasn't vaccinated. A muffled sob filled the clearing, and tears blurred her vision.

"Damn it, Kaegan." He'd teased her with friendship, and now he was leaving her worse off than when he'd entered her life.

Struggling with his body weight, she dragged him onto his stomach and pounded on his back. Over and over again, she punched him with every remaining ounce of energy.

Kaegan's body convulsed, and coughing wracked his body. He struggled to breathe, and she fell backward, watching in joy as he fought to survive. Gripping the sand and pebbles of the beach in her palms, she smiled behind the sopping muzzle. Slits of gray focused on her. Even pale and gasping, with sand plastered to one of his cheeks, the slow smile that took his mouth made him the most beautiful thing she'd ever seen.

He rolled over, pushed himself up and stretched his neck, offering his face to the clouds above. It was too much to resist. He sat there vulnerable, and even if it ruined everything, it would be worth it. She catapulted into his lap, straddling him, and threw her arms around his neck.

He was alive. Nothing mattered but the racing rhythm of his heartbeat.

Seconds ticked by, and he sat rigid under her hug until finally, he leaned forward and slow hands slid around her waist, encircling her completely. He wasn't gentle. His hug didn't coddle her or treat her like some fragile flower under careful fingertips. He squeezed her until she couldn't breathe, and he buried his head against her neck.

"Thank you for saving me," he said in a voice both gravel and satin.

She leaned back and gripped his steely shoulders. "You didn't make it easy."

His gaze dipped to her muzzle, and he ran his fingertip over the strap across her cheekbone. His gaze flickered behind her, and he frowned. When she turned, Deads bobbed in the river, sinking and clumsily resurfacing.

"They must've followed us over the cliff," she reasoned as she pulled away and sat beside him.

"We should go find Colten."

"Agreed, but it won't hurt you to rest for a few minutes first. I'm pretty sure you were dead for a while."

He stared at the gruesome bodies bobbing in the waves and nodded. A frown darkened his face. "Can you hold your breath for a long time?"

Leaning back on her palms, she shook her head. "No, why?"

"You could've died trying to save me."

Should she tell him she would've happily done so? That her life would feel like it lacked purpose if something happened to him? She'd focused on the cure for so long, she'd forgotten about having connections with people. Real connections. Her pants had been ripped up the side of her calf and she stared at the pale skin that glowed from beneath the sopping fabric. The muzzle on her face was heavy with water, an uncomfortable reminder of what she was. Nothing had changed. Kaegan would find a nice, unquestionably human woman someday, and she'd hover in the background of his life as that friend who saved him once. No, she couldn't tell him how she felt or that she'd drown a hundred times over if it would prolong his life. What she felt was wrong, and dangerous to his very existence.

A Dead clawed his way steadily to the beach where they sat, and together they watched his slow ascent in silence. When he was close enough, she stood and pulled her knife.

Kaegan would never know it, but in her heart, it would always be true. "He's mine," she whispered under her breath as she brought the blade down against the Dead's temple.

Chapter Nine

Colten splayed his hand reverently against the cinder block wall of the Denver Colony.

Soren stared at him with one blond eyebrow cocked. "We can leave you alone if you want to kiss it."

Kaegan pursed his lips and tried not to laugh out loud as Colten scowled at her.

"Look, Z, it's not every day a man gets to meet his idol."

"*Stop* calling her that," Kaegan said at the same time she said, "Stop calling me that." Really, the number of times Colten had used the taunt over the past two days was borderline ridiculous. He was even starting to shove the moniker in where it didn't make sense.

"This way," she said, leading them along the fence line.

The gate was huge and wooden, and two guards stepped through before they'd even reached it. What kind of welcome would Soren receive here? Kaegan cringed at the thought of watching her wilt like she had in Dead Run River. This stop would be a quick one, though, and he wouldn't have that sick feeling in his gut for long before they'd be on their way and to the shelter of the woods again, away from all the people who treated her like a pariah.

"Holy hell," one of the guards called with a beaming smile. "She's back. Teague, call it in. Tell Sean Soren is back." He was shorter, at five-six or so, and his chestnut hair was mussed. The man leaned his rifle against the fence and wrapped Soren in a rough hug. Whacking her on the back a few times, he laughed as they rocked, and she greeted him.

"Hey, Barret, long time no see."

"Hell yeah, too long. What is it, two years now? We were starting to think you'd never come back." Pulling back, he teased, "You couldn't send a messenger every once in a while to let us know you were still alive?" and then playfully punched her in the arm.

The other guard looked nothing short of shocked and confused as he talked into a hand-held radio. "Soren is at the front gate." His voice went up an octave at the end like he was really asking if he should let the strange looking creature in or not.

"New guy?" Soren asked with a jerk of her head toward the guard.

"Yeah, Teague came to us last year. He just finished his training a couple of months back."

"Nice to meet you, Teague. I'm Soren, and this is my team, Colten and Kaegan."

Colten snorted in derision, but she ignored him neatly.

"I know who you are," Teague said in a rush. "I just didn't expect—"

"The muzzle is throwing him off," Barret said. "What's up with it?" With a tug on the strap that dangled from the buckle, he asked, "Is this the latest fashion at Dead Run River? Because I have to tell you, I don't think it'll catch on here."

Swatting away his hand, she wrapped her arm around his neck and drew him close, making chomping sounds with her teeth. "It's so I don't bite the newbies like Teague over there. New people taste extra delicious and are super tempting," she clarified to the pale faced guard.

Kaegan stared at her in shock. Soren was joking. Not only that, but she seemed completely at ease with Barret. And then suddenly, something ugly burned in his gut, and he wanted to step between them. Not for her protection but because, well, he just didn't like her arm flung around the stranger's neck or his comfortable smile.

"Bite check," Barret said, interrupting his escalating plans. "Soren you're cleared. You can go on in if you want."

"Why does she get a free pass?" Colten whined.

Kaegan sighed and tugged his shirt over his head. "Because she has second generation immunity. Even if she were bitten, she wouldn't turn." He threw his shirt on the ground near his newly shorn boots and froze when he met Soren's gaze.

She wasn't boldly holding his gaze like she usually did. Her supernatural eyes had drifted to his neck and traveled downward, caressing his skin almost as if she could touch him with a look. His breath caught at her expression, open and intense. Hungry. Chills rippled up his forearms as he wondered what the desire in her expression could mean. Did she like the way he looked? Or was he food she was trying to resist?

"Z," Colten said, "if you don't want to see my giant dick, I'd suggest you avert your eyes."

Soren's eyes widened, and the barest hint of color crept into her cheeks before she turned away. "I'll wait inside the gates for you."

"Don't bother," Colten said, unzipping his fly. "We can find our own way around."

She turned narrowed eyes on him. "You want to meet Sean, right? Well, I'm your ticket."

Colten watched her disappear through the gate and yanked his pants down. "What does she mean, she's my ticket? Does she know Sean?"

"Geez, man, do you listen at all when she speaks? She's from here."

Holding his hands out so Barret could check his skin for bites, he frowned. "The bite on my leg is old and healing. I'm vaccinated," he informed Barret as the soldier unwrapped the crispy gauze. Colten turned back to Kaegan. "From here, like, she lived here?"

"You really are the worst listener."

"Not when it counts. And that was weird right? Her claiming us as her team? I mean, we're not really a team, you know. Me and you are, but her?"

Barret cleared his throat and eyed the torn flesh of Colten's calf. "If Soren claimed me as part of her team, I'd feel like the luckiest son-of-a-gun this side of the apocalypse, gentlemen. That woman will save your sorry carcasses more times than you'll ever know about, and she won't ever tell you or look for credit when she does. Don't talk ill of heroes, yeah?"

"Seriously?" Colten asked.

Barret clapped him on the back and offered an empty smile. "Serious as a Dead bite. You're clear."

"Thanks," he murmured and started redressing as Barret turned to check Kaegan.

Both cleared, Kaegan slipped through the open gate behind Colten and was flanked by the guards. Another wall stood between them and the Denver colony, identical to the imposing gray cinderblock one they'd just entered through. Soren leaned against the second fence and tossed a shredded leaf to the ground before motioning them to the left.

What must she be feeling, coming home after so long? She didn't show any signs of nervousness, and other than a definite focus on the upcoming second gate, she didn't seem overly excited either. Soren was a lot of things, and one of those was a tough read.

"I bet he's bigger than Finn," Teague said quietly behind him.

"How much you want to bet?" Barret asked.

Kaegan turned away as the guards threw a flurry of whispered negotiations at each other. A man kneeled on the ledge of the fence above them, a long range rifle limp in his hand. His expression couldn't be seen from the shadow that shielded his face, but the tilt of his head followed them steadily.

"Open the inner gate," Teague said into the radio as they stopped in front of another heavy, wooden barrier.

Soren stood small and stiff beside him, so close, he could almost feel her warmth. Unable to resist touching her, he reached out and fluttered his fingers softly against her hand. "You okay?"

Her chest rose and fell steadily as she turned her head and looked up at him. The sunlight made the color of her eyes more brilliant, and he swallowed hard as she held him there, frozen beneath her captivating gaze. "You don't flinch when you touch me."

The image of her straddling him by the river, of her arms possessively around him, and the lengths he felt he'd go through to touch her like that again rippled through his mind. Slowly, he leaned forward until his face almost touched the strap of the muzzle on her cheek. "I'm not scared of touching you, Soren," he said quietly, for her ears alone.

When he stood straight again, she looked at the gate with lowered brows. "You should be."

The wood groaned as the gate began to move. Through the widening opening, colonists stood gathered at the entrance, talking, laughing, smiling. Soren's eyes rimmed with the barest hint of moisture, and she ran through as soon as the opening was wide enough. A dark headed woman nearly tackled her, and they stood swaying in an unbreakable embrace as others crowded around. It would've been difficult to see them if he weren't a head taller than most of them. Colten stood off to the side, but Kaegan drew forward as if Soren was magnetic. Watching her reunite with her people opened something inside of him that tasted like happiness. Damn, it had been a long time since he'd felt anything but the grit that came with the obsession over the pursuit of survival.

A tall man with black hair and dark eyes pushed through the crowd and pulled the two women into his arms, laughing as a tear streaked down his cheek. It must be her parents, Laney and Derek Mitchell. Kaegan was staring at the woman who may have single-handedly saved the entire remaining human population with her struggles to sacrifice her body for the vaccine two decades before. He was in the presence of greatness—honest, decent, good-to-the-core people. Soren clutched onto her father's guard uniform with a white knuckled grasp. No wonder Soren was so strong. Her family tree was an oak.

She moved from person to person, hugging them, talking low enough for him to miss the words. Her eyes were crinkled like she was smiling. Her gaze drifted to him between greetings, and as time went on, she glanced back more and more often. Finally, she tugged on a man's hand and pulled him through the crowd. He was tall and lithe, with striking blue eyes and the barest hint of gray peppered through his short, dark hair. A scar stretched down the side of his face, giving him an air of subdued ferocity.

"Everyone," she called as the crowd quieted. "This is my team, Kaegan and Colten."

"You fighting now, Soren?" the man beside her asked.

"It's a long story. Team," she addressed them, "welcome to the Denver Colony. Colten, this is Sean Daniels."

Bounding forward like a stray dog in need of a scratch, Colten grabbed Sean's hand and shook it until his teeth likely rattled. The man gave him a hard look.

"Sorry," Colten breathed.

Soren whispered something into the leader's ear, and a smile stretched across his face. "Any friend of Soren's is welcome in my colony. Please, Kaegan and Colten, join us for dinner, and we'll talk more. Soren—" he squeezed her shoulder "—I'm glad you're back. This place hasn't been the same since you left." His voice cracked with emotion, and he turned abruptly and strode up a mountain trail that weaved through a grove of pine trees.

The crowd dispersed except for a few, and Soren introduced him to her parents and Vanessa. "Guist is on patrol with Finn, but this is his wife, Eloise."

He shook the petite, golden haired woman's hand and followed the slowly migrating group up the trail where Sean had disappeared.

Small log cabins dotted the landscape, and soon, the fence wasn't even visible behind the shield of trees that decorated the colony. It reminded him of Dead Run River, but the people here were much different. More open, affectionate, calling each other by last names and teasing, always teasing each other. He'd stumbled onto a giant extended family in the middle of the wilderness, and at the apex of it, was Soren.

"Where's Adrianna?" she asked Vanessa, Sean's wife.

"Off in the woods somewhere."

"On a run?"

The striking blond woman looked troubled and shook her head. "She's had a hard time while you've been gone. She spends a lot of time hunting now."

"How is Seamus?" Eloise asked.

A flash of worry crossed Soren's face before she smiled and turned to Eloise. "He's practically king of Dead Run River. Everyone loves him there, naturally. He's still working away on the cure. Dr. Mackey isn't doing so well, so he'll likely be taking over as one of the head medical staff."

"What's wrong with Dr. Mackey?" her mother asked.

And so it went, easy conversation catching everyone up about the last couple of years. She failed to mention, however, how hard the people of Dead Run River had been on her, how they treated her like a second class citizen, and when anyone asked about the muzzle, she batted the question away with a good-natured joke. Once though, she shot Kaegan a look, as if she was checking if he was listening or not.

The woman baffled him.

Soren's father, Derek Mitchell, turned to him and offered a kind smile. "I bet you want to clean up and get some rest. They'll be talking like this for a while. You want me to show you to your place? You'll be in one of the trailers we dragged in. A family just left to try to find their people they'd been separated from when they arrived, and the place is empty for now."

"That sounds great. Thanks, Mr. Mitchell."

"Dear God, man. Call me Mitchell, please."

"Yes, sir."

"Drop that sir crap too. You're making me feel ancient."

He chuckled and nodded. "Sorry. It's just not every day I meet famous people."

"Yet you're on Soren Mitchell's team. Rumors love her."

Heat crept up his neck. He'd heard some of those rumors himself, and had even been inclined to believe some of them.

Birds called out in the canopy above, and a row of small mobile homes circled a clearing. In the center was a giant fire pit and plastic storage containers that looked like they held kitchen utensils.

"We have water power, but we try to reserve it for the big stuff, so no stoves. Soren will show you where to get food tomorrow. In about an hour, we'll have dinner over at Sean and Vanessa's house, so you won't have to worry about tracking down food tonight. Hot showers worked at Dead Run River because they had a genius who ramped up their equipment for years, but we don't have anyone that crafty here, so no hot water. We altered a river and it flows through the north side of colony. Respect the ladies' privacy. If there is a woman bathing, come back later or find a spot farther down to wash up. If you feel desperate for an actual cold shower, there's a few stalls on the other side of the colony. You'll have to haul your own bucket of water."

Colten followed along quietly, two blades tied to his back knocking against each other melodically.

"Do you need any help with work around the colony while we're here?" Kaegan asked.

"How long are you planning on staying?" Mitchell said, pausing at the front porch of a single-wide, painted in blues and grays.

"Not long. We're headed to the coast."

"The war?"

"Yeah, you've heard about it?"

"We've had several messengers in here over the last two weeks talking about it. And Soren?"

"We've invited her to come, but it's up to her."

A frown shadowed Mitchell's face and he tossed Colten a set of keys. "Let me talk at you." He turned without a backward glance and strode toward the trees behind the trailer.

"Daddy is pissed," Colten drawled with a brightness in his eyes he only reserved for trouble.

"Dick," Kaegan muttered and followed Mitchell.

"I've seen the way you look at my daughter," Mitchell said as Kaegan caught up. The trail was thin and plagued with tree roots determined to trip him up. Mitchell, on the other hand, looked as sure footed as a freaking billy goat and dodged them easily.

"I don't know what you're talking about."

Mitchell spun. "Don't bullshit me, boy. I'm grown and settled now, but I was your age once. I loved the chase, back when Laney was dating her boyfriend before me." He sighed and the harsh look in his dark eyes softened. Gesturing to a fallen tree stretched across the quiet woods, he sat, then pulled out an old rusty knife that had seen better days. He picked up a branch and ran the blade down the length of it, as if testing its sharpness.

Kaegan sat, but far enough away to avoid an easy maiming.

"Soren's different," Mitchell said low.

"I know." His voice cracked but the slow rhythmic slicing of Mitchell's knife made his balls clench. They were utterly alone in the woods, and if he believed the rumors about the mighty Derek Mitchell, he could slit him from ear to groin and spit on his carcass without much thought about it. Soren's mom, Laney, was equally dangerous. "H-How different are we talking?"

A slow, knowing, humorless grin stretched Mitchell's jaw. "You're afraid it's wrong to like her."

"The thought has crossed my mind," he admitted. He just wouldn't admit how many times. Today had been a constant pulling of his emotions after she'd straddled him by the beach.

"She's human. You aren't enamored with some monstrosity, if that's what you're worried about. But —" Mitchell swung a dangerous gaze to him "— others won't see it that way. People are cruel. When it comes to Soren, they don't have much patience with accepting her. She's *other* to them."

"She seems accepted here."

"Denver colony is different. She grew up here, and the entire place was built around her acceptance. Sean is a good leader and was friend enough to Laney to protect us when Soren was born. How was she treated at Dead Run River?"

Kaegan swallowed hard and dropped his gaze. Awful. Horrible. They'd treated her worse than they did the livestock. He couldn't tell her dad that, though. Not after she'd worked so hard avoiding that conversation with her family earlier. Mitchell gave him a hard look and grunted like he knew.

Mitchell looked off into the woods just as a gentle breeze picked up and rustled the leaves around them. "She can't just do flings, you understand? She's tough when it comes to most things, but she'll expect a lot from a man. I taught her she should. It'll take a special person to pair up with her. You talking about taking her to war with you makes me wonder if you're the type of option she needs. You've made yourself a soldier, expendable, you've shortened your shelf life. Soren needs a man who will stick around, even when it's tempting to run off and join a cause like men your age tend to do. You could get her killed with this mission, Kaegan."

"Sir, that's not my intention. I'd never want to put her in harm's way. I owe her my life, I just— from the moment I saw her, she seemed important, you know? Like she was meant for more than what she was doing."

"Like war?"

"No. Yes. I don't know, maybe."

"I watched the way you looked at her when she was greeted by her people at the gates. You didn't look much anywhere else. I look at Laney like that, so I know. Just, don't hurt my girl, okay? If you care about her as much as I suspect you might, put her first. Put her before the war, before what others will say, before yourself." He stood and sheathed his knife, then dusted his pants. "She deserves that."

Kaegan sighed as Mitchell left the way they came. He was wrong.

She deserved so much more.

Chapter Ten

"That team of sexies you came in with are cute," Vanessa said, sipping the sauce from the wooden spoon she'd been stirring with. "Especially the shorter one, with the bright eyes."

Soren snorted and pulled a pan of rolls from the wood burning stove. "You would think he's cute. His eyes are almost the color of Sean's, and he's a total jerk."

"Hey," Sean said defensively. "I'm not a jerk anymore."

"I knew it," Vanessa breathed, ignoring her husband. "It's the big brute you like then, is it? What's his name?"

Opening her mouth, then closing it again, Soren kept very busy setting the rolls one by one into a wicker basket lined with cloth napkins.

"Ignoring me won't make me stop asking questions," Vanessa said.

Silence.

Vanessa was beautiful, and had aged gracefully. Her hair was pulled back in a plum colored ribbon, her favorite color, and her smile lines were attractive as they deepened with her mischievous grin. "Did you let him get to second base yet?"

"God, Vanessa, really? His name is Kaegan. And no. No bases. I'm not even up to bat."

Her perfectly arched eyebrows drew down in a frown at odds with her natural expression. "Well, why the hell not? He's studly."

"He's very human."

"What? What does that mean? So are you, young lady, and if this is some prejudice thing on your part—"

"No, nothing like that. I mean, he's fragile."

"What is considered second base?" Eloise asked from the table where she snapped green beans into a bowl. "Is that under the pants?"

"Someone kill me," Soren muttered.

"I thought it was making out and playing with the boobies," Vanessa said. "Under the bra," she specified.

"You let him touch your boobies?" Mom asked from her spot beside Eloise. Why did she sound so excited by the prospect?

"No! No one has ever done that. Or kissed me. Like I said, not even up to bat. I'm basically warming the damned bench."

"Pity," Vanessa groused.

Her mom's mouth took on a worried moue, and Sean leaned against Vanessa's back, hands slipping to her waist, and whispered something into her ear. She giggled and said, "Be careful what you wish for."

Yack.

"I'm going to grab some fresh air," she murmured as she side-stepped Vanessa and Sean's canoodling.

"I thought it was third base that was under-the-bra-boobies," her mom said.

Soren turned at the stairway. She'd missed this—this comfort and ease around her. Finn and Guist came through the front door below, stomping leaves from their boots before setting foot on Vanessa's swept floors, as the three women who'd raised her argued over bases. Sean watched her with a catching smile that said he understood her discomfort as he leaned against the kitchen counter.

The old house had belonged to a religious group before the apocalypse, but you'd never know it looking at the raucous group cooking dinner in it now. Cult symbols still clung to old wooden boards under carpet in many of the cabins in the colony, but any bad mojo had long ago been dispersed by the happiness and determination of the people who'd called it home for the last two decades.

A small play area, where she and Adrianna had spent hours together while their parents cooked when she was younger sat atop the landing and led into a spacious dining area and kitchen. And behind her was a small hallway with two bedrooms. This was where Adrianna had been raised, and when Denver had fallen to the treachery of Sean's troops at the time, her friend had struggled to assimilate at Dead Run River, until Sean had cause to take his colony back from the Deads that trolled the broken fences. That cause had been Soren.

The best people on earth chatted happily in the room before her, and she smiled as she turned. Guist ruffled her hair, and Finn slapped her on the back in a greeting that rattled her bones. On the last stair, she paused and kissed her fingers before pressing it to a small, worn picture of a woman with long, flowing gray hair Adrianna had scratched into the wooden panel when they were kids. It was an old habit, born from Adrianna insisting they kiss the picture in order for Mona's spirit to rest. Her friend had claimed to see the ghost of the woman when they were kids on several occasions, but she herself had never seen an apparition. Maybe the spirits of the damned didn't show themselves to murderers like her.

The air outside was much cooler than earlier in the day, and she tugged her cotton shirt farther down. She didn't feel the discomfort of cold, but it wouldn't do to get sick right now. Murmured voices sounded from farther down the main trail, and familiar deep tones floated to her on the breeze. Her heart fluttered as she recognized Kaegan's voice, but it sounded troubled, so she stepped into the shadows of the trees, not wanting to interrupt.

"It's not right," Colten said as quiet as a whisper.

"Man, I don't want to talk about her any more with you. You don't like the answers I'm giving you? Fine. Don't ask the questions."

"I have to ask these questions, Kaegan. If I don't, you won't even think about them. That much is evident from you ignoring every woman of your own fuckin' species, and going fuzzy over a Dead that looks like she'd eat a mountain of men before bedding one."

"Shhh," Kaegan hissed, throwing a glance up at the lit windows above them.

"Can she even sleep with a man?" Colten whispered, undeterred. "Her vagina probably has poisoned juices or some shit. Eyuch—" he gasped as Kaegan's fingers gripped his neck.

"Enough. I get that you're trying to protect me, but don't talk about her like that." Kaegan's grip loosened.

"Zombie dick." Colten rubbed his fingers over his neck. "You're probably going to get zombie dick."

Kaegan shoved him through the front door and closed it before Colten could utter another word. Soren froze in her shadowy hideaway as he ran his fingers through his hair and growled just loud enough for her to hear it.

She shouldn't have been here to hear this conversation. Embarrassed, she scanned the woods behind her for an escape. Dinner was still a while in coming, and she couldn't sit in there and make nice with Colten while they waited. She'd just swoop in there as soon as dinner was on, put in her required time, and slink off to her cabin as soon as it was polite to excuse herself.

As quietly as possible, she backed up. Kaegan didn't seem to notice her as he sank onto the front steps and snapped a defenseless twig in half. When she felt it was safe enough, she turned and bolted for the safety of the woods.

The stars were out in droves, and the moon hung low and bright in the night sky. For lack of direction, she pointed her feet toward an old root cellar. She and Adrianna used to play there as children, and it had always felt safe. Like their own secret place away from everything that was going on around them.

Someone had put a lock and thick chain on the doors, and she tugged it once to test it. Disappointed, she scraped caked leaves and dirt from the double wooden doors. Rot had taken some of the boards, and they'd splintered with age. It seemed smaller than when she was a child, but everything had a tendency to feel larger to kids.

Arching her neck, she looked into the infinite expanse of the night sky. It had been ages since she'd just appreciated its vast beauty, and she lay down on a bed of lush grass. Hooking her arm under her head for support, she breathed deeply the smell of home. Of cattle and fresh cut wood, of pine and the ever present scent of the Deads who lingered just outside the walls.

"What are you doing?" Kaegan asked.

Gasping, she nearly jumped out of her own skin. What a terrible monster she made if she let a man sneak up on her like that. Irritated at being frightened, she said, "Baking a cake. What does it look like I'm doing?"

"Watching the sky, but why?"

With a sigh, she stretched her neck backward until she saw his towering form, upside down from this angle. "When was the last time you just enjoyed something beautiful?" Her voice sounded muffled and small behind the muzzle.

After a long while, he said, "I can't remember the last time," then turned as if to leave.

She returned her gaze to the stars as a heaviness pulled at her, and the sound of grass under foot, crunching and giving, drowned out the sounds of a mockingbird trilling late into the night.

The air stirred as Kaegan lowered himself beside her in the opposite direction. His face rested on a patch of weeds right beside her cheek, and his hair tickled her shoulder.

His warmth reached for her, drawing her to him, but she stilled herself completely at the shock. "What are you doing?"

"Baking a cake." His whisper held the remnants of a smile.

Locking her hands across her stomach to fight the urge to reach up and touch him, she moved her jaw against the chafing muzzle. "I don't have a poisonous vagina, you know."

"I had a feeling you heard all of that."

"Dr. Mackey ran tests. It's only my mouth that's catching, so you know…"

"No danger of rotting zombie dick?"

The need to defend herself from Colten had landed her in a conversation she wasn't sure she was ready for. Kaegan wasn't hers, and she didn't owe him an explanation, but still, it was nice that he knew the truth. But the weight of their impossible future hit her like a sack of rocks. She'd never kiss him. Maybe she could kiss a boy if he was vaccinated, but Kaegan, for whatever reason, had refused. And suddenly the thought of kissing someone other than him gave her a sinking feeling in the pit of her stomach, like she was falling into a black abyss and wouldn't ever stop.

"My mom was different," he said, turning his head so she could see herself reflected in his eyes. "You aren't like anyone else, but neither was she, and maybe that's why you don't scare me like you think you should." He rolled his head until he was looking at the stars once again, but the faraway look in his eyes said he didn't see the star dusted night veil above them at all. "I was four when the apocalypse hit. I don't remember much about the world before all of this, but I remember running. We were living down in Oklahoma, and Dad was at work. I remember Mom talking on the phone with someone, and she kept asking them, *Should I go? Should I take him and go?* And eventually, she did. The only memory I have of my dad is of him hunting us. No matter how far away we ran from the city, from the hordes, he followed slowly behind. And when he finally caught up to us at the state line, we were hiding under a broken down car on the highway when he found us. Mom killed him, but it did something terrible to her. I try to remember the happy times that she tried to give me as we drifted, but visions of her crying are what stuck with me. She didn't really seem to try to shield me from her heartbreak, but I think maybe that's because she didn't ever think we'd last through the day." He swallowed loudly. "She slept with every man she thought would give us protection. When she started wasting away, getting sicker, she talked to herself a lot, didn't take care of herself anymore. Didn't take care of me. I remember her walking around one of the colonies we'd settled in for a couple of weeks with no shirt. I didn't care though because she was my mom, and no matter what, I loved her. It wasn't her fault she was broken. It was the Deads'."

"Is that why you want to join the war?"

"I want to join the war because the thought of no future terrifies me. Come on." He rocked forward and offered his hand. "Your dad told me Vanessa would skin me alive if I was late to dinner. You might be immune to her wrath because you know her, but I don't want to test it."

Sliding her hand in his, she stood as he tugged and stumbled forward with the surprising strength of his grip. Frozen, she stood against his chest, unable to pull away from his warmth that enveloped her like a childhood blanket. He slid his arms slowly around her waist and pulled her closer until his chin rested on the top of her head.

Her limbs tingled, and she inhaled his crisp, masculine scent as she rested her muzzled cheek against his taut chest. "Did my dad grill you?"

"A little." His deep voice vibrated against her cheek, and she closed her eyes to give her sense of touch more rein. "He thinks I might not be a good friend for you."

One hug and she was drifting helplessly into an addiction for his affection. Dad was right. "You aren't." She moved to pull away but he tensed.

"Don't." He brushed his fingertips against the skin of her arm, conjuring chills. Slowly, he intertwined his fingers in hers. "Don't push me away. I know the risk, and I'm still here."

"You know the risk, but do you understand it? Have you thought about what I could do to you if I slipped up even a little? You'd be gone forever, and in your place would be a raving Dead who'd look like you and eat up everyone's memories of the man you used to be. I'm poison, Kaegan, and I'll destroy everything you are on the way down."

He leaned forward until his lips brushed her ear. "Take the muzzle off."

Shaking her head in denial of his request, she bit her lip against the want to show him all of her. "I can't. I'm scared."

"That I'll run?" He brushed light fingers over her back, and they rested on the muzzle clasp at the back of her head.

"No, not that you'll run. I'm scared I'll hurt you."

"You won't," he breathed in a soft stroke against her earlobe. "I know you won't."

A vision of screaming, terror, blood on her face and hands as she stared at her horrifying reflection in a bathroom mirror slashed across the back of her mind, and she eased back. "You know nothing. You wouldn't even be my first victim."

She left him standing in the moonlit clearing. Even as she felt him watching her, she didn't turn back — couldn't turn back or she'd cave.

The cold had never bothered her before, but after the heat of his embrace, the breeze seemed bitter and stinging against her skin.

Damn it, he'd let it go too far. Kaegan ran his hands roughly over his face as he watched Soren leave. Why did he always do that? Push people until they ran. Was it some sick way of testing whether people would stick around? Why he'd told her the story about his mom, he couldn't figure out for the life of him. That story was private. Not even Colten knew about his mom, and his friend had been smart enough not to ask. And then he just blurted it out to Soren like she's ready to carry that burden with him. She was as skittish as an injured predator and dangerous to boot.

But, she'd let him touch her, hold her. He'd been this close to unsnapping that cursed muzzle before she bolted. He looped his hands around the back of his head and started the hike back toward Sean's house.

Everyone was warning him off her. Hell, she was even telling him to take a hike, and still, he couldn't manage to stay away from her.

Her pale skin contrasted against the dark night, like a beacon leading him to sanctuary. Why couldn't he just forget about her like everyone else on earth seemed to be able to do? Because she was different, special. He couldn't explain why, but she called to the parts of him that actually had a shot at being decent. She made him want to do better, to be better, and it had been a long time since another person had stirred up any kind of emotion in him. He liked the way he felt around her. The way she looked at him, it was as if he was a man who had a shot at surviving the impossibilities of this godforsaken world and doing so with some dignity.

She could try to scare him off of her all she liked, but the cold hard fact was that right now, he wanted nothing more than to be holding her hand, walking beside her as they picked their way through the dark woods to eat dinner with the people who meant the most to her.

"I'm sorry," he said, jogging to catch up. "I didn't mean to upset you. I shouldn't talk to you or touch you like that. You haven't given me any signal you want that kind of relationship, and I went too far. Please." He tugged her hand, but a snarl, long and low sounded from behind the muzzle, chilling his blood until nothing was left but ice and marrow.

"You can't touch me like that."

"Okay." Holding his hands up in surrender, he backed off. "I'm sorry. I don't take it back, though. Hell, I don't even regret it, but I am sorry I overstepped what you're comfortable with."

Confusion washed over her visible features, and she dropped her otherworldly gaze to the leaves beneath their feet. "I don't remember the last time someone apologized to me."

"Sit by me at dinner."

"Kaegan," she said, sounding exasperated.

"I swear I won't touch you. Not on purpose. The dinner guests at this shindig are intimidating though, and I'd rather have you beside me as a buffer. I'm headed into a room full of legends, Soren, and the only other person I know there is Colten."

"Colten," she said, though his friend's name sounded like a curse on her lips. She cocked her head. "I can't imagine you being intimidated by anyone."

He wasn't, actually, but right now he'd say just about anything to feed his desperation to be near her.

When he didn't answer, she grumbled, "Fine," ungraciously and spun for Sean's house again.

So he'd been banned from touching her, and she was stomping loudly through the woods in apparent frustration with him. He was still in the game, and about now, in a time where tragically few victories existed, this felt like a win.

Chapter Eleven

"Take that damned thing off," Vanessa said with a frown.

Soren looked around the table as the others settled themselves. Nearly every set of eyes was on her. Except for Colten. He was staring at Sean. Idiot.

"I'm fine with it on." Who was she kidding? The muzzle itched like a small army of fleas, and her skin was raw where it was chafing her. "Besides, I'm not eating here, so what's the point?"

Mom squeezed her hand from her chair beside her. "Why not, honey? No one cares about your diet here."

Soren shot a quick glance to Kaegan on her other side, but he shook his head. "Uh, uh. Don't look at me like that. It doesn't bother me either."

"It's—" she started, searching their faces for any hint of understanding "—it's not that I'm scared to eat in front of him. He's not vaccinated."

"What?" Dad said a little too loudly for politeness. "She's joking, right?"

"Derek," Mom warned.

"No, sir," Colten said, leaning back in his chair with a stupid grin on his face. "He's not vaccinated. I've been trying to convince him to take it for years, but he won't do it."

"Why not?" Dad barked.

Kaegan leaned his elbows against the table, the muscles in his arms flexing with a tension he wasn't voicing, and he looked up slowly, dangerously. "My choice. My business."

Vanessa passed him the basket of rolls amid the stillness of the room. "He's right. It's his choice." She gave Sean a loaded look, and he stared at her with an expression that softened to sadness.

Bang! The door below slammed open, ricocheting off the wall. "Honeys, I'm home," Adrianna's melodious voice sang from downstairs.

Despite the chill of the tense moment, Soren turned in her chair and laughed as her best friend rocketed up the stairs.

"Soren?" Adrianna asked in a small voice. "Soren?" she asked louder as she dropped her backpack by her feet. A string of rabbits hung limply from her hand, but apparently forgotten, they stayed clenched in her fist as she ran and threw her arms around Soren.

God, she'd missed her. She buried her face in her shoulder, the irritation of the muzzle secondary to her need for one of Adrianna's epic embraces. Rocking gently, Adrianna sniffled against her shoulder, and Soren squeezed her tighter.

"Adrianna," she said finally, "this is my team. Kaegan—" she gestured to him as he looked on with a dumbfounded expression; Adrianna had that effect on people "—and this is Colten."

She nodded a greeting and held Soren back at arm's length. "You look skinny. That's not a compliment, Soren. I mean you look sick."

She scratched her neck in discomfort as Adrianna studied her with wary, dark eyes. She'd changed in the years she was away too. She looked taller, stronger. She wore dark animal leather on her legs with thick, fur lined boots to protect her feet. Her belt was lined with small throwing knives—a gift from Vanessa, no doubt. A thin, cotton shirt the color of rich soil clung to her shoulders and her dark hair was long and wild, pulled back into a ponytail. Her dark eyes danced as she held up the string of game. "No worries. We'll get you fattened up again."

She tossed the rabbits onto Soren's plate and unsnapped the muzzle on her face in one smooth motion. Eloise gasped loudly, and Sean growled a warning to his daughter. "Adrianna, stop it," he said.

Naked. Soren had never felt more exposed in the entirety of her life as the contraption slipped from her face and bounced twice before settling on the wooden floor boards at her feet.

Kaegan half stood, as if wanting to help, but he froze when she turned. "Soren," he whispered, as he took in the pitiful state of her face.

Adrianna picked up the muzzle with a disgusted look on her face. "How long have you been wearing this?" Her dark, accusing eyes lifted to hers. "How long?" she yelled.

"Soren," Mom said. "Did they make you wear this at Dead Run River?"

Adrianna rattled the muzzle, her knuckles white from her unflinching grip on the strap.

Swallowing hard and turning to the table, Soren said, "Two years. I've been wearing it for two years, and yes, it was a requirement if I wanted to stay at Dead Run River."

Mom shook her head slowly. "I'm going to kill her."

"Laney," Sean warned.

"No, Sean. Mel strapped Soren into a mask made for a fucking animal. An animal!" Turning, she asked, "Did people treat you differently there because of it?"

She wouldn't answer, couldn't. How could she admit she'd let them treat her like they had and not defended herself. How could she tell Laney Landry that she'd let the whisperings of humans defeat her only daughter.

"They did," Kaegan said. He swung his gaze to Mom. "I only saw a fraction of it, but she had a handler who facilitated the colony's treatment of her, assigned to her by Mel. Mel herself warned me from going anywhere near her."

Why would he do that? Why would he betray her like that? "Stop," she whispered, pleading.

"No, they should know, Soren. Your family should have answers for why your face is bleeding. On why you don't want to take the mask off."

Anger flared, red and burning. "I already told them why I don't want to take the damned muzzle off!" Snatching the constraint from Adrianna's fist, she whirled and bolted down the stairs, then ran through the front door and out into the safety of the night.

Damn him for making her feel weak. For making her feel alive and mistreated and angry where she'd only felt subdued acceptance before. And double damn him for being braver than her—for having the courage to speak up in there when her tongue seemed cemented to the roof of her mouth, threatening to trap that dark secret in her throat forever.

Tears blurred her vision as she ran for the river. Hang her instincts — she wanted to wash the blood from her face before anyone else could see it. Dad's horrified look would haunt her for the rest of her life.

Avoiding the main trails, she eventually slowed as the river's gentle rapids drowned out the sound of everything else. The muzzle made a stifled thud onto a patch of grass, and after a quick glance around to make sure she was alone, she kicked off her boots and rolled her pants up, then waded into the gently lapping waters.

Scooping water, a hideous reflection looked back at her in the tiny pool in her palms. Frightening eyes, hair as pale as the stars were bright, and along her cheekbones, raw, open skin. Bloody crimson against alabaster. Squeezing her eyes tightly closed, she doused her face, over and over until her tears washed away down the current.

Drying her face on her arm, she let the water lap at her palms as she looked out over the water. How many times had she bathed in this river? She preferred it to the showers at Dead Run River, but maybe it was because the flowing water was a comfort that hummed of home. Of safety and acceptance.

She shouldn't have run out like that. It was cowardly, and after everything she'd allowed, it was time to start standing her ground instead of retreating. That had been her moment, and she'd let it pass, choosing instead the path she had taken constantly since she'd left here years ago. Ashamed, she dropped her head between her knees and watched a tiny fish keep pace with the current flowing between her ankles. How funny that the little fish came to her to seek protection.

A limb snapped. Kaegan stood on the bank of the river with the string of rabbits in his hand. His eyes, the color impossible to see in the shadows of the night, seemed riveted by her mouth. "I've wanted to see what you looked like without the muzzle since the first time I saw you."

"Are you disappointed?"

A smile, slow and alluring touched his too sensual lips. "No. You're beautiful."

This was the first time anyone had ever called her such a thing. Beautiful? Terrifying was the word that left people's lips when they spoke of her.

"Thank you." He'd never have any idea how grateful she was for those words.

He stepped forward, slowly, and she stood. "You say that like you're thanking me for a pity compliment. It's not. I've never told a woman that before."

He brushed his fingertips across the undamaged flesh on her cheek, and desperate not to lose the warmth, she pressed her palm on his knuckles to hold him there.

"Your lips are perfect." His steady gaze stayed on them, and when she smiled, the expression was reflected on his face, as if he were in a trance.

"Did you expect them to be rotted off? Did you imagine me with snaggled, yellow teeth?"

He ran a light thumb over the outline of her bottom lip and chuckled. "I didn't know what to imagine. I'm glad you finally lost the muzzle, though."

"I've killed people," she whispered. She grasped his hand tighter, hoping he wouldn't pull away from her. He needed to know what he was allowing himself to covet.

"I know. So have I."

She lifted her chin, searched his eyes, but they remained serious and haunted. "You mean Deads?"

"I've killed a lot of Deads, Soren, but no. That's not what I'm talking about. I've killed people too, so stop thinking you'll taint me."

"Did they deserve it?"

"Yes," he said.

"My victims did not."

He dropped his hand and pulled his shirt over his head. "Swim with me."

Muscle flexed and rippled as he tossed the rabbits and clothing to the beach. As he bent to remove his pants, he turned his head. A devilish smile crooked his lips. "You'd better hurry. I told your parents I'd bring you back to dinner, so we don't have much time."

Utter abandon filled her. How could it not with Kaegan stripping down to his bare and perfectly masculine form right in front of her? A breathless giggle escaped her lips as she pulled her shirt over her long hair. "I thought you couldn't swim."

He laughed louder. "Because of me almost drowning in the river? You just caught me on a bad day. It was the log's fault."

Unhooking her bra slowly, she turned away from him. This wasn't like bite checks. Kaegan had retreated until the waves lapped his hips, but he was unapologetically waiting for her to undress and suddenly she was consumed with shyness. She didn't look like other girls.

Over her shoulder, she asked. "Have you been with other women?"

"Yes," he said honestly. "Have you ever been with other men?"

Snorting, she shot him a look. The boys hadn't exactly been flocking into her pants. It wasn't surprising that he'd been with others, but it shot a pang of feeling through her chest. Jealousy or perhaps insecurity, she wasn't sure.

"Soren, you're stalling."

Sighing, she pulled down her pants and tossed them onto the pile in the sand. "Happy?"

He dropped into the waves until they brushed his chin, and his smile grew even naughtier. "Exceedingly. Come here."

"I can still turn you," she warned.

"I know, you keep saying that. I won't touch you."

That sounded disappointing, but okay. Slipping into the water until it flowed across her hips and then her ribs, she followed him deeper into the river, circling him as he searched her with the most covetous eyes she'd ever seen.

"Where did you get the row of scars across your hip?" he asked.

Lifting her feet from the riverbed, she treaded water. "From the tests Dr. Mackey was running on me. We were trying to find a cure to bring back the newly turned, remember?"

A touch as soft as butterfly wings fluttered across her scars.

"Liar," she accused. "You said you wouldn't touch me."

"What I meant," he said, gripping her side with a hand that nearly encircled half of her, "was that I wouldn't touch your lips with mine."

"Mmm," she said with a mock frown, allowing him to pull her closer.

"The rest of you," he whispered against her ear, "I'll only refrain from touching if you ask me to stop."

She tensed as he wrapped an unyielding arm around her ribcage and pulled her chest into him. His torso was warm and inviting, and she relaxed against him as he ran a hand up the back of her knee. The motion made her draw her leg up instinctively, pressing her against his rigid erection.

"Slow down, woman," he teased, nibbling her ear.

A needy noise came from her throat, low and growly, and he pulled back to study her face.

She squeezed her eyes closed. "Sorry. I've never done that before."

His chuckle was deep and reverberated from his chest. "Don't apologize. I like that you only make that noise for me."

"Cannonball!" Adrianna shouted from the beach as she catapulted into the waves near them. She was naked as the day she was born, and Colten followed shortly, also nude. Fantastic.

Gasping, Soren tried to pull away from Kaegan, but his grip tightened, and his eyes danced. It was becoming increasingly clear that he was a go-with-the-flow kind of guy.

"What are you doing here?" Soren asked as Adrianna broke the surface.

"Well Kaegan promised to bring you right back, but Colten and I didn't really trust him to get the job done—"

"And we were right," Colten chimed in.

"So we came after you ourselves," Adrianna finished with a grin. "I didn't know he was your lover boy, Sor! Happy day. Do you know, you might be her first boyfriend ever?"

"Ade!" Soren said. She was pretty sure an epic blush was trying to commandeer her face.

"What about you?" Colten asked.

"Oh, I've had dozens," Adrianna assured him, splashing him in the face.

Colten splashed back, and Adrianna cupped her hands and doused them all with river water. Kaegan laughed and let her go enough to join in the battle. Well, awesome. They were all completely naked, no one seemed to think it odd but Soren, and now they were having a splash war like a bunch of ten-year-olds. Well, why not?

By the time they'd tired of the game, Soren was breathless from laughing. They'd drifted downstream a distance. As she relaxed into the current, Kaegan rested his arms under her back as she, Adrianna and Colten floated.

"You know," Colten said. "You have a pretty normal looking body for a Dead."

Adrianna dunked him and laughed when he came up gasping. "You douchebag. She isn't a Dead."

"Normal looking doesn't even come close," Kaegan said, raking her body with a thirsty gaze. She was still mostly submerged in the dark water, but apparently he could see enough.

She'd remember to be more embarrassed tomorrow when everyone else wasn't naked right along beside her.

"Don't make me bite you," Soren muttered through a sleepy smile.

"Wouldn't hurt me," Colten pointed out. "I'm vaccinated, remember?"

"Oh, I bet it would still hurt," Adrianna said, relaxing into the waves again.

Massaging her back gently, Kaegan said, "We should probably get back to the house soon. Your dad is going to kill me. I told them I'd try to bring you right back."

Adrianna sighed dramatically and stood on the rocky bottom. "The giant is right. Vanessa is downright scary if someone messes up her meal. She doesn't cook often."

"Vanessa is your mom?" Colten asked. "You guys don't look anything alike."

"Blood doesn't a family make. When she and my dad hooked up, she adopted me and raised me just like a mom would. So yeah, she's my mom."

Adrianna had been haunted by memories of the day her dad shot her biological mom. She'd been watching that day on the roof as he ended her and had detailed the day often when they were young. It made Soren thankful that both of her parents had survived the chaos of the first years after the outbreak. Under Adrianna's tough exterior was housed a well of churning pain.

"Race you to the bank," Soren challenged. "First one to touch the pile of clothes wins."

"That sounds lame—" Adrianna started, then pushed Colten's head under water and tore out in the direction of the clothes.

"Freakin' cheater," Colten yelled, laughing, and then swam after her.

Kaegan waited until they were halfway to the bank and sank down, pulling her to him. His lips were so close, her breath hitched with wanting. Resting her forehead against his, she asked, "Why haven't you taken the vaccine?"

"For personal reasons."

"Reasons you can't tell me?"

His chest rose as he inhaled slowly, little water drops escaping down his smooth skin to the water below. "This will have to be enough for us, Soren."

"Okay," she whispered.

"I don't want you wearing that muzzle any more, though." Running a finger along the raw skin it had left, he shook his head. "It's not right."

"It might not be right, but it's safe."

"It feels like you're hiding from me when you wear it."

"I'm not. I just don't ever want to mess up again."

"Oh, lovebirds," Adrianna sang. "You lose big time."

"I mean, really, you guys have the worst swim time in the history of competitive swimming," Colten said, unashamedly standing against the stark woods with his hands on his bare hips.

"Family dinner, take two. You ready to do this?" Kaegan asked.

"Yeah. No more running."

His teeth were white against the dark as he smiled. "That a girl."

Chapter Twelve

Dad wiped his mouth with a cloth napkin and threw it over his empty plate as Soren topped the stairs. "We didn't wait," he said unnecessarily.

Adrianna pursed her lips and scuttled around her, taking a seat next to Vanessa with her eyes averted. Kaegan and Colten took their earlier seats as she sank into hers.

"Why?" Mitchell asked. "Tell us why you let them treat you badly, and I'll drop it. Tell us why you didn't just come home where you would've at least been fed properly. Did they shame you with that too? Or are you just watching your figure?"

"I had a handler who was trying to assimilate me into the population of Dead Run River better. At least that's what she told everyone. She was making me eat cooked food, and it made me sick. I'm not watching my figure."

"And the muzzle?"

"I had to wear it, or I couldn't stay within the gates."

"Honey, why did you stay?" Mom asked.

"Because I wanted to help find the cure. I really thought I could. I came into Dr. Mackey's office every day and like an idiot I thought, *today is the day*. And I thought if I just took one more insult, one more unfair rule, if I plodded quietly through the rumors and the dirty looks, at least I'd be there for the discovery of the cure."

"Did you know this was happening, Sean?" Mom asked. "I mean, you've visited Dead Run River so many times since she moved there."

"Yes," Sean said, looking sick.

"Mom, I begged him not to mention this stuff because I didn't want you to worry."

"Why is this cure so important to you, Soren?" Dad said, voice rising. "We have the vaccine. Your mother sacrificed so much to get it to the masses, and you're sacrificing your quality of life for what? A cure that might save a few more? This family has given enough."

"Because I want to use it on myself! I want to look like you and Mom, and I want to walk down a trail and have children not scream and run from me. I want to be *normal*." Her shoulders slumped as she felt a great weight of her admission press against her. "I want to kiss a boy without killing him."

A single tear slid down Mom's cheek, and it shattered Soren's heart with the tiny splat it made on the table. Her parents had worked so hard to give her a normal life, to give her the strength to bear this, and she was failing them. "I'm sorry," she whispered, her voice ragged.

Kaegan gripped her hand under the table, but she didn't deserve the comfort.

"What made you leave?" Vanessa asked quietly.

"Kaegan told me I deserved better. I don't know why it took a stranger saying that for me to accept it, but I was already at the end of what I could take."

"So now you'll go to war." Dad's chair creaked as he leaned back in it.

Adrianna had been picking at a hangnail with one of her smaller knives, but perked up, eyes wide. "What's he talking about?"

"We're going down to the coast. Something is brewing down there that has everyone excited. The Deads are migrating to the water, and forces are gathering to put a dent in them."

"That could change things, right?" Adrianna breathed.

Sean nodded. "This isn't the first migration—it's just the first one people have realized the importance of. They've been traveling in droves down to the coast for the past five years. No one knows what drives them, but a similar thing happened at Dead Run River before Mel settled it. Hundreds of Deads gathered at the river's edge, just waiting. There have been messengers for a while, but the migration won't peak for a few days yet. This won't be like Dead Run River though, Soren. I'm talking about the bulk of the population of Deads in North and South America being in one place. And they'll be hungry."

"Not for Soren," Adrianna said. "They've never gone after her for food." She swung her gaze to Soren, the same bewildered look on her face as when Kaegan began to figure out she wasn't just some mistake nature had made. She was a weapon. "I'm going with you."

"It'll be dangerous," Kaegan said. "There's little chance of survival out there."

"Sounds like my kind of party."

"Are you sure?" Soren asked.

"You left me behind for some mission I couldn't get on board with before, and it tore me up. I'm not going to be argued out of it. I just need a day to put together a bigger team for us because this—" she made a circle with her finger, gesturing to her, Kaegan, and Colten "—isn't near enough to survive the trip, much less take out a chunk of Deads before we go screaming into that good night. I might be reckless, but I don't have a damned death wish."

Vanessa sat silent for the first time in as long as Soren could remember, and Sean rubbed her neck and asked, "What do you need from us?"

"Sean," Vanessa whispered.

"She's going to go, Vanessa. She's grown, and I can't watch her waste away around here any more. We got to make our choices when we were their age." His voice cracked, and he turned his gaze back to Adrianna. "So what do you need from us?"

"Your blessing."

"Granted as long as you stay with the team. You stay with Soren, no matter what. You take care of each other."

"Done."

"Done," Soren agreed. "Guist, I wouldn't mind if you packed our go-bags for us."

He smiled and nodded. "I'll pick them up in the morning and see what they're lacking. You two are out in the trailers?"

Kaegan and Colten nodded in unison.

"We'll need more weapons," Adrianna said.

The chairs screeched against the floor as Sean stood. "Follow me."

The others stayed in the house, but Sean and Dad led the four of them to the old root cellar that had served as her and Adrianna's playhouse so many years ago. The heavy chains clanked as Sean unlocked it and pulled them off.

"Watch your step," he murmured.

The light disappeared altogether about ten steps down, and Soren felt around for each step before applying weight. A soft trill of metal sounded somewhere in front of them, and the glow of a newly lit lantern filled the space. The cellar had changed in the years she'd neglected it. Maps hung from the concrete walls like wallpaper, and a huge, crudely made table filled the middle of the room. Across it was strewn drawings and topographical maps. Ledgers were stacked on an old bookshelf against the wall, and a box sat in the corner. *Soren and Adrianna*, it read in dark thick marker. The top was open, and one of her childhood dolls was flopped over the cardboard ledge, waiting as if Sean and Dad had stored it for them in case they ever came back to play.

Sean held a door open and waved them forward. "This way."

It used to be a crude chicken house, filled with crates and grain feed and buckets to collect eggs, but now it was a chaotically organized storage room for a weapons cache. Pistols and rifles lined the wall, and boxes full of musty smelling hay housed shotguns and military grade weapons. Ammunition by the droves sat in boxes on shelves.

"I've never seen so many guns in one place," Colten whispered, like if he spoke at normal volume, it would suck the magic from the room.

"Sean thought it would be smart to start stocking up the second year of the migration," Dad said.

"I thought they didn't make guns anymore. Not since the outbreak, but some of these look new."

"Not new, just never been used." Sean grabbed a sawed off shotgun and tossed it to Kaegan who caught it deftly and checked the load. "We've been trading in secret for years, and the ammo was mostly made in-house." He gestured to a workbench with rows of bullet casters in the next room. Lead, oils, shell casings, and gunpowder dotted the counters.

"This one's yours," Dad said low, handing her a pistol. "It was Uncle Jarren's. I know you didn't ever get to meet him, but he'd want you going to battle with a piece of him. It's never jammed up in all the time I've used it. Look." He tipped it up and pointed to a tiny inscription on the barrel. *Until my last breath, I'll fight*, it read. "You remember how to use one of these?"

She swallowed the emotion that threatened to overwhelm her. Jarren's gun. She'd never met him, but from stories her parents had told her, he was her hero. He'd been everyone's hero. "It's been a while, but we'll go out to the range tomorrow."

"You each need a pistol," Sean advised. "Blades will be your go-to weapon, but when you're desperate, and those times will come, you pull the pistol. When you run out of the small ammo, you pull a shotgun."

"And after we run out of ammo for the shotgun?" Adrianna asked.

"You run like hell."

Suddenly, everything felt real. Going to war wasn't just a passing thought about what she'd do some day. It wasn't a bucket list dream. They'd be leaving in two days' time for something that would change her forever. She was human, but the virus was as much a part of her as anything else. It affected her looks, her healing, her ability to survive among the Deads. And in this moment, she was picking a side. No matter that she'd been treated like a disease at Dead Run River, she was choosing to fight on the side of humans. This moment, right here, was her declaration of her people. Adrianna, Colten, and Kaegan watched her silently as she holstered Jarren's pistol, now her own. Either way, she was a traitor. Either way she lost, but she couldn't ride the fence forever or good people would die. One or the other had to fall under her protection.

Her people were humans.

Leaving much heavier than they came, Soren led the way through the woods to Kaegan's trailer. She'd never slept much and had done guard duty when she lived here before, trolling the gates for any sign of trouble, but tonight was different. The Denver colony slept safe and sound under Sean and Vanessa's diligent protection. Tonight was her last night to relax before every moment would be devoted to the survival of her team.

"You want to sleep over at our place?" Colten asked Adrianna.

"No spank you, Romeo. I have a place of my own." As she broke through the trees to the trailers, Adrianna gave a little salute and drifted away. "Plus," she called over her shoulder, "somebody died in there a couple of years back, and I'm pretty sure it's haunted. Sweet dreams."

"Charming," Colten muttered as he picked his way around a giant tree stump.

Soren laughed and when she looked up, Kaegan was watching her with an unfathomable expression. "What?"

He shook his head and adjusted the strap of his shotgun.

"What?" she asked again, louder.

Twitching his head to the side, he said, "It's just nice seeing you in this place after seeing you in Dead Run River. You smile a lot. Maybe you did before, but I couldn't see it behind the muzzle."

"No, I didn't smile much there. But Denver is different. It's home, you know?"

"No, I don't. Colten and I have bounced around for so long, I can't remember staying in one place long enough to have that kind of connection with it."

"Where will you go if you survive the war?"

His smile didn't quite reach his eyes. "Best not to talk about futures we don't have."

At the top of the porch stairs, Kaegan turned as Colten disappeared inside. He pulled her in close and rested his chin on her head as she relaxed into his arms. "You want to stay over?"

She opened her mouth to answer but Colten beat her to it. "No! I don't want to be eaten in my sleep. My muzzle rule still applies here."

"You need sleep, and I'll only keep you awake. If I get tired, I'll crash with Adrianna."

"Ahh, I forgot the no sleeping part for you." He slipped his thumb under the hem of her shirt and gently fingered the puckered scars on her hip. "It feels strange being apart after the last couple of days."

He was right. Tonight would feel strange being any distance away from him, sleeping or awake. She'd spent hours the night before watching over his sleeping form. How could she feel so connected with a man she'd met such a short time ago? She'd even gotten used to Colten's obnoxious presence.

"Dude," Colten said over the creaking of the door. "Someone left a jar of moonshine under one of the beds."

"I'll leave you boys to it. I've got bunnies to eat."

"About that," Kaegan said, grabbing her hand as she turned. "I think you need to eat more."

"You don't like me this skinny?"

"I like you just fine any way you are, but Adrianna and your dad talk like this isn't a healthy weight for you. Should we be stopping more to hunt and eat?"

"Probably. I need as many meals a day as you guys, but I've been trying to be respectful of your eating habits."

"Screw that. I don't care."

"I do!" Colten called from inside.

"You say that, but it's not exactly pretty when I go all Dead on some raw meat."

Kaegan leaned against the wooden porch railing. "Does it bother you to eat in front of other people?"

He wasn't offensive with his questions, just direct, as if he was really interested in her responses. She liked that. "A little. Most are completely grossed out by me already. Snarfing down a raw flank steak in front of them just invites more judgment."

"I'm judging you," Colten called.

Kaegan looked heavenward, as if he were praying for patience. "We're your team now, and we'll have to get used to it just like you'll have to get used to traveling with us."

"You're stalling," she accused.

"Yep."

"Good night, Kaegan."

He stood on the porch with his hands in his pockets, watching her until she made her way into the trees. Out of sight, she squatted next to a giant live oak and rested her palm against the rough bark.

Kaegan didn't go in right away. Instead, he locked his elbows and gripped the porch railing until his arms flexed against the threadbare fabric of his T-shirt. Looking out over the circle of trailers, he shook his head at some mental conversation she didn't have a guess at, then disappeared inside.

Maybe it bothered him that he liked her at all. Or perhaps he regretted asking her to come along, but they were in it now. Good or bad, they were on a collision course. She just couldn't figure out if it was with each other or with a fighter's end neither one of them was ready for.

Soren shook the feed pail, and the chickens came running. Bigger livestock tended to stampede in the opposite direction from her, but chickens? Maybe they were too dumb to sense a predator. She'd always enjoyed taking care of them in her spare time when she was growing up. Mom even had favorites that she named, though all the ones she remembered seemed to have been eaten long ago. These squawking hens begging grain didn't look familiar at all.

Tossing it out by the handful, she hummed under her breath, a song about dapple and gray horses Mom used to sing to her and Adrianna when they had trouble sleeping.

"I should've known you were with the freaking chickens," Adrianna groused. "I've been looking all over for you. Come on. The boys are already at the range."

"Want to help me feed them?"

"I'm not going in there with those feathered devils." It wasn't the hens she was scared of. It was the roosters, which had a tendency to chase Adrianna in her younger days. They didn't much bother chasing Soren.

Soren bent down and let a few of the braver birds peck feed from her outstretched hand.

Adrianna's mouth puckered. "Gross. I'm sure you're about sixty-eight percent more likely to contract worms or botulism or something now."

Wiping her hands on her pants, she let herself out of the coop and replaced the empty bucket in the small storage shed nearby. "I have the Dead virus. I'm pretty sure that trumps botulism. Which isn't spread by chickens, by the way."

"Bird flu," Adrianna corrected with a sarcastic grimace.

Soren tried to wipe her grain-dusty hands on Adrianna's shoulder, but her friend ducked out of the way and made a disgusted noise.

"Stop that right now, Soren Leanna Mitchell, or I'll stab you." She pulled a blade for emphasis.

"Sorry, chum, I've already been stabbed this week. Somebody beat you to it."

"What?" Adrianna lowered the weapon. "Who stabbed you?"

"Colten."

"That jackhole. Do you want me to hurt him?"

Soren snickered. Not because she didn't think Adrianna would follow through. On the contrary, there was a high chance Adrianna would actually hurt Colten and enjoy it, but she laughed because she'd missed Adrianna being protective of her. She'd missed everything about her. "In his defense, he was close to death with a raging fever and was having some pretty interesting hallucinations."

"Still," Adrianna muttered. "A stabbing is a stabbing."

"Have you seen the boys this morning?"

"Yeah, Colten is hung over or maybe still drunk, I don't know. Your lover boy is actually a decent shot, though."

"Don't call him that."

"Why not? It's obvious you two like each other. Own it. Denying it only makes it weird for the rest of us."

"Whatever. Who are you dating?"

"Dating or banging?"

"Uhh, is there a difference?"

"Jack and Brock."

A redbird landed on a low-hanging branch farther up the trail, and Soren tracked it as they walked. They were pretty little creatures. "I don't know either of them."

"You wouldn't. They're new to the guard training program. Came here just to get a crack at Finn's training camps. He'll make men of them yet."

"Did they come here together?"

"Of course. They're brothers."

Soren had been right in the middle of swallowing and choked, coughing until she could breathe again. "You're date-banging brothers?"

Adrianna shrugged and waved to Mrs. Williams, who was having a time of it trying to corral her three children.

"Hi, girls!" she greeted them. "Soren, aren't you a sight for sore eyes. It sure is good to see you back here again."

"It's good to be back," she called. Really good. Perhaps she'd stayed way too long at Dead Run River without visiting home. She was actually starting to feel sane again, but maybe Kaegan had something to do with that too. She had an overwhelming urge to show him exactly where she came from when he was around. To show him how she'd grown up and what made her...*her*.

The closer she walked to the gates leading to the shooting range, the more her stomach did uncomfortable little flip-flops. He'd seemed at ease with her yesterday, but maybe he'd see things clearly this morning—see how wrong she was for him.

At the cinder block fence, she smiled at the guards as they opened the gates. Adrianna kissed one of them, but Soren hadn't any idea if it was Jack or Brock. Maybe it was neither.

Shots sounded from down the fence line. They were set up close so the guards at the front could help them pick off Deads attracted by the noise. Colten looked to be passed out in the sun without his shirt on, lying on his back on a burlap sack. Kaegan was on his stomach, firing a long-range weapon and taking instructions from Finn and Guist.

Adrianna was still talking to the guards behind her, so she stopped to watch. Sunglasses shielded his eyes from her, but his arms moved and flexed as he reloaded and took aim again. A target clung to a tree some two hundred yards off, and a tight grouping had been blasted in the bull's-eye.

"We'll have to put a target farther back and see what you can really do when you come back," Finn said with a toothy grin. He and Guist gave each other a loaded look, like they were impressed, and pride swelled in her. His skill with weaponry surprised her and made her realize that she only knew a tiny bit about the man her heart had latched on to.

"Soren," Guist called. "Come on over here, and we'll get you started with that pistol." He pulled a box of ammunition from a stack beside Colten's snoring form and started pulling bullets.

Kaegan's gaze arched to her, and the slightest smile stretched his cheeks. He lifted his sunglasses and said, "Hey. I was wondering if you were going to make it out."

"Is he still drunk?" Soren asked.

"As a skunk," Finn said. "Best he doesn't handle firearms right now."

Soren approached and stood over Kaegan so her shadow protected his eyes where he'd been squinting against the sun. "Are you okay?"

"I don't drink moonshine." He hefted himself up and dusted dry grass from his shirt. "That stuff will make you go blind."

"Smart man," Guist said with a frown at Colten.

His chest rose and fell deeply like he couldn't hear a word they were saying, but already his shoulders were showing signs of too much sun. "He's going to get sunburned laying out like that."

"It would serve him right, now wouldn't it?" Finn asked.

She kicked an empty burlap sack over him, then pulled at it until it covered all but his forehead. "Yeah, but I don't want a teammate

favoring another injury out there. You both already have gimp legs."
She picked up a large leaf and started shredding it.

"What are you doing?" Kaegan asked, watching her.

When she had the perfect shape of a penis and balls torn out,
she licked it and plastered it to Colten's exposed forehead. "Revenge
for the stabbing and constant barrage of insults."

Kaegan snorted and Finn covered a booming laugh with the
back of his hand.

"What did I miss?" Adrianna asked, looking from face to face.

"About an hour of target practice, ladies," Guist said in a stern
voice. "What does ten o'clock mean to you? To me, it means be here
at nine fifty waiting for me to arrive. I'm not here for my own health.
I know how to shoot a gun, and Finn sure as anything has better
things to do than wait around for you to finally show up. Surely you
can see what a time suck this has been."

"Don't bust my balls," Adrianna said, punching her fists on her hips.
"I was here, remember? Soren was the one who ignored pew-pew time."

"Damn it, Adrianna. *Yes, sir.* All I was looking for was a *yes, sir,*
like every other trainee in the entire colony can manage."

Swatting at a pestering fly, Adrianna stared at him like he'd lost
his mind. This—this was why Adrianna hadn't completed guard
training. Oh, she knew her weapons as well as any guard and had
practiced extensively. She could handle a blade as well as Soren or
any other fighter, but she didn't take authority well.

"Dead," Soren said.

"What?" Guist said, swinging an irritated gaze to her.

"I smell a Dead. A ripe one coming from that direction." She
pointed west with the barrel of her handgun.

"Oh." Guist handed her a fistful of bullets and said, "Well, load
your clip, and let's start you on moving targets."

Chapter Thirteen

Moving targets turned out to be much more difficult to hit than stationary ones, but maybe it was a good thing they'd tightened up their aim on the creatures they'd actually be fighting. Each hit gave Soren a sick feeling in her stomach, but it was the way it would have to be. Deads weren't people anymore, and they'd eat the ones she cared about in a precious heartbeat. She just had to remember that.

She'd spent the afternoon with her parents, and by dinnertime, the nerves had kicked in. She'd be leaving this place tomorrow, possibly for the last time. Drinking in every detail of her stay, she hoped it would be enough to draw on if she met disaster at the end of this.

"Hold this. And this," Mom said, stacking storage containers of beans and creamed corn in her arms.

The weather was perfect for eating outside, and Vanessa had suggested they take advantage of one of the giant fire pits for their last dinner in the Denver colony.

The smell of cooking meat turned her stomach as she followed Mom out the front door, and like a compass pointing north, her eyes were drawn to Kaegan. His back was to her as he flipped steaks. The aromatic meat sizzled on a grate a small distance above the simmering embers of the fire. Kaegan's shoulder muscles moved under his blue thermal shirt, and her fingers itched with the desire to trace the striations through the thin fabric. Memories of his smooth skin under her wet fingertips in the river slowed her progress, and as if he could read her thoughts, he turned stunning gray eyes on her. Everything faded—the noise of Dad and Sean's banter, Finn dropping tinder and branches onto the small woodpile, Guist and Eloise tossing clanking horseshoe irons at a metal stake. Laughter died to nothing but a murmur as Kaegan's partially hidden face stretched with a languid smile, spreading until it reached his eyes, brightening them somehow. God, he was the most beautiful thing she'd ever laid eyes on.

"You gonna eat him?" Colten asked from right beside her. "It looks like you're gonna eat him."

She turned narrowed eyes to Colten, who seemed quite pleased with yet another jab. His eyes were bright as if he was waiting for her to snap at him, and his forehead sported the tan line of an impressive cartoon erection.

Apparently, no one had felt inclined to enlighten the idiot.

"Colten, I can't take anything you say seriously when you have a dick on your forehead," she said.

"Three hours," Adrianna sang from her seat on a tree stump that had been carved in the shape of a crude chair.

Colten fingered his forehead with a frown. "Three hours for what?"

"Three hours before anyone spilled the beans that you have the tan line of a tiny wiener on your face." Adrianna held up her pinky and wiggled it.

"Wha—" He swung a cold gaze to Soren. "You?"

"Yup."

His eyes narrowed to slits. "Nicely done," he conceded as he stalked off.

"Here, let me take those," Kaegan said.

Stretching her neck back to take in his full height, she released the containers of food to his care and thanked him. The warm, sweet smile from earlier still clung to his lips, and she wanted to lick it off.

Lick it off?

What was wrong with her? She needed to put the damned muzzle on again and save herself temptation. The way he leaned forward when she handed over the food with his mouth slightly parted did nothing to sway her sudden need for more from him. Nor did the attractive stubble that shadowed his jaw, or the riveted attention he gave her as the words, "Thank you," left her lips.

"Hey," he said, leaning so close, she could feel the warmth of his broad chest. His fingers gripped her waist, and her stomach clenched with longing. "I saved a couple of steaks to the side for you." He twitched his head to a plate of raw beef that sat near enough the fire to warm up, but not to cook. Breath tickled her ear, and a curious warmth emanated from her stomach, lower and lower until it reached the deepest places within her, simmering until the heat surely matched the smoking remnants of the fire.

He accepted her. Here he was, declaring he didn't care what she ate or that she was different. Before she had time to think or change her mind, she turned her head and brushed her lips lightly under his jaw, reveling in the feel of his stubble against the tender flesh of her mouth for a moment before pulling away. She shouldn't have done it. Even if he couldn't be turned like this, she was tempting them both to get too close.

Sidling around him, she looked back once she reached the fire, but he stood frozen, looking after her with wide, serious eyes and animated dark eyebrows that had drawn together like she was a puzzle he hadn't all the pieces to.

Heart pounding, she sat next to Mom, who was shoving potatoes into the charred logs of the fire. She tried to help, but really, her focus was on Kaegan as he knelt beside the fire pit again and checked the steaks. He seemed to be having the same problem, because his eyes drifted to hers twice.

"Soren!" Mom yelped, yanking Soren's fingers away from the flame. "You have to be more careful. Look there, you've burned yourself."

The tips of her fingers were indeed red and angry looking. "Sorry, I didn't feel it."

Mom sighed, and shot Kaegan a troubled look. "You can't afford to lose your head," she said softly. "It'll be different for you, more dangerous. You have to think when you're around him, or neither one of you will survive this."

Soren opened her mouth to answer, but Adrianna whistled a catcall. "The dream team is here."

Three figures emerged from the trees, two men and a woman, all around her age.

Colten came from behind, wearing a baseball cap that covered his forehead. "Who are they?"

"They," Adrianna said with a Cheshire cat smile, "are the second half of our team. This is Ben Cavenagh, recruited for his brawn." Adrianna pinched Colten's bicep and made a squeaking sound. He yanked it away, and Ben laughed.

"She really recruited us because we're the only ones dumb enough to join the crusade." His voice was friendly and his smile easy. He was handsome, with chestnut brown hair and dark eyes. Only a few inches taller than Soren, his muscular arms threatened to cut through his T-shirt like glass. Brawn indeed.

"This is Lauren," Ben introduced the blond haired girl next to him as she shifted her weight uncomfortably, like she didn't like the attention. "She don't talk, but she understands just fine."

"And," Adrianna drawled as she stepped behind a tall, lanky man with glasses, "you probably recognize this guy from before."

He did look familiar now that she mentioned it. His mouth was set in a grim line, and his hazel colored eyes were hard as he stared back, unblinking.

"Adrianna," Sean warned. "I don't think Mark is a good fit for this mission."

Mark. Why did that name sound so familiar?

"Surely you remember me, Dead," the man said. "You killed my best friend. Or are your victims so easily forgotten?"

Mark. Mark Greenfield. Her mouth suddenly went dry as a desert in the wind, and she took a step back. "Why would you want to come with us?"

"It's not to play power squad with you, princess zombie. It's for the research."

"Mark's a scientist," Adrianna explained in a bland tone. "Or tech groupie? I don't know. He likes to study shit, and he wants to come along for the learning side of things. Plus he might come in handy if we need something fixed up in a hurry. Plus he knows first aid."

Sean stood to the side of their little group, shaking his head. "We've been burned bringing an unprepared civilian with us before. Can you shoot?"

Finn cleared his throat and handed him a Glock he pulled from a holster tied to his leg. Mark pulled it back as Finn chucked a log far into the abyss in front of them. Pulling the trigger, a crack echoed through the clearing as a chunk of wood exploded from the spinning propellant. In one smooth motion, he clicked the safety into place and handed the weapon back to Finn, grip first.

Well, fantastic. If the hordes of Deads they were about to fight didn't kill her, Mark-freaking-Greenfield would surely finish the job.

Mark glared at her, and Kaegan at him as she withered under his hateful stare. Lauren shoved Mark in the shoulder and mouthed, "Stop it," and to Soren's unending surprise, he softened, if just slightly.

"Dinner is on," Eloise called in a sing-songy voice, breaking the spell of utter discomfort.

Turning, Soren bit her lip and shot Mark one more sidelong glance. Well, this is what they'd come here to do. Stock up on supplies and weapons and find a larger team. She just hadn't imagined a team quite like this.

The sound of the subtle slide of leather filled the dark as Soren checked each of her blades and sheathed them. She'd sharpened every one of them on a wet stone in the night and now stood in the crisp, early morning air waiting for the rest of the team to meet her at the front gates. She'd said her good-byes, and the flutters of sadness at leaving home after such a short time were replaced by dragon wings, flapping around inside of her as her thoughts turned to the uncertain future. Only a vision of Kaegan, smattered in blood and looking ferocious as he had the day she'd first seen him, calmed her nerves. Whatever was going to happen would happen beside him.

Adrianna slid out of the trees, then Lauren, quiet as hunting cats. Soren bent to secure the holster of her pistol more securely on her waist and tied it steady around her upper thigh. She wasn't used to the weight yet, but she would be soon enough. Her battle swords clanked against her back with the movement, bringing her comfort. Lauren carried an assault rifle across her shoulder blades and a foot-long bowie knife was perched on her hip. Adrianna's belt housed the smaller throwing knives that she'd grown most comfortable with growing up, a gift from many hours of lessons from Vanessa, no doubt. Soren hadn't checked the satchel that rested against her hip yet, but she would when they made camp later that night. She trusted Guist to have packed everything just the way she needed. The man had an instinct for it.

She heard the men before she saw them thanks to Colten's voice, which seemed to carry for miles when he was riled up.

This morning, the argument seemed to be about her wearing the muzzle or not.

"Look, we voted, man, so suck it up," Colten said. "She wears the muzzle or this thing doesn't work. We have enough to worry about surviving the trip to the coast without wondering if one of our own will eat us. You heard what Mark said. She killed his friend. What's the difference between that boy and us? I'll tell you what it is. Nothing."

"Colten, if you don't drop this, I swear —"

"You swear what?" Mark asked. "Three against one. The vote was fair, so get over it."

"She's already wearing it, you dunces," Adrianna called testily. "And, Mark, your argument is ridiculous. A fair vote would've included the entire team, which it didn't. Lauren, did you get a vote?"

Lauren shook her head.

"I know I wouldn't vote for something so ridiculous," Adrianna said. "We haven't even left yet, and you're bickering. Kaegan, you're awesome. You others can jump in a lake of piranhas, or I'll push you in one myself if I have to hear you bashing on Soren the entire way to Mexico."

"She's not a morning person," Soren explained in a muffled voice.

"I wish you wouldn't wear that," Kaegan said, worry swimming in the gray depths of his eyes as they raked over her covered face.

She shrugged. If it were just the three of them and Adrianna, it would be different. But the new team members, Mark especially, changed things. She didn't want him hating her any more than he already did, and if wearing the muzzle took the sting off teaming up with the murderer of his best friend, then it was a burden she could bear.

The black of night had relinquished the horizon to the deep blues and subtle oranges of sunrise, and Soren nodded a good-bye to one of the night guards she recognized. When they were outside of the colony gates, she turned and inhaled, pinning to memory the smell of home.

The others had set out, but Kaegan lingered. "I'll bring you back here," he promised. "When this is through, you'll see it again."

She smiled sadly at the promise he had no control over keeping, but his face, heavy with the shadows of the lingering night, stayed focused on her, serious. "You kissed me yesterday."

"On the cheek."

"Don't diminish it. The kiss counted. Does it mean you care for me?"

She shouldn't answer. Instead, she should forget about the feelings that churned inside of her, creating a hell for both of them and casting them into dangerous waters.

"Soren," he growled, stepping closer until the coming sunrise was blotted out by his imposing frame. "Do you care about me like I think you do?"

"I shouldn't."

His voice dipped low, deep and sensual. "But you do?"

Unable to find her voice, she nodded.

He placed a gentle finger under her chin and ran it over the strap of her muzzle. "You're mine then."

"Yours?" Tears burned her eyes, and she blinked them away. "How could I ever be yours? I can't even kiss you. Not really. I can't be with you. I can't touch you like I want to."

He cupped her face with the palm of his hand and kissed her forehead. His lips lingered there, and she closed her eyes and sighed. Nothing could touch her when he held her like this.

"We'll find a way to be together."

Shaking her head in denial, she whispered, "Not without the muzzle. We're a package deal if you really want to be with me. I hate it. I hate wearing it, but I will if it'll keep you safe."

Resting his forehead on hers, he squeezed his eyes tightly closed. "I miss seeing you. It feels like you're hiding behind it. I don't ever want you to hide from me."

Sliding his hand up the back of her neck and tugging her hair until she looked up at him, he searched her eyes before leaning forward and kissing her on the cheek. For such a hard man, his kiss was unexpected. His lips softened, hesitating for just a moment before he pulled away. When he eased back, his eyes seemed to question if what he was doing was all right. His grip on her hair tightened, and he dragged her waist to him with the other hand, then dipped his mouth to her neck, where he nibbled his way down the length of it.

Frantically, she gripped the fabric of his shirt as his lips traveled down her collar bone. She was melting. At any moment, she'd disappear into him, and she couldn't find it in her to care.

Click. The snap on the back of her muzzle loosened, and the contraption fell away.

"Kaegan," she whispered against his neck. God, he smelled so good. "Kaegan?"

"Mmm?" His teeth grazed her shoulder, and she bucked forward with a gasp.

"Kaegan!" The word had come out a snarl, gravelly and inhuman, and she ducked his embrace and snatched the muzzle from the patch of weeds it had fallen into. As fast as her shaking hands could manage, she fastened it in place and rounded on him. "Don't manipulate me again. I'm not asking for much. You can get the vaccine and have all of me, or you can deal with the muzzle. It's your choice, but stop testing my strength. You don't have any idea what I can and can't handle, but I can tell you this." She spun on her heel and said over her shoulder, "I can't handle killing you." She stomped off in a fog of worry and irritation. Did the man have a death wish?

The others were easy enough to find because Colten and Mark were arguing over coordinates and maps.

"You're both wrong," Adrianna said. "The goal's to get to the Crow, right?"

"What's the Crow?" Soren asked as she leaned against the tree near Adrianna, who was tying her boot.

"It's what will get us the greatest distance the fastest."

"And safest," Kaegan agreed, coming up behind her. "They got the trains running ten years back, but nobody rides them. They are just black market supply trains that run near some of the biggest colonies. They call it the Crow Train on account of all of the scavenger birds following the Deads attracted to the noise on the tracks. The conductors are all hellions and criminals, so how do you propose we convince them to board us? We have nothing of value to trade."

"Let me worry about that," Adrianna said, standing. "First we have to get ourselves to the La Junta colony if we're going to have a shot at jumping it. The trains have to stop there to refuel. And if we're lucky, we can get one to take us within a few days' walk of the coast."

"I don't know," Mark drawled. "If the Crow Train is black market, it will have attracted a seedy population. Are we sure we want to risk getting that close?"

Adrianna sneered. "I suppose we could just walk the entire way, you wuss, but keep in mind, Deads aren't the only dangers hunting in these woods. Not anymore. The longer we're on foot, the bigger the risk."

Kaegan clicked on a flashlight and pointed the beam down a mountain pass on the plastic protected map. "There's our best bet to get to La Junta then. It's the right season for traveling it, and we won't be scaling any hills on the way down."

Colten turned the map and set a handheld compass on the edge. With a frown of concentration, he pointed east. "This way, but we'll have to be quiet about it. The monsters will be looking for an easy way up and down this mountain too, and this is a natural trail."

Mark folded the map, and Soren sidestepped the group and led the way through the brush. She could almost feel Kaegan's gaze on her back. If she'd angered him earlier, she didn't know, nor did she purport to know the inner workings of a normal red-blooded man.

All she knew was he scared her, now more than ever.

Chapter Fourteen

Adrianna stood above Soren, pulling her hair back with one hand and swatting at a mosquito with the other. River water rushed through Soren's fingers as she refilled her canteen, refreshing after the long afternoon of walking. On the edge of civilization, or the remnants of it, they'd stopped to rest before making their way through the Dead zone. The monsters still hung around old cities. Maybe they had lived there once, and when food became scarce, they migrated back to where their instincts deemed comfortable. Or perhaps it was the disease telling the deteriorating brain the best chance for finding food was around buildings built by the meat bags they dined on. Either way, the ruins of the damned housed horrors, and they were on a war path to blaze directly through the fray.

"Do you hear that?" Colten asked from his seated position against a towering pine.

"No," Adrianna said, then took a long drag from the canteen Soren handed her.

"You shouldn't drink after that," Mark said.

"Well, given that I've been drinking after *her* since I took the vaccine when I was seven, I'm pretty sure if I haven't croaked and turned into a moaner by now, I'm good."

Ben kneeled beside his pack, zipping up the largest compartment. "Whatever that sound is, it's creepy. Do you think it's from a colony?"

Low metallic groaning echoed off the mountain, stopped, then screeched to life again like some haunting apparition singing her discontent with her demise.

"Have you ever been to the cities before?" Soren asked.

Shaking his head, Ben said, "Never. I was born in a colony up north and only traveled to the Denver colony for training. We didn't see any cities on the way in. Have you?"

"My dad and Sean took us on supply runs when we were old enough. I've seen the Denver ruins but that's it."

"Mark," Kaegan said coldly, "If you call Soren *that* again, I'm going to lob your head off." If it weren't for the calculating expression on his stony face, Soren would've thought he was joking.

He arched an eyebrow. Nope, not kidding.

Mark stood, his dark eyes narrowing to slits. "I don't get you. Of all of the virile women on the planet, you pick a genetic dead end. She's not even hot, Kaegan. She looks like one of those corpses we're always braining. You can't tell me when you look at her you see someone attractive."

Kaegan's jaw ticked. "Keep talking, Mark."

"It's the muzzle isn't it? It adds a little mystery? A little danger? Or maybe you like banging murderers, I don't know. I can't figure —"

Kaegan's fist connected with Mark's nose, and a disgusting crack of broken bone filled the clearing. Mark hit the ground hard, and Kaegan was right there, pummeling him before Soren could even register that he'd moved from his casual stance yards away. Gads, he was fast. Cobra strike fast, and if she didn't do something, he was going to kill the insulting little weasel.

Apparently Ben and Adrianna thought the same because all three of them dove for Kaegan at the same time. Ben was bucked off easily, but even through a haze of blood lust, Kaegan seemed to have enough of his head that he didn't fling her or Adrianna with the same brute strength.

"Stop. Stop it!" she said, steel in her voice. "Let him say what he wants. They're just words."

"No!" Kaegan said, pushing off Mark's coughing frame. "They aren't just words to me. I've had to watch people talk to you like this since the day I met you. We left Dead Run River, and I thought we'd be clear of it, but then Colten mouths off too much for his own damned good…"

"Hey," Colten said halfheartedly. He still hadn't moved from his seated position by the bank, like Kaegan beating the peas out of someone was just another Tuesday.

"…And now I have to listen to this asshole insult you? No. I'm not doing it anymore, and anyone who doesn't like it can turn back." He jammed an accusing finger at Mark. "This team isn't a team if you're relentlessly bashing what you perceive as the weakest link. Which she's not, by the way. I've watched her fight—you haven't had the privilege yet. Your taunts are on borrowed time, my friend, because she could gut you quicker than you can snap your damned fingers, and if she doesn't feel like it, I'll do it myself if I have to hear you cutting her down at every turn." His voice dipped to a growl. "Don't…test me."

Adrianna had dug an apple from her pack and crunched into it. Around the bite, she said, "Soren, your boyfriend is hot."

"He's not my—"

Kaegan threw her the coldest glare over his shoulder. Oh, hang it then.

"You broke my nose!" Mark clutched the injury with two cupped, blood covered hands.

"Surely you see you had that coming, right?" Adrianna asked. "When a furious looking giant tells you to *keep talking*, it's a warning, not a dare."

"If you knew the truth about Soren, you wouldn't defend her!" Blood gushed from Mark's nose as he used his hands to push him up.

"Mark," Adrianna warned, stepping toward him.

"No, I want to hear this," Colten said, dusting leaves from his pants as he stood.

"You should. All of you should know exactly what you're traveling with. What you're sleeping next to and trusting with your lives in battle."

Kaegan turned, his throat working as his eyes landed on her.

Horrified, she whispered, "Stop."

"When we were little, vaccines were scarce. The only people vaccinated were experiments to determine the side effects, so most of us were still exposed to the virus—to Soren. Drew Jacobs was a kid, a ten-year-old boy, and you turned him. We knew what you were, what you were capable of, because the teacher talked to us all about you in meetings each year before school started. She talked like you were special, but you weren't. You were just a killer they were warning us to stay away from."

"Please," she breathed, shaking her head against the onslaught of memories.

"I found her," Mark said, voice cracking as his eyes rimmed with moisture. "I came to find Drew because we always walked home together, and she was eating him from the neck in. Her mouth was covered in his blood, and he was staring at the sky with this horrified look. I'll never get his expression out of my head as long as I live. He was terrified when he died. I screamed for the teacher, and she told me to run and get help, but I knew he was already gone. He woke up and turned the teacher, a mother of two and the nicest lady in the world. She killed two of her students who'd lingered in the school yard, and they killed their friends. All kids in my class." A single tear streaked through the gore on his face. "I can still hear the echo of the shots as the guards put down my friends, my teacher. If that's who you want, Kaegan, you're just as messed up as she is."

The taste of him. Soren still remembered what he tasted like. It was the only thing she'd put in her mouth that tasted right. The horror on everyone's face as they realized what she'd done had tainted the taste and sealed her fate as a monster, deserving of human scorn. Drew's empty gaze still haunted her. He'd pleaded after she'd nicked his jugular, but there was nothing she could do. He'd gone violently, and at the memory of it she swallowed bile that threatened to grapple its way up the back of her throat.

Staring at the riverbank pebbles near the toes of her boots, she bit her lip against the sting of shame and wished she could be anywhere but here, under the appalled stares of teammates who would never accept her now.

And Kaegan. *Kaegan.* The affectionate feelings he had would be tainted with the bloody knowledge of those children's deaths. Of the children of the teacher, Mrs. Parker, who had to grow up motherless because a monster had killed their parent. They'd thought they were safe inside those cement fences, but they hadn't realized the real threat walked among them.

She'd wanted to tell Kaegan, but not like this. Honesty was important, but this should've come from her. Unable to look at him, she shouldered her satchel and said gruffly, "Now you know why I wear the muzzle," then sidled past the imposing man who would now be a stranger.

Adrianna squeezed her shoulder as she passed, but she shrugged it off. She didn't deserve comfort for something like that. Mark had a right to be mad. She'd ruined a lot of lives, and his was apparently one of them. The others followed slowly, and she was glad to be in front. She couldn't bear to see the disgust on their faces.

She was so lost in her own turmoil, she didn't realize the eerie noise was getting louder until she broke through the clearing. An old farmhouse with a collapsed roof stood in the shadow of a windmill. The blades turned, influenced by the breeze, and sang a haunting song of the ghosts who used to live in the ruined house behind it. Chills lifted the hair on her forearm. Six Deads stood under the windmill, looking up to where the sound was coming from. Just staring.

None moaned or moved. Maybe they'd been there for months, drawn to the noise. The wind dropped, and the blades quieted, and the Deads dropped their empty gazes until the wind picked up again.

"Do you want to leave them?" Adrianna asked, sympathy lacing her voice.

Leave them to this empty life of waiting for the breeze to make a melody? "No. It's war, right?" she asked in a flat tone. "Every Dead at the end of our blades now is one less threat later. I'll do it. You wait here for the others."

Grass tickled her waist and flowed like river waves as air currents caressed it, urging her forward. The clearing stank of rot, but other than the walking corpses, this place was probably once beautiful. A paradise. She ran her hands over the soft blades of pasture and closed her eyes for a moment, imagining what the home looked like before the end of the world. Children playing in the yard, hanging from the frayed rope swing that still clung stubbornly to a giant oak out front. The paint had been stripped by Mother Nature, but maybe it was white before. Perhaps pastel blue to match the sky. A cloud covered the sun, dimming the field and casting gray over everything.

One of the Deads, a man with a missing eye and stringy hair down to his shoulders, turned at her approach. His clothes hung in tatters, and his skin had turned a greenish hue. Strips of flesh were missing from his neck and face, and his ribs were exposed, like he hadn't turned fast enough before another ate him. Poor sod. What an awful way to go. A flash of Drew's face on the Dead made her stomach clench, and she pulled her knife from its sheath on her leg.

She'd sat there shivering after Drew had died, knowing she should kill him completely before he woke up, but she'd been too shocked. Too weak. There was no more room for fragility now. The Dead stumbled toward her, attracting the attention of the others, who then followed him. At least they weren't waiting on the wind anymore. And soon, very soon, they'd be put to rest, like what should've happened the day they died. Killing them was an act of kindness; she just hadn't realized it until this moment.

Drawing her blade back, she thrust it into the Dead's temple and kicked him away. Jamming the knife upward, she caught the next through the jaw and pulled her battle blade with her free hand. The blade shone in the remnants of hidden sunlight as it arced against the neck of a female Dead who looked on the verge of starvation. Recovering the blade from the limp Dead, she spun and hit the next two in the throats as they lined up, and she gritted her teeth as her blade sunk to the hilt in the skull of a young girl, taken too young by a disease that should not have existed.

It wasn't until she stood panting over the bodies that she noticed the rope tied from the girl's wrist to a woman, whose severed head stared back at her, teeth clacking rhythmically. Kneeling, she touched the blood stained rope and frowned. Any similarity between the two Deads had faded over the years of their decay, but they had to be related. Mother and daughter, perhaps, who'd got in a bad spot somewhere and been cornered. Tied themselves together so they'd stay side by side forever.

She wanted to weep for them.

Instead, she drew her dagger upward and freed the mother's snapping jaws from an unfair afterlife.

She didn't know how he'd approached so quietly, but Kaegan unhooked the small shovel from her satchel and started digging without a word. Dropping to her knees, she scooped dirt with her hands until there was a shallow grave made for two, and wordlessly, they dragged the mother and daughter into their final resting place. She cradled the child in her mother's embrace and Kaegan covered them with the rich, black earth.

When she turned, the rest of the team stood in a quiet line near the grave, but she didn't offer an explanation. She wouldn't bury every one — couldn't bury them all like they deserved — but she'd bury the ones she couldn't live without doing it for. If the team didn't like it, tough. She was through with apologizing for who she was.

Glaring at Mark, with his face still caked in blood, something loosened deep within her. She'd been sorry for so long, but what for? She was a monster, trying to be human, and damn it, she'd succeeded for the most part. She was a killer, the daughter of the infamous Laney Landry and Derek Mitchell. She'd been trained to fight by Finn and learned survival from Aaron Guist himself. Vanessa had gifted her speed with a blade, and she'd been raised as a daughter of the heart by the greatest leader in the known world, Sean Daniels. She was warrior, friend, ally, and enemy. She was Dead and human, and no matter which side she chose, she was traitor. Tired of apologizing for being different, this was where the winds of change turned into a fucking tsunami. She was a weapon, and they didn't even know it.

She.

Was.

Soren.

Chapter Fifteen

Castle Rock—A Nice Place to Live, a sign on the visitor's center read. They'd ghosted the tree line as long as they could, and now all that lay before them was city. Dead city.

Gutters sagged from paint-stripped buildings, lush overgrowth had taken over the once manicured lawns, and leaning street lights dotted crumbling sidewalks. Power lines that had once carried the convenience of electricity snaked the street under their felled poles. Cracks that spider-webbed the pavement told of the earth's unrest in the wake of the apocalypse. Debris littered everything. Piles of dirt and leaves higher than a man's shoulders shadowed corners of most of the buildings, and climbing ivy crept over houses, threatening to consume them completely. A mangy looking dog stood in the middle of the street with a snarl on his lips and a cocked head, like he was deciding if they'd make an easy meal or not.

Maybe at one time it had been *a nice place to live*. Now, it was ashes of the city it had once been.

Soren skirted a huge chunk of rebar-laden cement that must have been washed out by a flood. Colten climbed to the top of the rubble and scanned the area, assault rifle in hand. He didn't have his finger on the trigger, but instead it brushed just above it, not ready, but close enough.

"Anything?" Kaegan asked. He hadn't said a word to her in the hours they'd been walking, and the absence of his attention left a lonely, gaping hole in her.

"Nah. Nothing moving that I can see. They must be gathered farther inside of Denver. That or the bulk of the Deads here have already migrated south."

"Let's keep moving then," Kaegan said. "It'll be dark soon and we need to keep an eye out for shelter. A house or building that looks secure."

The dog vanished behind what looked like a crumbled grocery store. The animal was a good sign. They didn't tend to stay where Deads were dense unless they wanted to get eaten. The world didn't house many weak animals anymore. Everything alive was still breathing because it had fought to survive.

"There," she said, pointing to what looked like a thick grouping of trees. The branches of the crepe myrtles were heavy with flowers and sagged just enough to show the stonework of a building behind it. The roof seemed to be mostly intact from where she stood, and the one window she saw had been boarded with thick plywood in recent years. Someone had stayed there. With a little luck, they were long gone and not pointing the barrel of an old Winchester rifle at them right now.

"Good," Kaegan said, approaching the building with long, confident strides. With the barrel of his shotgun, he moved branches of some sort of giant shrub aside.

Castle Rock Museum, the hand painted cream and black colored sign read.

"Let's go see if anyone is home," Adrianna said, stepping around the corner of the building.

So overgrown was the side yard, Kaegan had to hack it with his machete to blaze a trail, and the door stood crooked in the grips of a giant vine that was wrapped around it.

"Well," he muttered, prying it open for Colten to enter, "I don't think anyone has been here for a while."

Colten banged on the wall and waited quietly as Soren squeezed through the opening. A shuffling sounded from a back room somewhere, and she clicked her flashlight on. The ground was covered in a thick layer of dust, but a wide, bloody trail led to a hallway at the back of the main room.

Colten looked at her with somber eyes. "Oh, the owner is home. He's just not human anymore."

The others filed in as they followed the trail, careful to search every room on the way, until finally they came to a closed door. A soft scratching sounded from the other side near the bottom.

"He's probably starving and so weak he's on the ground," she breathed, and Colten nodded.

One, he mouthed.

"Two," she said, gripping the hilt of her knife.

Three.

Shoving the door open, she ran the light over the room.

Four pairs of white, searching eyes fell on them and the instantaneous noise of the groans became deafening.

Colten cursed and pulled a display table over in front of them. It slowed the monsters down, but something latched onto Soren's ankle as he lunged at the first Dead. Cold claws scrabbled at her leg, but she couldn't drop the light, or Colten would be fighting blind.

"Kaegan!" she yelped, falling backward and kicking her leg to dislodge the scrabbling claws. The tiny flashlight clattered to the floor behind her and flickered out.

The door flew open the rest of the way and slammed against the wall, and a new, brighter light arced over the room. As Kaegan's large frame hurtled over her to join the fight, she stabbed at the Dead, still shrouded in darkness. How terrifying that she couldn't see him! Horror seized her throat as the hands reached higher. He was coming for her, and at any moment her leg would be close enough to his mouth that she would feel his gnashing teeth.

In one last effort, she closed her eyes and tried to imagine where his head would be. Thrusting down with her blade, the clammy hands stilled, and she stifled the scream of relief that filled her lungs.

Strong hands pulled her backward against a wall. "Are you okay?" Kaegan asked, eyes wide.

"Yeah," she said, breath heaving from the rush of panic.

Under the beam of his flashlight, her attacker lay facing them with empty eyes that seemed glued to her leg, as if even in death he hungered to hurt one last thing. He wasn't long decayed, a year maybe, unlike the others in the room. Also unlike the others, he was missing the bottom half of his body. Bile stung her throat, and she looked away.

"Soren," Kaegan whispered. "What did you do?"

"I didn't do that to him. It was them." She pointed to the pile of bodies Colten was standing over.

"No, not him. Your leg."

Confused, she followed the flashlight beam. Blood gushed from a gash in her pant leg, and she held up the knife she still clutched in her hand. Oh, she'd brained the Dead all right. She'd also done a bang-up job of stabbing herself in the process.

"Gads," she whispered.

Kaegan scooped her up on one swift motion and barreled out the door. Damn, he was strong. Her weight didn't even seem to bother him in the least. Neck craned, he searched for something. Just as she was about to ask, Adrianna said, "This way. There's light coming from upstairs."

Scaling the stairs behind Adrianna, a single bead of perspiration streamed down Kaegan's clenched jaw.

"Do you hate me?" she asked.

Adrianna turned the mattress of a small bed over, dislodging a dust cloud into the air, and he set her down on top of it.

Pungent with the smell of mothballs, the mattress sunk in under her weight, springs creaking with the motion.

"We'll talk about this when you're not bleeding, yeah?"

His clipped tone made it hard to ask. Closing her eyes so she wouldn't see his anger, she asked, "So that's a yes?"

"For crissakes, no! No, I don't hate you. I don't know what that says about me, and frankly I'm tired of thinking about it. I can't hate you, Soren. It's…" His chest heaved as he searched her eyes with an intensity to rival the sun. "I can't…" He sighed explosively and dropped his head. "Shit."

Adrianna was working furiously to get the bleeding stopped on her leg. "Think he loves you, Soren."

Kaegan flicked two fingers at Adrianna and nodded. "That."

"Just say it, you giant moron," Adrianna advised. "You're screwing this all up."

Soren went completely still. It couldn't be. After what Mark said, it couldn't be possible that he felt anything toward her but disgust and distrust. Right? But no, the silver in Kaegan's eyes filled with emotion — rage, worry, and something else that brought flutters to her stomach and made her heart feel like it was too big for her chest.

Dust motes swirled around him in the rays of sunlight that filtered through the dirty window as he searched her eyes. "I haven't ever said that to anyone."

"You don't have to say it to me," she said, giving him an out.

"I love you, Soren," Adrianna said in a deep voice.

"Stop," Kaegan drawled.

"Stopping," Adrianna said, zipping her lips, then ripping into a baggie of bandages.

His eyes stayed on Adrianna's work for a long time before he turned to her. Instead of saying anything, he took her hand and placed it on his chest. His heartbeat was strong, steady. "It's yours."

And somehow that small gesture meant more than any three words ever could.

She parted her lips to confess just how much he affected her, but Adrianna said, "Kaegan, I need you to hold her together while I stitch or we'll never get this stopped. You nicked yourself good, girl. And where in the fig is Mark? That little douche. He's the one with the medical experience."

"I don't want him touching her. You're doing fine," Kaegan murmured, pressing her opened skin together.

Soren watched in wonder. It looked like it should really hurt. Times like these made her thankful she was a freak. She didn't feel anything from the long, open gash, not even a dull ache.

For someone who swore up and down she didn't know much about medical stuff, Adrianna sure did stitch her up swiftly enough. The stitches didn't even look that crooked. She frowned thoughtfully at Adrianna, whose dark hair hid her face as she wrapped gauze around the clean wound. Her friend had changed since she'd left. Grown stronger, more secure with herself. Pride swelled in her chest as she smiled down at the feather laden braid that twined down her tresses. It looked like her own, but dark, where her pigment was light. It still struck her sometimes how alike and dissimilar they were all at once.

"All right, Sor," Adrianna said, patting her good leg. "If your super special zombie healing abilities are going to work on this, you need to eat, which means…" She pointed to Kaegan and waited.

"I need to hunt."

"Bingo."

"Colten," he called.

Steps sounded off the stairs, and Colten popped his head around the corner. "What?"

"You want to go hunting with me?"

"For what?" Colten asked.

"For Soren."

Colten looked at her with a confused knot in his brow. "I already stabbed her once."

"Not hunting *Soren*, you idiot," Kaegan growled. "She needs to eat."

"Fine. Do you like dog?" Colten asked, eyebrows almost to his hairline like he was asking how her day went.

"She's not eating dog meat," Adrianna said with a shake of her head. She was grinning, but Colten couldn't see it from his place on the stairs.

"We'll hit up the tree line again and see if we can get lucky," Kaegan assured her, squeezing her hand.

Worried, she said, "If you're going that far, take Ben with you too. Just in case. And don't let Colten spit on my food."

"I heard that," Colten called from below as Kaegan chuckled warmly.

Leaning forward, he kissed her forehead. "We'll be back soon."

"Kaegan," she said as he left.

He turned and jerked his chin in question.

Her heart hammered away, rivaling its speed during the fight below, but this fear was different. "About what you said earlier."

"Yeah?"

"Me too."

A slow smile spread across his sensual lips, and he winked. "I know." Turning, he left without a backward glance.

She sat with her mouth hanging open, then clacked it closed. That cheeky man.

Adrianna's gaze followed him out with a toothy grin. "I like him."

"Of course you do. You like Colten too," she accused.

"Don't. Don't play matchmaker with me, Soren Mitchell. I would chew that boy up and spit him out and ruin him along the way. He's too good to get mixed up with me."

"You think Colten is good?"

"I do," she said softly. "And someday, you will too."

With that, she turned on her heel and left.

Huh. Soren lay back, sinking into the old mattress. The ceiling was cracked, resembling a map of rivers and highways as the damage stretched from wall to wall. She supposed if it was a choice between Mark and Colten, she'd pick the latter. His insults were losing their sting lately, though why that was, she hadn't any idea.

Testing her injured leg, she stood and scanned the small, dusty room. The previous tenant, likely the one who had been clawing at her leg a half an hour before, had kept a tidy home. Why anyone would live on the fringe of a colony alone was beyond her. Survival rates were grim if you didn't have the safety of numbers, and looking around the room, it seemed like such a lonely existence. A bedside table housed an old paperback book, the cover so layered with dust, it was unreadable. The single window was adorned with a thick panel of fabric, and she pushed it aside to see the street below. In the waning light, the dog stared up at her with a tilt to his head. The shepherd looking mutt had one ear that flopped, making him cute if one could ignore the snarl on his lips. Maybe the owner hadn't been so alone after all. If it was indeed his dog, what kind of loyalty did a creature have to possess to stay around for months after his master died?

A knock sounded, light but firm, and she turned. Lauren stood with her hands clasped in front of her, looking decidedly uncomfortable.

Soren smiled encouragingly, but then remembered the girl wouldn't be able to see it behind her muzzle.

The girl's mouth moved, as if she wanted to say something, but nothing came out. Her honey-blond hair was pulled back, and her soft brown eyes studied her. A smattering of dark freckles graced her cheeks. Why hadn't she ever noticed them before? Now they seemed like the most obvious and endearing of her features.

Lauren sat on the bed and pulled a small chalk board from her pack. The chalk made a soft screeching noise as she scribbled across the dark panel.

Was the boy an accident?

Soren sat on the bed and nodded. "He was unkind to me, and one day it got to be too much. It wasn't like Mark said. I didn't just eat him because I was hungry. He was choking me after school because he said his father would be proud of him. I thought I'd die, so I bit into him as hard as I could."

Erasing the board with the sleeve of her green hoodie, she wrote even faster than before.

> That's what I thought. You don't seem to be the type of person to kill someone lightly. I can tell these things.

Relief swelled and stretched until she sighed. Lauren probably didn't know it, but her belief in her was a rarity. "Are you and Mark together?"

> Sometimes, but not right now.

She didn't explain further, and Soren didn't push. Instead, she asked, "What happened to your voice?"

> It's broken. I'm not some sob story with a traumatic experience that made me clam up. I just don't have a sound. Sometimes I scream and scream, desperate for anything to come out, but nothing ever does.

Out of the corner of her vision, Lauren stared at her while she read the chalk board.

As soon as she looked up, Lauren wiped it clean and wrote:

> It doesn't bother me except when I want someone to listen to me. I get overshadowed in groups.

"I bet. I'll try to listen better."

One nod and Lauren pointed to the floor beside the bed.

"You want to sleep there tonight?"

Yes, she mouthed.

"You're not afraid of me eating you in your sleep?"

She snorted and shook her head.

> You won't. I'm too gristly.

Ha. Lauren put the chalkboard away and stood.

"Wait. You can have the bed with Adrianna if you want it. I don't sleep much, so the mattress would be wasted on me."

The ghost of a smile took her lips, and she mouthed, *thank you*, before she disappeared down the stairs.

Kaegan could hear them, smell them even, but so far hadn't caught a glimpse of the beast they hunted.

"This is a bad idea," Colten warned.

"You have any other ideas on easy game that's active this time of the evening?" Ben asked.

"Easy? Have you ever hunted boar before? They're mean as sin, especially if you sneak up on them."

"Soren needs red meat and a rabbit or two won't do," Kaegan whispered. "We could use the protein too. Don't go for the big daddy. Just pick off a smaller one, and get out of the way."

Colten muttered, "I can't believe we're reduced to feeding a freaking zombie now. Some fighters we are."

Anger coursed his veins, red and blinding until all he could think about was wrapping his fingers around Colten's throat. Closing his eyes, he counted to ten, and then ground out, "If you call her a zombie again, your nose will match Mark's."

"Geez, man. You're so touchy now."

"He's got it bad," Ben said.

Bad? Nah. He'd liked girls before. It had been a few years since he'd had any kind of steady relationship with one, but bad? So he thought about her more than was maybe healthy. And he worried about her wellbeing. And when people insulted her, he wanted to kill them slowly. Okay, so maybe he did have it worse than he ever had before, but it was Soren. She was different. Not just the way she looked, which enamored him more every time he saw her, but she was kind. Not polite-kind to trick people into liking her, but she was someone who honestly cared about the feelings of others. And she did what she thought was right no matter what anyone else thought of her. She was respectable, beautiful — this gorgeous warrior who had consumed him, mind and body, without any effort at all. And when she fought? She was an artist.

"Hello," Colten said, waving his hand in Kaegan's face.

Irritated, he swatted it away and ducked a low hanging branch. The end of the world had been bad for the humans, but for nature it was a triumph. Animals had made a comeback as their natural habitat ate at city ruins. Packs of dogs ran wild; boars had pushed their way into the mountains in giant groups; and he'd even seen a tiger once, probably the offspring of ones escaped from zoos or personal, rare animal collections. Deads were the biggest danger, but they weren't the only risk out in these woods.

A musky smell permeated the woods, and grunts filled the evening air. They were running out of daylight and fast, and no way did they want to be stuck out here longer than they had to.

A great crashing barreled through the woods, and Kaegan tensed. "Get back," he shouted, gripping his machete. The last thing he needed was a teammate in the path of his swing.

Big. The tusked beast was so large, the giant ferns and brush shook in his wake as he bore down on them.

This was going to hurt.

Chapter Sixteen

"Soren," Kaegan whispered, shaking her shoulder gently.

She opened her eyes and didn't recognize where she was for a moment. Moonlight streamed through the window, illuminating Adrianna's arm hanging down from the mattress above her.

"I must've fallen asleep," she breathed, pushing herself off the floor and locking her elbows behind her. That was strange. She felt as if she'd been asleep for a long time, but that wasn't usual for her.

Ben and Colten shuffled in and collapsed on the floor. They looked exhausted, and Colten smelled like blood.

Kaegan leaned over her, his hand brushing her hip as he jerked his head toward the stairs. "Eat and then you can go back to sleep."

The deep blue light illuminated one side of his face and made his eyes look brighter. A strand of hair fell forward, and she brushed it behind his ear with a grateful smile. He was tired, and still, he'd gone into the night to hunt for her. People like her just didn't get this lucky.

The palm of his hand was rough against hers as he helped her up, and she followed him down to the first floor. He favored his injured leg more than he had earlier, and when he turned toward a crackling fire in the fireplace, he grunted.

Pulling him to a stop, she probed his ribs and he winced. "What happened?"

"Rough hunt. Probably just a couple of cracked ribs. It doesn't feel so bad."

Unthinking, she lifted his shirt and exposed bruised flesh over his rib cage. "Can you breathe all right?"

"No punctured lung here. I'm breathing fine."

From where she stood, she could tell each inhalation pained him, but he wasn't gasping for air. She ran light fingertips over his flesh, hands adjusting to the shape of each rib, and Kaegan stiffened, then shivered under her touch.

The look in his eyes was nothing short of ravenous. Gripping her hand in a move so fast it startled her, he leaned forward. The shimmer of the flames glowed across his skin in waves. "Until you are comfortable enough to take your muzzle off, until you are comfortable enough with me, I'm not pushing you for intimacy."

His words stung. It wasn't discomfort with him that made her wear the damned thing. "Did you not hear Mark's rather loud tale of my murders?"

"Murder is premeditated, and I doubt you meant to kill that kid. You were just a child."

Pressing her shoulders back, she lifted her chin. If he was going to set ultimatums, then she could too. "I'm not fooling around with you without the muzzle on." Cocking an eyebrow in victory at the blank expression that took his face, she turned to the slabs of meat that sat atop a plastic bag near the fire.

Hesitating for only a moment, she unsnapped the mask and sank her teeth into a rather large boar's shoulder. Stifling a groan at the relief of food hitting her taste buds, she ate quietly as he watched her. She couldn't imagine what she looked like in his eyes, eating raw like that, but he'd have to get used to it eventually. Her entire team would, because she sure as pig pebbles wasn't going to hide what she was anymore.

With a knife, Kaegan cut thin slivers of ham and slid them onto a spit carved from the woodpile. His skin glowed as he sat next to the fire and cooked his meal. Except for an occasional spark throwing a pop from the fire, the room was quiet. Moments like these were rare, meant to be savored and tucked away to remember later when things looked bleak. His lips puckered slightly as he blew steam from the meat. What she wouldn't give to be able to touch her lips to his, to lose herself in his touch and forget everything that had ever happened.

Unable to eat more, she washed her face with canteen water and settled against the wall while he ate. Between bites, he said, "I dated a girl once who was addicted to pickled beets."

"Beets?"

"Yeah, those little red vegetables? She ate them at every meal. They smelled terrible."

"Hmm, still not as weird as eating raw meat, I'd guess." Imagining another girl touching Kaegan brought something ugly and dark to the surface, and she turned away so he wouldn't see her jealousy. She suddenly wished she had an ex-boyfriend story to punish him for making her feel this way.

"What's wrong?"

"I don't like hearing about other girls," she blurted. Angry at her mouth, she muzzled it, clicking the contraption into place.

Kaegan set the empty skewer down and wiped his hands on a cloth. Slowly, as if he were hunting her, he stood and pulled her up with him. "If you want to know me," he said, tilting her head back, "you'll know all of me. Girlfriends, friends, family, I won't keep my life from you, Soren. You shouldn't be jealous of others or angry with my past." He laced his fingers around her knuckles and drew her hand upward until it rubbed the length of his hard erection through his pants. His voice dipped to a whisper as he said, "No one has ever affected me like you do." His other hand gripped the back of her neck, daring her to pull away. "Take the muzzle off."

Nothing sounded better in that moment than giving in to him, but the memories dredged up from Mark's tale of her downfall were too fresh. She wasn't scared of much, but his loss to her bad decision wasn't acceptable.

"Guist packed a vaccine in my pack," she breathed.

Searching her face, his eyes went cold, serious. "That's not a solution for us."

"Why not?" She didn't understand his reservations. All he had to do was take the vaccine and they could be together.

Releasing her, he frowned. "It just isn't, Soren. And it doesn't matter how close we get to each other—it won't change. Just...just know I'm doing this for us, okay?"

Turning, he kicked his bag against a wall and lay down with his back to her. Stunned, she stood watching him until his breathing became less ragged and angry. He'd explained this more than once, and what did she do? She kept pushing him on something he didn't want to do. She didn't know his reasons, but whatever they were, they were important to him.

The stairs beckoned her, an escape from the discomfort of his anger, but she couldn't go back to sleep like this. Clenching her fists against the fear of rejection, she lay down behind him, closed her eyes, then ran her palm under his arm until she rested her hand on his taut abdomen.

Kaegan went still beneath her touch, stiffening until he was a stone statue under her hands. With a sigh, he relaxed and placed a big, warm hand over hers, as if to keep her from pulling away.

"I'm sorry," she whispered onto the back of his neck. "I won't mention it again."

He stroked her hand gently, slowing as he relaxed into sleep, and miraculously, against the safety of his body, she fell under the deep folds of slumber too.

Kaegan's movement woke her. He jerked his arm, now wrapped tightly around her, as if he were dreaming. He frowned in his sleep, and she gripped his bicep. His eyes flew open, wide and furious, and for seconds, he just stared at her as if he'd never seen her before. Little by little, the tension seeped from his body, and the stony muscles under her hand relaxed.

"Bad dream?" she whispered.

Gray dawn light stretched through the cracks in the boarded up window and lit the devastated expression on his face. "Yeah," he said, soft voice trembling slightly.

His unshaven jaw was deliciously rough as she ran her palm over the sharp planes of his face. "Whatever it was, it's not real."

His gaze drifted somewhere above her. "It felt real."

"What was it about?"

"My mom. Losing my mom. We weren't in a colony when it happened, so I wandered around alone for a few days before I was able to find help."

"Oh my gosh. Kaegan." What else could she say? A ten-year-old boy had walked Dead infested woods all alone, mourning the person he loved the most. He must have been terrified. She tried to imagine what she would do if Mom had died outside of colony, and swallowed the heartache. It was too hard to even think about, and Kaegan had lived it. From the faraway look in his soft gray eyes, he was still reliving it.

"It's over now. It was a long time ago." His lips pressed against her forehead but the sound of his voice still held phantoms of a past more painful than she'd even thought existed for him.

"Hey," she said, desperate to ease the pain of his memories. "You know how I know you like me?"

His arm tightened around her waist, and his leg came to rest between hers. "How?"

"Because you hug me in your sleep." It was impossible to pretend during sleep, but in the middle of the night, he'd rolled over and scooped her up like it was the most natural thing in the world.

A deep chuckle bubbled up from his throat, and she gave a little sigh of relief that the spell his mother's loss had cast had been broken. "Maybe I'm just a cuddler."

"No. I've watched you sleep next to Colten before, and you two can't seem to get far enough away from each other."

"This is wrong," Mark said from behind her.

Tilting her face up, she squinted as Mark's tall frame blocked the wisps of sunrise.

"There's nothing wrong with me sleeping beside him," she said, confused.

"Not you, Dead. He's wrong for encouraging this. It's instinct for you to find a healthy host, unvaccinated and easy. You are doing exactly as your disease intends. I can't fault you with doing what you are programmed to do. But you," he said, glaring at Kaegan. "You should know better than to play house with a fucking Dead."

"I don't know how I feel about this," Colten said from the doorway. "Ripping into Soren is my gig. What you're saying doesn't sound right. If she wanted to eat Kaegan, she could've done it ten times over."

"Oh, she's a patient hunter," Mark said. "She waited years before she killed Drew. Sat in our classes like she was one of us. Watching us. Picking her victims."

Rage moved her, rocketed her up until she stood face to face with Mark. "Drew, your best friend, was an evil little shit who tried to kill me. Kill me! It was a choice between his life or mine, and I was the better monster. Your memories of Drew have blurred over time. He taunted me every day, pushed me, goaded me in front of the class, and I wasn't the only one. He was a bully like you are now. Drew wasn't some innocent little human who I ate for giggles, Mark. He was a murderous little weasel who sat on my chest and choked me nearly to death with a smile on his face."

Mark's snake-like eyes filled with fury, and red crept up his neck, flushing his cheeks. He shook, but she didn't care.

"I'm not even sorry for him. I was defending myself. My guilt is over the people he took with him. Their loss is on me. His loss is on him."

"Bitch," he yelled, grabbing her hair and yanking her neck backward.

The cold barrel of his gun jammed into her jaw, but the deafening crack of a weapon being cocked wasn't his. It was Kaegan's, and at that moment, it rested against the throbbing vein in Mark's temple.

"If you pull that trigger," Kaegan breathed in a terrifyingly calm voice, "I won't shoot you. I'll make sure you're bit, and then I'll rip your limbs from you, one by one, and feed them to the Deads. I'll watch you turn and leave you to flop around on your fucking torso until you starve to death. Put. The gun. Down."

Mark's smile was nothing short of twisted as he lowered his weapon and held it up in surrender. His eyes never left hers. "He won't always be around to protect you, Soren."

Colten lowered a Beretta she hadn't even noticed him draw, and Adrianna cursed softly under her breath. "Mark, I went out on a limb to bring you with us, and you've made me regret that decision in record time."

"Seriously? Are you all blinded by her? For what? What possible advantage could you have for championing her? You're all as worthless as the Dead you've put on a pedestal." He spat on the floor at Soren's feet and shouldered his backpack, then shoved the front door open and disappeared.

Lauren clung to the stair railing, her doe eyes wide. Frantically, she scribbled something on her chalkboard.

You shouldn't have done that.

"Done what?" Soren asked.

Taunted him.

The door creaked in the breeze where Mark had escaped, and Soren bit her lip behind the muzzle.

"Cheer up, Soren," Colten said, clapping her on the back so hard she pitched forward. "His bark is probably worse than his bite."

From the bleak expression on Lauren's face, she knew that Colten was utterly wrong.

"You okay?" Kaegan asked. His gaze, like hers, was riveted on the door, but he wrapped his arm around the back of her neck and pulled her close. His heart hammered away, though from his calm demeanor, she'd never have been able to tell he'd been spooked. His gun rested on her shoulder, and she inhaled deeply. She'd never had a gun shoved at her before. Not that she wasn't threatened regularly, but guns had become rarer over the years, survivors choosing blades instead. Knives never ran out of ammo, after all.

"Yeah, I'm fine. Maybe Lauren's right."

"Maybe." He dipped his head until his lips brushed her ear. "But I have to admit I liked watching you tear into him like that."

"We should get going if we're going to reach La Junta in two days," Adrianna said. "If we time it right, we should hit it by nightfall on Wednesday, but we can't afford to fiddle-fart around."

Breakfast was a quiet affair. When stomachs were filled and an extra leg of meat was packed away in plastic to temper the smell, they set out.

Mark leaned against the corner of the museum with a scowl on his face. No one spoke to him, and he followed some distance behind them, but who cared? Lauren was the only one who seemed concerned, and even so, not enough to fall back and hike beside him.

The city was a maze of rubble, matted with human trash from years before, and everywhere, trees and plants poked up through the earth. In another fifty years, the buildings here wouldn't even be standing. Maybe they'd be swallowed up completely.

The smell of animal wafted to her on the breeze, and she paused, wiping a hand across the back of her neck to warm the chill that had settled there. But when she turned, nothing seemed amiss.

"Deads?" Adrianna asked.

"No, just my imagination."

"All that sleep you got last night messed you up," she said with a smirk.

"It must've."

The city seemed unnaturally empty of Deads, so they avoided the woods and traveled with wary eyes scanning their surroundings. By the third hour of hiking through city streets, the only corpses they'd seen were the ones that had starved to death sometime since the last freeze. Shrunken bodies peppered the streets, and bone piles dotted dilapidated doorways. Everything smelled like Deads, so she couldn't pinpoint the danger she felt. Still, the feeling of being followed haunted her, and she turned for probably the tenth time in an hour. Nothing. Just Mark, following up the rear and offering a dirty look for her troubles. Maybe having him at her back was what left her unsettled, and she shook her head to ward off the cold.

As she turned a corner, her attention on a piece of plastic draped across a downed light pole that was flapping loudly in the wind, a clawed hand reached out and brushed her cheek. She jerked back. Groans grew louder as a swarm of Deads rattled a chain link fence they seemed to be trapped behind. There had to be twenty bodies or so, and the more that flung themselves against the fence, the more the metal pole that held it upright leaned.

"Let's go," Kaegan said, and she followed them at a jog. Could they take on twenty? Maybe, but not without a risk of injury and loss. Best to pick their battles, and this was not it.

When she turned back, the fence was bending dangerously forward. She pushed her legs harder to keep up with the others.

A lone Dead stumbled in a circle down one of the side streets and took chase when she spotted them. Adrianna peeled from the group and pressed her forearm on the Dead's chest before thrusting a knife through the top of the corpse's head. It dropped like a sack of stones.

"This way," Adrianna said when she caught up.

Ahead of them was a pileup of old, rusted cars, so they ran down a thin alley and hit a park on the other side. The playset still stood with a single swing clinging to its position by one chain. A filthy baby doll lay under it, and its open eyes seemed to track them as they bolted across the clearing.

This way, the wind seemed to whisper.

The deeper they fled into the park, the denser the brush became, thicker and thicker until it was a prison, and the only way to escape was to go back the direction they came. Kaegan and Colten chopped at the vines with their machetes until a thin path, the width of a deer trail, was made. Everywhere, the sweet rotting scent of Deads clung to the air, unescapable, and so thick, it seemed to settle on Soren's skin.

"Aaah," a Dead yelled, as it stretched its neck toward Adrianna, who ran directly in front of it. The Dead was tangled in the vines, but Adrianna stumbled in her shock, and Soren lurched forward, thrusting her readied knife upward, through its jaw.

It hung limply from its forest prison, and Adrianna stood clutching her chest, frozen. "Geez, I didn't even see that thing."

"Come on," Colten said in a grim tone. "This place is peppered with trapped Deads. It's creepin' me out."

Lauren tugged on her sleeve, and what Soren saw in her face froze her blood. Following to where she pointed behind them, she cursed softly. "Guys?"

"What?" Mark griped.

"We have company."

The fence had broken, and the newly freed Deads were loping toward them faster than they were hacking a path. Soren looked around, panicked as they stumbled through the small opening. The brambles were still so thick, there was no way to run for fear of being ensnared with an ill-placed foothold.

This way, the wind repeated, and the hair on her arms electrified. No, it wasn't the wind directing them to safety. It was an emaciated boy, eighteen or so, with dark hair and bottomless eyes. He stood twenty yards ahead and pointed to the west.

Ben didn't hesitate. Bolting in the direction the boy pointed, he shoved his way through the vines, hacking a pathway.

The boy didn't move, just stared with those empty eyes, and the uneasy feeling in her gut intensified. The monsters were coming, but Dad had taught her something valuable. Something she drew on right now, in the heat of the moment when a split second decision would save or kill them all. Deads weren't the only monsters. Humans could be even more dangerous.

"Ben," she yelled. "Don't!"

He turned, only yards from the boy with a confused frown on his face.

"There," she said, pointing her battle sword the opposite way.

The boy's face transformed into something fearsome, and a slow, yellow toothed smile took over his face before he bolted for the dark shelter of the vines.

"That boy doesn't have salvation for us," she hissed, turning to check the horde's progress. Too close. "Let's go."

"But he's human," Ben breathed. "He could have a shelter around here."

"Soren just saved your life, newb," Adrianna said, slashing at the brambles in front of her. "Not all humans are helpful." And Adrianna would know because she'd told Soren horror stories about the humans they'd fought when Sean took the Denver colony back.

Over and over Soren tripped on the looping, thorny foliage, but at least it seemed to be slowing the Deads as well. The disadvantage? Deads didn't feel anything and just kept coming, crawling over each other in their attempt to reach the team.

"Come on, come on, come on," Colten said, sweat pouring down the sides of his face.

Soren dropped back and brained the two closest Deads to give the others more time. Holy fuck, the forest was thick here. This was a fighter's worst nightmare—being trapped without an easy escape route. Hopping over heavy cords of brush, she could almost feel the Deads breathing on the back of her neck. The sound of their groaning excited others who'd been hung up in the vines and were now struggling and reaching for them.

"Through here," Kaegan said, hacking away at the growth. An old road cut directly through the woods, and as Soren followed the others out of hell, she turned at the opening and waited. The last thing they needed was a group of hungry Deads trailing them, and the opening had created a bottleneck.

A woman stumbled out of the fray, rotted teeth clacking and filmy eyes riveted on Kaegan, who'd come to stand beside her. Fury filled her, pumping through her blood until she couldn't see anything but the Dead's kill zone. She wanted to end the life of anything that looked at him like that, gnashing its teeth with the need to kill him. With a grunt, she pinned the creature against an old tree just as the second Dead emerged. The Dead was old and her bones brittle, and Soren barely had to use force when she jammed her knife downward. Kaegan beheaded the next, and as the third and fourth Dead stumbled out of the tree line, Adrianna and Colten had joined the fight.

Lauren kicked in the clacking heads they'd severed with a grim look of acceptance.

When no more Deads came through the opening, the team stood there, panting and waiting.

"The rest must be caught up in the woods," Kaegan said, shooting her a wide eyed glance.

"Well, let's make tracks," she said. "The more space we have between them and us by evening, the better a chance we'll have for them to lose our scent if they escape."

Mark was already farther up the road, jogging away like he didn't give two waltzing horsefly farts about their fate. MVP did *not* go to him today.

Kaegan shook his head, his mouth set in a grim line. As her strides lengthened to catch up with the rest of the team, he placed the barest touch of his fingertips on the small of her back and looked over his shoulder with a wary frown.

"I feel followed too," she admitted quietly, as the warmth of his touch spread through her back and settled her roiling stomach. It was impossible not to feel safe when he was so close.

Their boots made matching echoes off the cracked concrete as she matched her pace to his. Dark hair had fallen out of its binding and fell forward into his face, but it didn't hide the haunted look there. "We'll feel better when we get away from the city."

His voice rang strong with confidence, but he tossed another worried look at the woods they'd just escaped.

At least she wasn't going crazy.

Kaegan felt it too.

Chapter Seventeen

Soren hacked away at the magnesium fire starter with the blunt end of her knife until a nickel sized pile of shavings sat under a small pile of tinder. It was strange to be away from Kaegan now, but the separation was necessary. He'd volunteered to go with Mark and Ben to refill the canteens at a nearby creek while the rest of the team set up camp.

Colten was rifling through his pack, Lauren was tying a rope between two trees to set up a shelter, and Adrianna had gone off into the trees because she had to *piss like an aquatic camel*. Her words.

Turning the fire starter over, Soren rammed the striker down the ferro rod in a practiced motion, igniting the small pile of shavings to a blinding, tiny flame. Pulling the dry tinder and small twigs over the top, she blew on it lightly, shielding the newborn fire from the bigger breeze with her cupped hands.

"Nicely done," Colten said.

"Thank you. I think that is the nicest—"

"I thought for sure I'd have to watch you try to start a fire for the next hour and a half."

"Asshole," she muttered under her breath. The man just couldn't let her keep a compliment.

Lauren seasoned dried beans while Colten boiled a pot of water over the growing fire. She scoured the nearby woods for dead, dry branches and made trips until the pile was big enough to last through the night. Adrianna returned and scaled a large pine, took her time securing a harness where she'd be sleeping that night, then jumped down just as Colten dropped slivers of ham into the simmering beans. He tossed Soren the bone, still heavy with meat, and she caught it deftly. She chose to ignore that he'd thrown it to her like she was a dog. At least he wasn't shoving cooked food down her throat or insulting her while he was at it. Baby steps.

Night had fallen while dinner cooked, and the only light in their camp was from the flickering flame. The murmur of conversation was soothing as they gathered around the warmth of the fire. Lauren sat next to her and watched intently as she picked meat from the bone and devoured it unashamedly. She'd get used to her eating habit eventually—probably.

Licking the iron flavor from her fingers, she looked up just in time to catch the movement. Reaching back, she drew her battle blade and stood.

"What is it?" Adrianna said, scanning the woods.

Lauren stood beside her and drew her own knife, then pointed.

She saw it. Two eyes reflecting in the wavering orange glow. A wolf. No. The animal slunk closer, eyeing the bone in her limp hand. Not a wolf, but a dog. The dog that had been near the museum.

She almost laughed out loud. Of course he was following them. That's why she and Kaegan had felt hunted the entire day.

"It's the dog from Castle Rock," she said as Colten drew his Berretta. "Don't shoot."

Bending at the waist, she offered the bone the animal couldn't seem to take his focus from. It still had enough left on it to feed a hungry stomach, and she could share. No other dog had ever come this close to her. Attack or run was usually the reaction she got.

The dog growled and backed up as she approached slowly, and she paused, offering the bone farther in front of her. Crouching, she waited as he eased toward her on his belly. His ear was flopped, and his mouth set in what seemed to be a permanent grimace. His teeth were bared, but his dark eyes were still on the bone. He was big, but she could count his ribs, and his hip bones stuck out. A deep pity took her. She'd known hunger like that too. "Easy," she crooned, stretching her arm as far as she could.

In a rush, he bolted forward and took her offering in his powerful jaws, then disappeared into the forest like he'd never been there at all.

She remained, the stretch through her heels feeling good after a long day of walking, and Colten said, "I thought you didn't eat dog meat."

She was able to contain her eye roll, but just barely. "I'm not hunting the dog. Just feeding it."

"Great, well now he'll follow us around looking for a hand out."

"I'll share my food if he does. You won't have to share a single bean." Standing, she said, "It's been a while since the boys left. Do you think they're okay?"

Adrianna shoveled a steaming bite into her maw and said around it, "They're probably bathing in the creek. They're armed to the teeth, so we'll hear if there is a scuffle. Settle, Soren. Your man is fine. I mean, hell, he's built like a freaking mountain. It would take a horde to do any damage."

Adrianna was right. Colten didn't look worried at all as he leaned back against a log he'd dragged up and set his plate on his lap. And she didn't know what Mark was to Lauren, but she looked as if she couldn't care less if they stayed out all night. She was just anxious and for no good reason. Kaegan fought with the violence and unleashed fury of a storm. The man could more than take care of himself.

But as an hour came and went, and then two, she couldn't help the feeling that something was wrong. Even if they'd bathed and filled the canteens ten times over, it should not have taken this long. She tried to stay in the here and now, joining in the soft conversation when she could and helping Adrianna sand the fire until it was nothing but embers to keep dinner warm for the others. Nothing took her mind off Kaegan. What if they'd got trapped somewhere and hadn't had time to pull their weapons, or what if they were treed and needed help?

Her heartbeat had been pounding a steadily climbing rhythm for the better part of an hour, and at this rate, the damned thing would just fling itself from her chest. She stood abruptly. "I'm going to go find them."

She turned and came face to barrel with the north end of Mark's pistol. "No need," he gritted out.

"What are you doing," Colten barked out.

"That's close enough," Mark said, raising what looked like Kaegan's sawed off shotgun in Colten's direction.

"Where's Kaegan," she whispered.

"Don't you worry about him, Dead. He'll probably live. And if he doesn't, well, you won't have to mourn him where you're going. Lauren, don't fucking move, or I'll blast them both."

Dread socked her in the stomach, threatening to bend her in half.

Mark leaned forward, his dark eyes churning and a muscle in his jaw twitching under the tight clench. "Do you even know what you did to me all those years ago, Dead? You ruined everything. I had to drop out of school because of the nightmares. Because you were there, haunting me except you weren't a ghost. You were sitting in the seat next to me while I tried to control the panic that seized me every time I saw you. I've played Drew's death over in my mind a million times, and for the rest of my life, I'll remember the savage look in your cold eyes as you ate him. He was a kid. I was a kid. And everyone just went on like nothing happened. Like someone didn't die inside colony gates to the gullet of a monster. Didn't matter what he did to you. You know why? Because you're a Dead. You don't count. You never did, and for the life of me, I can't figure out why everyone rallies around you like you're some hero of the apocalypse." He cocked his weapon, but it wasn't the pistol in her face that drew her attention. It was the caress of his finger on the trigger of Kaegan's shot gun. The one pointed at Colten.

Oh God, he didn't mean for any of them to make it out of this. They couldn't if he was to join civilization again. Massacring teammates couldn't be hidden if someone still existed who had witnessed what he'd done. His secret would have to go to the grave. Their graves.

The dog barked from behind Mark, so loud it echoed, and she took the split second of his orbiting focus to jam her hand upward, jerking the shotgun's shell into the branches above. The sound was deafening in the quiet of their intended graveyard. Twisting out of the path of his pistol, she rammed her shoulder into his stomach and slugged him across the face before he even hit the ground. The air whooshed out of her lungs as she landed hard on top of him, but she recovered enough to pin his wrists with her knees, and wrap her hands around his throat.

He bellowed in pain and bucked her off of him with surprising speed, and just as Colten and Adrianna reached Mark, he pulled the pistol to her temple and growled, "Don't. Move." The full weight of him pressed against her chest as he settled over her.

"Mark, think about what you're doing," Adrianna pleaded. She, Colten, and Lauren all had weapons cocked and pointed at him. "If you pull that trigger, you'll die within seconds. Is this really how you want your life to end?"

"Oh," he said, panting. "I've thought about this for a decade. If I die tonight, I can die happy knowing I took her with me."

Chaos and yelling broke out around them, but all Soren could focus on was the dark, empty smile that stretched Mark's face until it was almost unrecognizable. She'd die here in the woods, never knowing if Kaegan was okay.

Mark slid his fingers around her throat and tightened them until she couldn't inhale. "Is this how Drew did it, Soren? He was only a boy and didn't know you'd need a bullet through the head, but I'll avenge him and do one better. I'll do both. Good-bye, Dead."

Panic seized her as she fought for breath, and just as blinding pinpoints of darting light blurred the edges of her vision, Mark pulled the trigger.

Nothing happened.

His smile faded, and he pulled the trigger again.

Silence. Not even the wind dared whisper through the tree branches above. And just like that, his weight was gone from her chest.

Kaegan towered over her and lifted Mark until his toes scrabbled for solid ground. Blood ran rivers from a deep gash over his eye, and his hair had come loose from its tie and was littered with leaf matter. He didn't have a weapon, but from the unwavering grip he had on Mark's neck, it was a safe bet he didn't need one.

"You should've killed me," he said in a low, dangerous voice.

Mark pulled a knife from a sheath on his hip, but Kaegan threw him down so hard, his body made a dull thud against the earth.

Gasping and crawling like it would help his lungs recover, Mark tried to escape, but Colten stood in front of him and kicked the knife away. "You'll pay for your treachery, Mark." Colten jerked his head back toward Kaegan. "Be a man about it, yeah?"

"Or," Adrianna chimed in, "a woman about it."

If Soren wasn't still trying to convince air molecules to force their way into her crushed throat, she would've laughed. No it wasn't a funny situation in the least, but she was pretty sure she was in shock.

Kaegan pulled a length of rope from his pack and approached Mark with the look of a Death Bringer in his gray eyes.

"What're you going to do?" Mark asked.

"A life for a life. It's only fair."

"But I didn't actually kill anyone!"

"You killed Ben!" Kaegan roared. "He bled out while you were bumbling around the woods trying to find the camp again. You didn't have to tie him up, Mark. You bashed his skull in."

"Oh my God," Adrianna said in horror.

"No. No, no, no," Soren chanted softly as tears stung her eyes.

"I removed the firing pins from your pistol last night," Kaegan said, hauling Mark upright.

"What? Why? What if I needed the weapon in a Dead fight?"

Kaegan shrugged like he couldn't care less and pulled a hidden knife from Mark's ankle. "I told you I'd let you turn. Warned you if you touched Soren. I don't bluff, Mark. I'm going to tie you to a tree in the woods, and then I'm going to cut you to attract the monsters you hate so much. And when they've had their fill of you, you'll spend the rest of your miserable undead life tied to a tree. You'll starve to death, but the rate is...what?" He frowned at Colten.

"About three years," Colten said with a nod.

"Three years."

Mark's face went pale and sweat dotted his forehead. The whites of his eyes were visible in the muted ember light, and a small whimper wrenched from his throat. "I want her to do it. I want Soren to bite me, it's my last request."

"You don't get a last request, asshole," Colten murmured.

"Please," Mark begged. "I know she won't eat me, and I'll go quickly. Have mercy."

"Soren?" Kaegan asked, cocking a dark eyebrow as if he already knew her answer.

Ben. Ben hadn't done anything wrong, just been in the path of Mark's insatiable wrath, and now he lay cold in the woods somewhere. They'd all be dead if he'd had his way. Every drop of blood that seeped from Kaegan's wound filled her with vengeance, black and bottomless. She dragged her gaze away from the fire in Kaegan's eyes to meet Mark's. "I don't eat dog meat."

Before he could respond, Kaegan shoved a wad of gauze in Mark's mouth, then tied a bandage around his head until the only noise that came from the man was muffled yelling. He struggled, but Colten stepped forward and held him firm.

Steady tears made tracks down Lauren's face, but she stood stoically, gun limp in her hand. Whatever she and Mark had been, she didn't move to defend him now.

Kaegan dragged Mark by the collar until he reached the edge of the dull firelight. "Soren," he said gruffly, "I can handle a lot of things, but I can't handle being away from you right now. Could you please come with us?"

She stood and followed behind Colten, boots crunching through the leaves. Lauren and Adrianna followed closely behind her. Splitting up now that their numbers were dwindling suddenly seemed like a terrible idea.

Kaegan picked a wide tree near the creek. He and Colten tied Mark as if he were hugging the trunk, doubling up on the rope in case he rubbed one free on the rough bark.

Lauren turned away, and Soren wrapped an arm around her shoulder as they made their way to Ben's still body. The moonlight reflected off the shallow waves and illuminated his face in tones of soft blue.

Soren sank to her knees beside him. It wasn't fair. She hadn't known him that long, but he should've gone to war with them and died honorably, not been snuffed out by some messed up revenge trip that had nothing to do with him and everything to do with her. His death was on her. She didn't hit him over the head, would never hurt him, but she'd taunted Mark, and Ben had become collateral damage during his rage. Lauren covered her face with her hands, and her shoulders shook with quiet weeping. Soren held her close, resting her muzzled chin on her shoulder.

The rhythmic *snick, snick* of the handheld shovel sounded behind them as the boys dug a grave for Ben.

Adrianna stood by the creek, watching the water flow by. It was her way. She wasn't good at farewells.

Silently, Kaegan and Colten lifted Ben's body and set him in his final resting place. Adrianna found a large river rock and placed it as a marker at the head of the grave and one by one, they touched it and trailed back toward camp.

As they passed Mark, Kaegan followed through on his promise, pulling his machete and cutting into his forearm until it ran red.

For the first time in her life, the smell of fresh blood wasn't enticing. Now it turned her stomach. Tonight never should've happened.

Colten dropped back, waited for her to catch up, and slipped an arm around her shoulders. Leaning his temple against hers in a move that shocked her to her bones, he whispered, "I saw what you did back at camp. You went after the gun pointed at me instead of the one that would've saved you, and that says something about the type of person you are. I'm sorry I stabbed you when I first met you, and even if we die out here, I'm glad I got the chance to know you." He reached back and unclipped the muzzle. "Don't wear this anymore. It upsets Kaegan, and he's struggling enough with all of this. Hell, I can't stand to see it on you anymore either. You aren't a monster, Soren. People like Mark are the ones who deserve to be muzzled."

Perhaps her emotions had been amplified with the loss of Ben, but the streaming tears down her cheeks were all Colten's doing.

He brushed a knuckle across her damp lashes, his smile white in the moonlight. "I'm still calling you Z, though."

She laughed thickly and nodded. "I don't think I hate it so much anymore."

Chapter Eighteen

K aegan watched her and Colten with an unfathomable expression, and Soren slipped her hand into his when they caught up.

Colten stoked the fire when they arrived back at camp, and the glow lit the woods, flickering off tree trunks and brush. The first aid kit was in Adrianna's satchel, and she handed it to Soren without her asking. Kaegan's face was a gory mess, and they didn't need the smell attracting things that went bump in the night.

"Come on, sit down," she said, gesturing to the dark side of a large evergreen.

Grunting, he slid down against it and sighed heavily. He wouldn't meet her eyes, so she straddled him and cupped his cheeks. "Mark's death isn't one that you should carry. He killed Ben. He would've killed all of us."

He blinked slowly, drawing his dawn gray eyes to hers. "I should've seen it coming."

"You did. You took the firing pin from his favorite weapon. Kaegan, you saved us."

"No, I should've seen the ambush by the creek. Ben had gone quiet, but I just thought he shoved off for a piss. He was dying instead." He hissed as she dabbed the gash on his head with a cloth she'd doused with canteen water. "He hit me with a branch. Looked like he used the same one on Ben. I think I only blacked out for a minute, and when I woke up, I tried to revive Ben, but his face—"

"I know. I saw it." She wished she hadn't, wished there was a way to erase the memory from her mind, but it was there, bright and unavoidable. Maybe it was a good thing she didn't dream.

Brushing his finger down her jaw, he whispered, "You did good. I saw you fight Mark."

"He still bested me."

"Only because you were focused on protecting the others. You were beautiful. Lethal. But when Mark pulled the trigger against your head, it did something awful to me." His voice trembled. "I wanted to rip his head from his body with my bare hands for trying to hurt you."

The firelight on the other side of the tree cast quivering shadows across the woods as the others prepared for sleep. One half of Kaegan's face was illuminated in the soft glow, enough for her to see the hunger that churned in his eyes as he dropped his gaze to her lips.

"I want to kiss you so bad, sometimes I can't think of anything else," Kaegan said, focusing on her parted lips.

It was hard to breathe, hard to think when he looked at her like that. As if he were hurting and the only thing that could relieve the pain was the taste of her. She lifted a curved, threaded needle to his wound, but he grabbed her hand and shook his head.

He gripped her waist so tight, his fingers dug into her flesh as he pulled her forward until she was crushed to his hips. Even through the thick canvass of her pants, she could feel his rising excitement against her.

"I've worried half my life that I'd never find someone to match me," he rasped. "I was scared I'd walk the earth alone and never really be affected by anyone, and then I saw you, and now I don't even feel like the same man anymore. You're different, deeper. And the more I'm around you, the more I want to be different too. My life is yours, Soren. My body, it's yours. I trust you with all of it."

She kissed his neck lightly and whispered against it, "My body is yours too, Kaegan, just not my lips. I'll get the muzzle."

"Don't," he said through gritted teeth. The tree was wide, and the team had settled near the fire. The murmur of their conversation had died until it felt like they were alone with the wind.

"What do you want from me?" she asked.

"Tonight, I don't want anything from you." Slowly, he untied the leather string of her pants, loosened them until they lay open.

Glancing around, she said, "We can't do this here."

Pulling her close until her chest brushed his, he slid his hand down the front of her, cupping her, silencing her denial as the warmth of his hand met the wet heat he'd created with the intensity of his admissions. Her body hummed as she wrapped her arms around his neck. She could never be close enough to him, and as he slid a long finger inside of her, she gripped his shirt and stifled a groan of ecstasy. Rocking against his touch, she set the pace, slow and languid at first, but faster as tension filled her. He nibbled on her neck, sucked and kissed in turn, and as climax built, he pulled her tighter and tighter against him until there was no ending to her and no beginning to him. His arms flexed and shook, his breath trembled against her neck, and she bit her lip against the scream building in her throat. She shattered, and the only thing holding her together was Kaegan's embrace.

"Kaegan, Kaegan, Kaegan," she breathed as she buried her face in his shoulder.

A deep chuckle filled the quiet night and he eased her back. "Don't hide it from me, love. I want to see the face you make when I touch you."

She tried to steady her breathing, but anything more than simply existing seemed impossible. The smile dipped from his face as he studied her, and by the time he slid out of her, she was no better than mud in his hands.

God bless that man, he tightened and tied her trousers when her fingers didn't seem to want to work and then pulled her beside him into the shelter of his arm. Cocking his head, he said, "I like the way you say my name."

She smiled into the darkness, heat flooding her until it reached the tips of her ears as the shudder of aftershocks pulsed against where he'd caressed her.

"I was afraid…" he started. "I was worried you wouldn't be able to feel anything inside of you either. Since you don't feel pain, I didn't know what pleasure would be like for you."

Pursing her lips against a smile of pure satisfaction that threatened to take over her entire face, she snuggled against his ribs. "Pleasure won't be a problem for us."

His lips were warm as they pressed against her hair. "Good."

Kaegan lay below Soren at the base of the tree, on a worn blanket with his go-bag propped under his neck like a pillow. He was on his side, with his arms crossed in front of him as if he were cold, but when she searched for gooseflesh on his skin, she could find none.

Maybe she should put her blanket over him. She was lookout tonight, so she wouldn't need it. No, she was just obsessing. He was fine, and if she covered him up, he'd only wake. Even in his sleep he looked exhausted, or haunted, or maybe a disturbing combination of the two. She could tell being with her had only been a temporary escape, and that his thoughts had drawn inward, to Ben, when he sat beside the campfire to eat the leftover dinner that had been warming there. His silence was deafening as she'd searched for something to say to take the burn of Ben's loss from their shoulders.

No, she wouldn't risk waking him. He needed the rest as much as the others did.

Dragging her gaze away from his sleeping form to the moonlit forest, she leaned back against the trunk of the tree she'd scaled for a better vantage point. Frogs croaked, but it was an unusual sound. Sometimes it was akin to screaming, and at first it had rattled her. And why wouldn't it after the long night the team had? But time healed all, and in this case, settled all, and she had grown used to the screaming frogs as the hours dragged on.

In a few hours' time, it would be dawn, and they could break camp and escape the haunted woods where they'd lost a chunk of their team to betrayal. The urge to hurry from this place was so thick it was almost tangible.

Movement caught her eye, and she squinted, waiting for her eyes to adjust to the darkness below.

Another blurred movement, but this time, she caught a flash of brown fur. The dog was back.

They'd discussed a name for him. Lauren had written *Maynard* on her board, and when Soren had agreed it was the perfect name for him, Colten started calling him Nards for short, so they re-cast their votes. Instead, his name was now Max.

She climbed down the tree and dug a piece of dried venison from Adrianna's satchel. Slowly, she approached with her offering, but Max didn't seem interested in food at the moment. He slunk back and forth, tail tucked.

Soren frowned and cocked her head. Maybe he was agitated by the Deads Mark had likely attracted near the creek. "They're far enough away they won't pay attention to us tonight, Max," she said soothingly.

A high pitched whine wrenched from his throat as he looked behind him and jumped at some disturbance beyond her senses. A twig snapped and Max bolted.

Drawing her battle sword, she listened for a groan, a shuffle, anything that would point her in the right direction. She didn't smell Deads, and she should at this short a distance. She wrinkled her nose and sniffed, but still nothing.

As quietly as she could, she crept through the woods in the direction of that small ruckus. It was probably an animal. A rabbit or deer. Even a boar, perhaps.

The camp was far enough away she could barely make out the fire. It was nothing. She scanned the woods, but everything was still and quiet except for the screaming frogs.

"Geez, Mitchell," she muttered. "Get ahold of yourself."

As she turned, she ran into a solid wall of muscle. A man with a tattoo across the side of his face gave her a cold smile, and then threw a black bag over her face before she could scream. She fought like a wild, injured animal, but as soon as she thought she'd made ground, the crack of her skull sounded like gunfire in her ear.

A dull ache spread from her temple to behind her eye, and her legs seized and refused to work.

This was it. This was the part where she died.

Chapter Nineteen

Adrianna's cursing woke Kaegan up from a deep sleep. Dawn had broken the horizon, and the sun now hung heavy in the eastern sky. He would've been more concerned with the late hour if it wasn't for Mark-the-Dead, standing at the edge of a branch Adrianna was pushing on.

"Hurry up, Colten," she groused.

Colten rubbed his eyes sleepily, yawned, and pulled his machete. One languid thrust and Mark fell to his knees, limp but propped on the branch. The ropes still hung from his wrists, and Colten lifted one up to examine it. "Son of a bitch, someone cut these."

Kaegan looked around, the feeling of unease pushing him to action. "Soren?"

The morning light sifted through the trees, leaving the ground speckled around him. Leaves lazily rustled in the wind and branches swayed. Nothing more.

Adrianna dropped the branch and yelled, "Soren! Where are you?"

"Why would Soren cut Mark free?" Colten asked, still staring at the sliced rope.

"She didn't," he said bolting for the woods. "Someone else did, and I bet this has something to do with that kid we saw in the woods yesterday."

Turning around and around, he searched the woods. Damn it! Where was she? No way in hell would she let Mark slip past her when she was on watch. Dread slammed into him like a glacier, and his chest constricted until it was hard to breathe. She was gone. Every instinct in his body screamed it was so, but still, he searched the woods.

A flash of brown ran between two trees, and he pulled his gun and aimed.

"Don't," Colten warned. "It's just Max. Don't waste your ammo on him."

Kaegan lowered his weapon as the mutt slunk from the tree he'd hid behind and sniffed at something on the ground. He looked up and then sniffed again, repeating the gesture until Kaegan surged forward. The dog had found something.

Skidding to a stop, he brushed leaves away from a single curved blade in the dirt, the smaller of the pair Soren carried on her back. The ground was torn up, like she'd fought, and branches had been snapped where something big had been dragged away.

"Pack camp fast," Kaegan breathed. "They could have hours on us."

He stared in horror at the fallen blade as Colten sprinted for camp. He didn't matter without her. Nothing did. She was everything good, and now she was in danger. He wouldn't, couldn't believe her already dead. His heart would've felt it if she didn't exist anymore.

"Hold on, Soren. We're coming for you," he breathed.

"Check its back. Does it have wings?" a man asked from somewhere far off.

Opening her eyes made her want to retch, so she pulled her knees up to her chest and tried to stay asleep instead.

Rough hands pulled at her shirt, and she gasped. A shrill and constant noise rang against her eardrum, irritating and grating. A breeze caressed the bare skin of her back, and a calloused hand rubbed down the length of it. Not Kaegan's hand.

Squinting against blinding sunlight, her cheek brushed against splintered wood as she tried to turn her head. Light streamed in through a crude, glassless window, and large, untied boots echoed across the floorboards in front of her face. She tried to rub her temple, but her hands seemed to be tied behind her back.

"Where am I?" she asked softly, so as not to add to the shrill alarm rattling her brain.

The man with the tattooed face leaned down in front of her and smiled, exposing two missing teeth in front. "Well, darlin', you're in hell. That's where you are. Don't worry yourself none though. You won't be here for long."

Thank goodness for small blessings. If she had to exist in the cloud of that man's fetid breath much longer, she'd lose her sense of smell.

"'Cause we're going to kill you," he clarified.

Oh.

"Can you tell whomever is rubbing my back to lay off?" she asked sweetly. "I'm not a fucking kitten."

"What are you?" the man behind her asked.

Soren gritted her teeth. If they wanted answers, she wasn't giving them lying down and vulnerable to their groping.

Tattoo Face yanked her into a sitting position and dragged her backward until she leaned against a wall. "If you're smart, you'll answer Bossman. Or," he said, pulling a knife from his belt, "I can start cutting off fingers until you talk."

She wouldn't exactly feel that, nor was it likely to entice her to talk, but he didn't have to know that.

Bossman wore hunting garb, and his camouflaged boots squeaked as he knelt. Intense, dark eyes studied her like she was a lab rat.

"I'm a hybrid. My parents are human, but I have second generation immunity."

"Do you have any superpowers?" a blond haired boy of sixteen or so asked from behind Bossman.

"Would you consider sarcasm a superpower?"

"No," he answered seriously.

"Then no." So it was a lie, but they didn't need to know any of her cards.

"She's lying," Tattoo Face snarled. "She's had fight training. Nearly gutted me when I took her."

"Everyone alive has had fight training," she said blandly. "I wouldn't consider something so common a superpower. And I'm pretty sure anyone would try to gut someone who was attempting to kidnap them."

"Shut your smart mouth."

"Why do you wear feathers in your hair?" the boy asked.

"Michael," Bossman warned.

"Can I open my smart mouth to answer?" she asked Tattoo Face.

He only scowled so she said, "Because I like the way they look."

Good lord, her head ached something fierce. And if she could feel it, she probably looked like she'd been trampled by a horse.

"Where were you and your team headed?" Bossman asked.

"Mexico. We heard the weather is lovely this time of year."

Bossman spat on the floorboards and narrowed his eyes. "You're joining the war, ain't you? Hippy dippy idiots think you're going to change the world by offing a few walkers. Well I've got news for you. There are way too many of them and too few meat bags. You'll only feed the horde and keep them alive longer."

She shrugged. "Noted. Can I go now?"

His dark eyebrows shot up as he laughed. "Go? Dead, you ain't goin' nowhere. 'Cept maybe the bottom of a shallow grave. Old Troy here would've shot you down in the woods, but I was curious about what one of our boys told me yesterday. Said some team of fighters had a pet Dead with them, and that the Dead was giving the humans orders. Imagine my surprise when I heard this. I mean, humans bowing down to Deads." He grinned at Tattoo Face Troy. "Now ain't that the damndest thing? But rules is rules, and we have a strict no Dead left behind policy. Why did you think Castle Rock was so empty of zombies?" He thumped himself on the chest and beamed. "That's our territory, just like the woods you was campin' in was ours too."

"It didn't have a sign."

"Oh, it did, you just missed them. We had graffiti painted across the whole dadgummed city. Coffee?"

He stood and sauntered over to a French press, poured dark, pungent liquid into a dirty looking tin cup and offered it.

Why did she get the feeling that telling him she only ate raw meat would shave minutes off her already short lifespan? "I can't hold the cup. My hands are tied."

"Duh," he said with a self-deprecating smile. She got the feeling he was much more intelligent than he was putting on, and it made him seem more dangerous somehow. "Here, let me." He leaned forward until the cup was within an inch of her lips. His hand was so close, if she could only bite him. He didn't smell vaccinated. Just a nip from her would be enough to turn him in minutes, but the man kept his hand just far enough away to make her hesitate, as if he expected it. His eyes swam with triumph as she sipped the scorching liquid that tasted like burned bark and dirt. Hell, maybe it was. Gulping it down and praying it would stay put until he wasn't looking, she gave him a stiff smile and said, "Thank you."

His eyes were hard and humorless as he said, "My pleasure. We'll be executing you at dusk. My boys have been working so hard and deserve a break, so I think we'll make a little party out of it, what do you think, Troy?"

"I think they'd love that, sir."

"Good. Let's get our creative minds into the think tank and come up with some fun ways for her to die, shall we? Meanwhile, you sit tight and let us know if there is anything we can get you." He stood and strode to the door. "You're our guest, after all."

Troy followed and the door slammed, taking the wind right out of the room. She bit back a curse as the coffee she'd ingested made its way back up, coloring the floor beside her.

"I don't like that stuff none either," Michael admitted from his seat on a crude wooden bed across the room. "You want some water instead?"

"Please, can you untie me so I can hold the glass myself?"

"Mmm, I don't think my uncle would be too happy with me if I did that. I'll just have to feed it to you like he did. If you got away, he'd kill me and spit on my carcass."

"But he's your uncle. Why would he do that?"

"He's got a colony to run, and he didn't get to where he is by letting people cross him."

"Please," she pleaded. "I have a family. A man is waiting for me back where I come from. Please, just let me go." The boy seemed soft, and this was the only chance she'd get to bargain for her life, so there it was. Everything was laid out for him. All he had to do was cut her loose, and she could do the rest. Yes, she'd happily take out the entire colony if it meant she could see the people she loved again, but Michael likely wouldn't want to hear that.

"You're a tricky one," he said with a grin. "But Deads don't love people. You might think you do, but it's not the same feeling as humans have about other humans."

"I am human!"

"Then why do you look like a Dead?" He walked crisply over to a canteen and poured water into a cup, then allowed her a drink. "You ain't a human any more than I'm a Dead. Best you accept that, or your fate tonight is going to be mighty confusing for you."

The boy hummed to himself as he put away the cup, and she searched the tiny room for anything she could use as a weapon.

Dusk. She had until dusk to find a blade. All she needed was one blade, and she could wreak havoc on this colony. If she was going to die tonight, she didn't want to do it tied like an animal in some sick death game one of Bossman's psychopaths had concocted.

She wanted to go down fighting.

Chapter Twenty

The sinking sun cast lengthening shadows across the floor. They reached for Soren, and an irrational fear seized her that when the shadows touched her feet, her time would be up.

So far she'd only managed to fight the ties that bound her hands enough to do damage, and now the entire room smelled strongly of iron. Swallowing the whimper that scratched its way through her chest, she wiped the emotion from her face as the door handle turned.

"Do you hear that noise?" Bossman asked as he entered.

A clank, clank of metal resonated through the open window, and she nodded.

"They are hammering two stakes about a body's width apart, and the echo you're hearing is from the manacles dangling from them. I wouldn't want you to be unprepared when you see where you'll die. It seems our boys have been very frustrated by the amount of hunting they've had to do with all these Deads migrating through our territory, and they've been planning all day for your demise. We're popping popcorn as we speak for the festivities. You should consider this an honor. No other Dead's death has been revered so much in the history of the apocalypse. Are you ready?"

No, she was not freaking ready to die for show. Time was up. He approached with one corner of his thin lips turned up in a smile that she'd only seen on Mark. Hands down, this was the worst twenty-four-hour block of time ever.

Limply, she contorted her face until she hoped he would read defeat, and as she rocked back, she kicked her legs out, battering his chest, which sent him sprawling.

Good thing she wouldn't feel this. Grunting, she pulled her tied wrists underneath her bottom, and squirmed until they were in front of her.

Bossman roared and untangled himself from the table of clutter he'd blasted into and charged.

Weaponless, she turned and jumped out the window.

And right at that moment, she realized the room she'd been locked in all day was in a damned tree. A tree! Panicking, she flung her hands out and hooked the zip tie onto a sturdy wooden peg on a crude wraparound porch. Panting, she looked down. From here it was a good thirty foot drop between her dangling feet and the unforgiving ground. The colony didn't have gates, from what she could see, but they didn't need them. Almost every building had been constructed in the canopy, and Deads couldn't climb.

Boom! An explosion rocked the tree, loosening the peg. She yelped as the warm air brushed her skin and stared in confusion at the blazing building on the edge of the grove.

"What the hell?" she breathed.

"Find out who set that fire," Bossman barked at a trio of guards on the ground. He turned a frosty glare to her. "I have something to take care of here." His boots made a hollow sound against the porch.

Arms shaking, she grunted and tried to haul herself higher to lessen the strain on her fatiguing muscles.

"Looks like you got yourself in a little spot, Dead. Pity the boys will have to miss their fun."

They won't have to miss their death game, Bossman, she mouthed.

"What's that?" he asked, leaning closer.

"They'll have Deads to play with after all," she whispered, then used every last ounce of upper body strength she possessed to pull herself up and kiss his mouth.

The peg gave under the strain, and she watched his face transform with the recognition of what she'd done to him as she fell to the earth. Her death would come, and she wouldn't fight the inevitable, so she swam in his fear filled eyes as he wiped a hand across his mouth. Her final revenge was bittersweet. She'd enjoy it, but not for long.

Closing her eyes, she waited for impact, and it came sooner than she'd expected. Except she flew sideways into the tree and grasped a branch out of instinct. When her body stopped pummeling the rough bark, she opened her eyes. Colten's furious face was inches from hers.

"What are you doing here?" she asked.

"Saving you, obviously. You couldn't wait five freaking minutes, could you? You just had to jump out of the damned tree."

"Where's Kaegan?"

A pepper of gunfire trailed down the tree, shooting shards of bark at them as the bullets barely missed. Another louder shot rang out, and the gunfire stopped. Probably because the man holding the weapon had dropped like a sack of stones.

Kaegan sat atop a ridge with a long range rifle, lining up his next shot.

"He's a better shot than me, and I'm better at climbing trees so I had to play rescuer. Should we kiss now?"

"Stop messing around, you asshat," Adrianna called from below. She and Lauren were sprinting from the direction the fire was raging.

"Right." Colten leaned against the trunk he'd tucked into and pulled his machete. In one swift stroke, the zip tie was cut and fell to the forest floor below. Soren reached for a lower branch just as a bullet ricocheted off where she was about to put her hand.

Another shot rang out, deep and short, signifying Kaegan had hit something. Soren grabbed the branch and flung herself downward, and Colten followed closely, weaving in and out and letting gravity rush them.

Panic spurred her faster, and when she reached the last branch, she jumped to the ground and rolled to ease the impact. Colten almost landed on top of her, and before she was even on her feet, he was dragging her toward the woods.

Four armed guards were sprinting after them, and Colten turned long enough to down two with his Berretta. A knife whizzed past her face, and the *thunk* of a body hitting dirt sounded behind her. Adrianna stood ahead of them with a look of fierce concentration, and another deep boom made her cover her ears in shock. Pushing her legs faster, she climbed the hill behind the others, clawing at dirt and rock and propelling herself upward until her legs burned with exhaustion.

"Don't stop," Kaegan ordered. "Just keep going." He let off two more shots, then hoisted himself up and ran beside her.

The next hour was consumed by ducking low branches and watching for uneven terrain to keep the pace. Kaegan favored his ankle but didn't slow until they were miles away. He grabbed her shoulder and held her still. "Quiet," he panted.

Her chest rose and fell so fast she thought she'd pass out if she denied her body oxygen by quieting her breathing, but she stilled her feet and hoped that's what he meant. Colten had doubled over, and Lauren retched behind a tree. Adrianna pulled her arms over her head like that would help her catch her breath, and every single one of them dripped with perspiration.

"I don't hear 'em," Colten said between gasps.

"I think we lost them, but we'll have to be careful," Kaegan rasped.

Soren gripped his shirt in her clenched fist. "You came for me."

He moved from side to side, like a racehorse asked to stop running too soon. His eyes never left her, but his head shook slowly. "I can't…" His lips pursed to a thin line at odds with his normally relaxed features, and his dark eyebrows drew down, brightening the intense color of his eyes. He was beautiful and terrifying, all at once.

"Soren," Colten said low. "Let him go."

Kaegan brushed past her and strode away. With a confused glance over her shoulder, Adrianna followed, then Lauren.

"I don't understand," she said.

With a pitying look, Colten turned and jogged to catch up.

Had she done something wrong? She hadn't asked them to come after her, wouldn't have ever put them in danger like that, so what? The woods suddenly felt stark and lonely, and she dug the toes of her boots into the dirt between ferns and bolted after them.

Kaegan wouldn't talk to her, wouldn't even look at her in the hours that followed. They hiked long into the night, and every passing mile brought silence to spur her agony. Hungry and exhausted, a chill crept into her bones and she couldn't seem to warm up. And just as she thought her legs would lock and refuse to take another step, Colten jerked his head and pointed his flashlight at an old cabin.

"Anyone here?" he called. "We're looking for shelter. Tell us the cabin is occupied, and we'll move on, no trouble."

Nothing stirred, and the frogs screamed on.

"Thank God," Adrianna muttered. "I can't feel my legs."

The door was locked, but all of the panes of glass had been broken, so Kaegan reached in. The *snick* of the lock was the most beautiful thing she'd ever heard.

A quick sweep of the house revealed they were alone, and when the door was locked behind them, Soren nearly collapsed on the dusty couch. She blinked, and when she opened her eyes, Adrianna and Kaegan stood over her.

"You need to eat," Adrianna said.

"Eat what? I'm too tired to hunt right now. What I need to do is sleep."

"You've been asleep for two hours," Kaegan said quietly. "Colten found a couple of ducks in the pond behind the house." Indeed, a limp mallard hung from his outstretched hand.

Eyes on the stitching of the worn blue couch, Kaegan dropped it in her lap and turned for the door. "When you're done eating, come outside, and I'll stitch you up."

Stitch her up? He shut the back door a little too firmly behind him, and she shot Adrianna a questioning glance.

Swirling her hand in the vicinity of Soren's head, Adrianna said, "You need like twenty of them, Sor. Your face looks like a crime scene."

Ah, the gash on her head, compliments of Tattoo Face Troy.

When her stomach was satisfied, and her face washed clean with canteen water, she stalled at the fire Lauren stoked in the stone hearth. Kaegan was angry, and a wise woman didn't storm a battlefield confused. Nothing in her wanted to endure his wrath right now. She was raw and so tired her bones didn't want to work, and hurt, if she was completely honest. Kaegan's aloofness stung, and quite frankly, she didn't want to do what he said until he started making sense. Determined to tell him just that, she stomped out the door, threw it open, and froze.

Kaegan leaned against the dilapidated porch railing, arms flexed in the moonlight, and the muzzle hung from his left hand, bumping the wooden posts in the breeze.

The implications cut her worse than any ever knife could.

Closing the door gently behind her, she stood beside him and watched the full moon's reflection on the rippling waters of the pond.

"I saw you," Kaegan said low, his voice cracking on the last word. "Why did you kiss that man?"

Baffled, she studied his tense profile. A muscle twitched in his clenched jaw, and she fought the urge to touch it, to soothe it away.

"It wasn't what it looked like."

He turned so fast she jumped. Gripping both sides of her face in an unbreakable grip, desperation tainted his gaze as he studied her for something she couldn't fathom. "Tell me he wasn't your first kiss. Tell me you didn't give away what was mine to some guy you didn't know."

God, she wanted to cry for their loss. "Kaegan," she murmured, rubbing her hands down his forearm and resting them on his knuckles.

He gripped her hair and leaned forward until his forehead rested on hers. "Tell me it wasn't."

"I killed him." Her whisper was ragged and laced with tears. "I hated him for what he was going to do to me, and he wasn't vaccinated. I could smell that he wasn't. I was going to die, but I wanted to take him with me, so I kissed him to murder him."

A desperate sound came from deep within his chest, and he pulled her against him. "I can't do this. I had all these ideas about how easy this would be when I found the right person, and it's not like what I thought at all. You'll have to do things that hurt me to survive. It won't stop. People will try to kill you, and if I can't get to you, I'll have to watch you fight for your life, and it guts me, Soren. Watching you come flying out of that window, watching you fall, seeing you get peppered with gunfire and running for your life, and if I missed, just one hair off on my aim, you'd be gone forever. I don't think I can do this. I can't go to war with you." He dropped to his knees, pressed his head against her stomach and gripped her legs. "I'm not strong enough to lose you."

Even kneeling, his dark hair brushed her chest. Running her fingers through his silky tresses, she said, "You were the one who convinced me I was strong enough to leave Dead Run River. You gave me something you'll never know the worth of. I appreciate who I am now because of the way you look at me. You were right, Kaegan. My destiny was bigger than that small-minded place. I was meant to be with you." She tilted his face up. "If you don't want me to fight, I won't. But I'm still going with you. I'm not asking you to give up your mission because it's who you are. You spill your own blood to give others a chance. It's part of the reason I fell in love with you. But I want the same trust. I won't always make the decision you want me to, but you can't control that. Thinking you can will only drive you mad when I do something different, and I can't have you in my head when I'm making those decisions. If I worry about what you'd want me to do, my end will come sooner than either of us wants."

Kaegan stood slowly, never taking his eyes from hers, and as he towered over her, he leaned down as if to kiss her. An inch from her lips, he closed his eyes and said, "Fight if you must, but don't kiss another. It's all I want, Soren. I want to taste your lips so bad I'm losing my mind. I know what I can bear, and I can't take your lips on another man."

Without another word, he stepped around her and disappeared down the porch stairs. Tall marsh grass hid him as he strode toward the lake. He didn't get to walk out on a conversation. He was supposed to stay and fight for them with her, and anger surged through her, making her arms tingle with the adrenaline. Stupid man, drawing her out here only to leave her alone.

"Kaegan," she called, jogging the trail he made through the weeds. Where had the man gone so fast? "Kaegan!"

An arm reached out and grabbed her by the waist, and she stifled a yelp. Kaegan's hand went over her mouth as he dragged her against him. "Put this on," he growled, holding out the muzzle.

"No! You've been trying to make me get rid of the stupid thing this whole time and now—"

"It's your damned rule, Soren, remember? God, can't you see I'm burning here. Put the damned mask on so I can touch you like I want."

"Oh," she said meekly. Well, that changed things. Her fingers shook as she fumbled with the clasp, and with a growl, he turned her and clicked it into place. Spinning her hard enough to make her dizzy, he yanked the tie on her pants and pulled her hand against his long shaft, hardened beneath the fabric of his trousers.

His hands were everywhere, pulling, caressing, tugging clothes off until she stood naked in the marsh grass. He eased away only long enough to pull his shirt over his head and throw it in the grass behind her. Muscles rippled under tanned skin as he moved, and she couldn't take her eyes from him if her life depended on it. Her skin grew cold in the moment he was away, but he returned and drew one of her hardened nipples into his mouth. She could feel the vibration of his groan against her breast, and a tremor ran up her spine. She watched his movements in a haze, still in disbelief that a man like Kaegan would want to taste her, would want to touch her.

Hurried, he pulled her down onto his lap and gripped her hair until her neck arched toward the moonlight. "You're mine," he rasped against her throat. "Swear to me the only man you'll ever kiss again is me."

She squeezed her eyes closed against the urgency of the oath on her lips. "I can't ever kiss you, Kaegan. Will you never be satisfied?"

So fast, she gasped, he rolled her over and slid into her. "Satisfied?" he asked, easing out slowly. "No. I could be buried inside of you every day for the rest of my life and still not be satisfied. Don't ever ask me that question again, Soren. The answer will always be no—I can't get enough of you."

She was lost as he thrust into her again, riding a wave of feeling and emotion and sensation. Gripping her hands, he lifted them above her head, pinning her under him as he claimed all of her. He dragged her waist closer, filled her, pressed into her, asked for more, and she gave eagerly because with every touch, she came closer to something important. Something she'd share only with him for the rest of her days.

The muscles of his back flexed under her fingertips, and his grip on her hair tightened as their rhythm became frantic. Release filled her like the pin being pulled from a grenade, and at the explosion, she screamed his name.

He cried out at his own climax and shifted her farther back into the grass, pushing her as if his breath had been stolen and only ramming forward would save him. Warmth spilled into her and he froze and buried his face against her shoulder.

His dark, chin-length hair fell out of its binding as he eased back and looked down at her. "Shit," he rasped, eyes intense. "That wasn't how I wanted our first time to go."

"I'm not complaining," she said, surprised by the husky tone her voice had adopted.

"I just imagined making it," he looked around the small clearing they'd made in the grass, "more special for you. But you've been driving me crazy, and then almost losing you today…" He shook his head. "I'm sorry for coming at you like some rutting animal."

"Mmm," she said, stroking his jaw with the tip of her finger. "I think I like the way you came at me just fine."

With a sigh, he rolled over and pulled her into him until she rested her head on his shoulder. "Remember when we watched the stars at the Denver colony together?"

"Mmmhmm," she hummed.

"That was the moment for me." He turned his head and watched her. "That was when I knew what I wanted."

"And what was that?"

"You. All of you."

She turned and smiled in wonder. "How can you look past everything and see me, Kaegan?"

"There is nothing I have to look past, Soren." He brushed a finger down the strap of the muzzle, trailing heat wherever he touched her skin like the tail of a meteor. "I love every single thing about you."

The breeze caressed her bare skin, and a shooting star streaked across the ebony sky. She pointed, and he entwined his fingers with hers.

"Make a wish," he breathed.

She thought about the bleakness of their future—the obstacles they had to overcome and the war that sat just on the horizon, and she dismissed any wishes about their future. This falling star was special and meant for only them, and she didn't want to waste it.

Her hope was for the present.

She wished this perfect moment could stretch on and on.

Chapter Twenty-One

"Could you be any more obvious?" Adrianna asked grumpily.

Soren didn't know what she was talking about. She and Kaegan were on opposite sides of the room and hadn't even touched each other since breakfast. And yes, that was only half an hour before, but to her, it felt like three and a half years.

Adrianna bent forward to tie her shoe. "Whenever you're ready, could you please stop rubbing it in the faces of the rest of the team who aren't getting any, hmm?"

"Ha," Colten said, leaning back on the couch and throwing an old, discolored tennis ball at the ceiling, then catching it. "I offer to have sex with you like, every fifteen minutes, Ade. You have no one to blame for your sexual frustration but yourself. Carry on you two."

Kaegan snuck her a secret smile and went back to packing the pots into his backpack. Soren turned and handed Lauren a rolled blanket to strap onto her go-bag.

Lauren scribbled across her chalkboard:

We should make it to La Junta today.

"Agreed," she said, grabbing her toothbrush and small jar of home-made mint toothpaste.

Lauren grabbed hers too and followed her outside. It was still dark, but likely that was due to the storm clouds that swirled overhead.

"If we can avoid any big skirmishes, I think we'll make it there by midday."

A nod from Lauren, and she scooped toothpaste and started brushing.

The sky to the west was filled with circling black birds and Soren pointed. "Look."

Lauren grimaced and spat as Soren started brushing beside her. She couldn't smell the carnage yet, but if the Crow Train was anything like Adrianna described it, she would soon enough.

The others emerged from the house, ready to go, and Kaegan plunked her satchel over her shoulder. He'd brushed his teeth earlier, and Soren didn't like to be rushed, so she waved them on. Lauren held back and gargled canteen water with her, then wiped her sleeve over Soren's mouth with a wry smile. The fabric of her hoodie came back covered in toothpaste.

"Mmm, thanks for the save," she said, wiping her chin again for good measure.

Kaegan waited up ahead and she smacked her lips and said, "Minty," as she passed.

He looked distracted and happy as he pushed brambles out of the way with his machete. "Yeah? Let me taste." He leaned forward and she stretched on tippy toes to reach him.

Lauren shoved him in the chest, hard. It wasn't until Soren saw the angry confusion in her friend's face that it hit her. In a move so casual she hadn't given a thought to it, she'd almost killed Kaegan. His face went ghostly white as he stood frozen in front of her, the lingering pucker of their almost kiss still upon his lips. After what they'd shared last night, it had been so natural to draw his kiss from her forehead, from her cheeks and neck, to her lips, and that one moment of comfort had almost snuffed his life from existence.

"Kaegan," her voice shook like a flame on a candle wick as she realized what she stood to lose in a single moment of distraction. Something so simple could ripple through their lives forever.

"What in the actual hell are you doing?" Colten barked. The furious look on his reddening face said he'd seen the entire thing. "Have you two lost your freaking minds? It isn't going to be the Deads that kill you. It's going to be some Romeo and Juliet bullshit, isn't it? Soren, I actually like you. I like you for Kaegan, but I swear to all that is dark in this world, if you turn him, I'm going to slit your freaking throat."

"I'm sorry," she whispered.

"You know, this wouldn't be an issue if you'd just take the stupid vaccine," Adrianna said, doubling back toward them. "Then you two could suck face all you wanted, and nobody would have to die over something so trivial. What's the holdup?"

Colten and Kaegan shared a significant look, and though Kaegan's glance looked like a warning, determination slashed through the blue of Colten's eyes.

"The holdup is, our boy Kaegan here is a breeder."

The woods dipped to complete silence, and Soren look from face to face with a frown. "A breeder. What does that mean?"

"Good gravy," Adrianna breathed. "Why?"

Kaegan stared at an overgrown glob of moss on a tree like it held the answers to the universe, and Soren asked again, louder in case they didn't hear her the first time. "What does that mean?"

Colten sighed and rested his hands on his hips. "He wants kids, Soren. And I don't mean it's a dream for his future, I mean, he's wanted to be a dad since we were fifteen years old."

"I don't understand." Her voice sounded frightened and small.

"Soren," Kaegan said in a gruff voice. "You worked closely with the vaccine. What is the infertility rate for people who've taken it?"

The number brushed her mind. Two numbers that had never meant a thing to her until this moment. Numbers that had become a suspicion when the first human to take the vaccine, Vanessa Daniels, tried for years to conceive and couldn't. Numbers made more real when the first round of test subjects suddenly couldn't get pregnant after becoming immune to the Dead virus. "Seventy-six percent chance of infertility," she whispered. "More if both parties are vaccinated."

"If I take the shot, our chances of starting a family dwindle to nothing."

"But, you're going to war," Adrianna said, anger lacing her voice. "What does it matter? You're most likely not coming back from this."

"And if I do?"

"And if you do," Adrianna said in a shrill voice, "it still doesn't matter because Soren won't have children."

"What's she talking about?" he asked, his intense gray eyes freezing her into place.

"Look at me. Take a long hard look and not just as someone who loves me, Kaegan. If you were me, would you risk passing this on to a child? To your child? Would you want your baby to go through what I did? You want a child. I never, ever did. And I never will."

She felt like she stood in quicksand and everything around her pressed against her. This couldn't work, and from the destroyed look on Kaegan's face, he was coming to the same realization.

"We can talk about this," he said, palms down like he was soothing a wild horse.

"Would talking about this include you trying to convince her to try for one?" Adrianna asked. "Because you weren't there when we were growing up. You don't know what it was like for her to come to this decision. You didn't see the kids taunting her, throwing stones at her as she walked home from school—and she was supposed to be safe in our colony. It was built around her, for chrissakes. Do you know what Dead Run River tried to do when she was born? They wanted to cull her, Kaegan. They wanted to murder a little baby because she was part Dead, and it won't be any different for her children."

Kaegan's eyes stayed wide and steady on Soren. She watched his heart break through those glassy gray windows to his soul. "So I have to choose," he murmured. "You or a family."

"No," she said in a low voice to hide the agony of her words. "I'll choose for you. This doesn't work for me anymore, Kaegan."

"Soren, stop it. Stop it!" he yelled. Red tinted his neck and cheeks as he glared her down. "You don't get to bail on our first argument."

"This isn't an argument," she said, fighting back burning tears. "Our lives have been on completely different paths from the beginning. I just didn't see it until now. You want a family so bad you risk your life every day. You chose wrong when it came to me, Kaegan. I can't give you a family. I won't. Not now or ever. Compromising means one of us gives up something vital to who they are and we'll grow to resent each other. You say you've accepted what I am, who I am, well this is part of the package. I won't steal your dreams for my own selfish ends. I can't do it. I'm not it for you, and someday, a long time from now, when you have a normal woman and a babe clinging to the leg of your pants for one last hug before you go to work, you'll look back on this moment, right now, and thank me." She bit back a sob that threatened to bring her to her knees. "You'll be glad one of us had the foresight to stop our destruction before we drowned in our bad decisions."

Dashing the back of her hand over the two traitorous tears that streaked her face, she straightened her shoulders and lifted her chin, then stepped around him. The birds in the sky in front of them circled round and round, mirroring her swirling emotions, and she gasped at the pain in her chest. She felt it, harsh and jagged, like some serrated knife was sawing her heart from her torso. It hurt to breathe, to move, to exist, and she squeezed her eyes closed at the onslaught of tears that streamed down her face.

The others followed behind her quietly, and for blessed hours she was allowed to wallow in what ifs and memories of the night before in all of its perfection. She'd let this go too long. Her instincts had been screaming at the danger all along, and she'd ignored them because Kaegan was kind. He was masculine and rugged and caring and gave everything to the people he cared about. He was too good to throw away something he'd so obviously cared about for half a lifetime, all for the sake of love. He'd find someone else who would affect him, and she'd be good enough. His love for a child would overshadow any shortcomings in their relationship.

How had she not seen it before? He was made entirely of fierce loyalty and protective instincts. Someday, he'd make a wonderful father.

The pain inside became unbearable as she thought of him with another woman. Holding hands, touching her. Kissing her.

Of course there wasn't a happily ever after for her.

She'd been so stupid to think good things could happen to monsters.

Kaegan was falling. He stared at the ground as it passed beneath his feet and wished he could sink and never surface. Why had he kept it from her? Because some instinct told him if she knew he wanted a child, he'd lose her, and now it had happened. Up ahead, he could almost hear her thoughts as she pulled her soul away from his. They had been made of the same matter, but now, hers was turning to stone and his was disappearing altogether.

Did she know she'd wrecked him? This mythical woman she spoke of him meeting and starting a family with didn't have a chance at comparing to her. He'd have to settle to get what he'd dreamed about, and even then, it would only be a shell of what he'd imagined growing up.

He'd grown up fatherless, and his mother was sad and didn't know how to care for a kid. He'd sworn to do it differently and make a child feel loved and safe. And when he'd stumbled out of the woods after Mom died and into the Carson City colony, Mr. McTavish, Colten's dad, had taken him in and treated him like his own get. He'd taught him how to be a man and how to take care of his own, and he thought, *someday I'm going to be this kind of dad to my kid.*

On dark days, and there were always plenty in a nomadic lifestyle, fatherhood was what he'd envisioned when he needed to escape. What his child would look like. Holding his son, or naming his daughter. It had been a part of him for so long, he didn't know how to be different.

Adrianna, Colten, and Lauren plodded on in front of him, quiet and somber, and he wanted to scream to fill the silence. It wasn't fair for him to find her, and then lose her like this. Not after what they'd been through.

The first drops of rain pattered against his face, and he stopped and held his arms out. Perfect. Stretching his face to the storm clouds, he let the water pelt against his skin. At least the stinging of the rain meant he still felt something, and right now, that seemed vital.

Kaegan knocked at the giant iron door and stood back, waiting.

Soren stretched her neck to look down the length of the chain link fence nervously. The station was fenced in for loading, but the noise would attract the horde. They'd waited until the train trilled and pulled the bulk of the Deads' attention before they'd sprinted from the woods like their tailbones had been lit on fire.

"Come on," Colten muttered, glancing behind them and hopping from one foot to another.

Kaegan knocked again, harder this time, and the door echoed under his pounding fist.

Two Deads wandering the line of the fence picked up their pace, altering their path until they were stumbling their way.

"Oh, for crap's sake," Adrianna said, pulling a small knife from her belt. "Knock again. Soren and I have this."

Pulling the smaller of her swords, Soren loped behind Adrianna and rammed it through the first one's temple while Adrianna shoved the second against the fence. The Dead on the ground looked newly turned. His skin was only in the beginning stages of sagging and transforming into the bluish hue of death. Even his clothes were mostly intact. Maybe he was trying to make it to the Crow too and was overtaken.

Pity. He was so close.

"Guys," Colten said.

Adrianna's Dead went limp against the fence, and she turned with a glower. "I said we got this."

One Dead appeared out of the tree line, limping badly. A moment later, two more stumbled out of the shadows, and six more after that.

"Ade," she whispered, tugging her shirt.

"What?"

Soren pointed, and Adrianna swore under her breath. "We don't got this," she called. "Fall back."

The train whistle blasted again from behind them, and the Deads broke into a run, pouring from the woods like relentless waves lapping a shore.

Colten took over beating on the door, and Kaegan pulled the rifle from his back, checked the load and pulled the scope up to his face. His hands were steady as he followed the movement, and when he pulled the trigger, the closest Dead dropped. Lauren pulled her pistol when they got close enough and popped off two rounds, dropping one and blasting another in the jaw.

The sound of screeching metal was barely audible over the groans of the hungry Deads and gunfire, but Soren dared a glance back.

A small window on the door was open.

"Please," Adrianna begged. "We're here to barter. Let us in!"

The window slammed closed.

The Deads were coming up fast, and they were out of time. "We have to go," Soren said, and just as the team began to back away, the door clanked and jerked open.

She covered the others until even Kaegan had disappeared inside, then jumped through the door as it began to close. Darkness swallowed her as the heavy door slammed, and the cold metal of a gun pressed against her temple.

Sometimes she really wished people would quit threatening to kill her.

Down a corridor, the flickering light of a torch lit the dark, brick walls, and the sound of water dripping echoed down the halls.

"Let me guess," the man said. "You're headed to the Boneyard."

"The what?" Adrianna asked.

"I've had fifteen fighter teams at least come through here this week, bartering Crow rides for a lift down to Albuquerque to join the war. Walk."

The barrel of the pistol shoved Soren's head forward, and the others followed, their footsteps bouncing off the dark brick.

"Is the gun necessary?" Kaegan growled. "She's not even resisting."

"Sorry, old chap. I heard her talking out there like a human, but she looks Dead to me. You got a problem with it, you can go back the way you came."

The clawing and scrabbling of Deads was loud against the other side of the door, and she swallowed hard at the image of them being thrust back outside. "It's fine."

The hallway stretched forever, and eventually they came to a halt at a dingy yellow door. The man behind her leaned forward and knocked. He was a tall man, but slight, like he'd never had a decent meal in his life. He smelled like the sweet smell that preceded rot, and the torchlight cast shadows against his hairless dome. He looked to be in his sixties, but when she looked closer to the smooth skin of his face, he was likely no older than thirty-five.

"You're sick," she said.

The man sneered, his teeth perfectly straight and white. "Not as sick as you. Larry," he called. "We got more riders."

The door opened, and a squat man with a frown and serious paunch glared at them. "I hope you came prepared," he griped. "Because if you don't have something worth my time, I'll feed you to the Deads myself."

"Let's get crackin' then," Adrianna said blandly, shoving her way through the door.

Larry's smile matched the door color and was nothing shy of wicked, and suddenly, worry torpedoed through Soren's chest. Adrianna was brash and loud, but someday it would get her into trouble, and that man's greedy gaze on her as she walked past said today could be that day.

Soren opened her mouth to protest her going alone, but Larry slammed the door, and the man with the gun pushed her against the opposite wall. He slunk down into a creaking wooden chair beside the doorframe and waved the gun at them nonchalantly. "So, where you from," he asked in a sing-songy voice.

"No," Kaegan gritted out, cutting off the small talk. Apparently, they weren't playing story swap with Crazy Eyes today.

Colten stared at the door with a look she could only describe as worried fury. A new expression she'd never seen on his face before. Huh.

Minutes dragged on, and her concern deepened until even the torchlight seemed to dim with her dread. What was taking so long? Cracking her knuckles, she paced to try to rid herself of the nerves.

At last, the door opened, and Adrianna slunk out, wiping her mouth with the back of her hand. An ashamed blush tinged her cheeks, and she looked down at Colten's feet.

Colten's breath shook. "Are you serious, Adrianna?"

Ade snorted, a grin cracking her face right open, and she said, "No, but you should see your faces right now. I had vaccines to bargain with. One for each of us. I even had one for Mark and Ben if they'd made it that I threw in for goodwill. Larry said he'll get us food for the trip. I'm kind of offended you guys bought it. My BJs would be worth way more than some stupid train tickets."

Crazy Eyes snickered from his seat against the wall, and Soren made a conscious effort to close her gaping yap.

Colten grabbed her arm, yanked her against his chest, and kissed her, hard. "That wasn't funny," he murmured harshly as he pulled away.

Kaegan shot Soren a wide-eyed look, but she was swimming in the sea of confusion right along with him. Adrianna's eyes had taken on a drunken quality, and Colten stepped around her, striding off in the direction Crazy Eyes pointed with his pistol.

Vaccines. Adrianna had bartered with the one thing Soren hadn't thought to offer. Of course they were worth more than she could even imagine on the black market.

In a perfect world, everyone would be vaccinated and immune and live happily ever after. That wasn't how life worked, though. Not anymore. Instead, the vaccines had been shipped to the big colonies, while the humans living on the fringe were out of luck. Probably only half of the human population was lucky enough to get their hands on a vaccine.

Kaegan had no excuse not to be vaccinated. Mark either. They'd lived where they were readily available, but Bossman's tiny colony likely had no access to the shots unless they bartered them on an underground market.

"Quit staring at me like that," Adrianna snapped. "You look like I just saved your puppy."

"I'm just impressed," Soren admitted.

"Well, don't be. It's the way of the world. I shouldn't get a pat on the back for common sense."

"You like him," she whispered.

Adrianna hadn't taken her eyes from Colten's retreating back. "Worry about your own boy problems," she muttered.

Kaegan shouldered his pack and shot her a long glance over his shoulder before he disappeared in the shadows between torches.

One look. One reminder of what she'd lost, and the pain was back, aching deeper and deeper until she bit her lip against crying out. The Dead fight had been a beautiful distraction, but nothing more.

She was broken.

Maybe she'd always be broken.

Chapter Twenty-Two

T hree days by train and they would be within walking distance of
the Boneyard. Until now, the actual battle had seemed far away,
but as the train engines roared to life, it all became real. Nervous,
Soren fidgeted as the train lurched forward by inches.

Wooden boxes had been thrown in as make shift chairs, and
someone had thoughtfully tossed a wad of musty blankets into the
corner. Adrianna stared out of the holes in the train car and clutched
the bag of food she'd been given on the loading dock.

The car had probably been used to transport livestock, because it bore
large air holes every few inches, giving an easy view of the world outside.

Dock workers, drenched with perspiration and donning filthy
white tank tops hurried to load the car behind them with heavy looking boxes reading *Explosives.* Comforting.

Layers of mold and moss draped from the cement loading area,
and the smell of Deads and human sweat was pungent against the
sensitive lining of her nose. Swaying in the breeze was a site safety sign
that read *0 Days Accident Free.* What on earth would possess a man to
work such a job?

Her gaze drifted to Kaegan as he sat talking quietly to Colten
and Lauren on the other side of the car. He could've ended up here
so easily when he'd lost his mom.

"Keep your fingers inside the Gory-Anna if you want to keep them," a loading hand advised and gave a shrill whistle. "All loaded up," he yelled.

The phrase was echoed and repeated down the line and in a few minutes' time, the train lurched forward again. Slowly, they passed one fence, then another, and by the final gate, the groans of the Dead were so loud, it was impossible to hear anything else. The wheels had been modified, and the tracks were covered in the carnage of monsters too dumb and slow to get out of the way. The smell was awful, and one by one, the team placed cloths from their packs over their noses. Lauren looked like she was going to throw up, and Colten handed her a rusted bucket that had been littering the floor. More proof he did have a heart.

The car rocked as Deads threw themselves at the sides. Clawed, bleeding fingers reached into the holes, and Soren moved to the center of the car with the others. The metal screeched under the weight of the desperate creatures, and Soren crossed her arms over her chest to ward away the cold that seemed to seep from the corpses' bodies.

A large hand, warm and comforting, squeezed her shoulder. "It'll be okay," Kaegan said.

His eyes tightened as if he'd noticed his mistake. They had no future. How could anything be okay again?

His fingers slipped from her collarbone, and he stared at the clawing undead.

Why hadn't these migrated like most of the others? Perhaps some of them didn't have the instinct, but more likely, they were kept in place by the whistle of the train and the smell of humans just beyond the fences. Like the Deads who'd stayed frozen in time, slaves to the movement of the windmill, these weren't ever going to leave. They'd spend their entire miserable lives chasing sustenance they'd never taste.

How could she not feel bad for the mindless creatures, stripped of their souls and given only the basest purpose to drive them?

Maybe they had the right of it. The Deads probably had it good and didn't deserve her pity. No emotion, no heartache, no insecurity—just survival.

"Come here, you," Adrianna said, pulling Soren into her side. Adrianna made a single clicking sound behind her teeth and rested her head against Soren's.

Together they watched the horde thin and the horrifying faces disappear to reveal trees and mountain paths that had been cleared long ago to make room for the tracks. Standing, she clutched the wall, unable to take her eyes from the mesmerizing sight. Cliffs and crags, streams and valleys passed just outside the car. She'd never traveled at this speed before, so fast. Or if she had, she didn't remember it.

"Can we talk?" Kaegan asked from right beside her.

"I suppose we should."

He gripped two holes above him and leaned against the wall, watched the passing forest. "I should've told you my reasons for not taking the vaccine. I kept a big part of myself from you, and it was wrong."

Leaning her cheek against the cool metal she shrugged. "What does it matter now? What's done is done."

"Don't do that, Soren. Don't act like everything is over—because I'm still standing right in front of you. I'm still your teammate. I still care about you, and I'm not going anywhere."

Her throat constricted until it was hard to breathe. "Why are you doing this," she whispered. "Can't you see this is already impossible? I won't ask you to give up the family you've always wanted, Kaegan. Will you ask me to change for you?"

His mouth twitched, and he looked away. "I don't think we should make a decision this big this early on."

"Answer the question. Would you ask me to change for you?"

"Yes! Yes, okay? I want you. I want the family. I want it all, Soren, more now than ever, and it's because of you. You don't want a kid right now, but that doesn't mean it'll always be that way."

"Yes it does. I've made up my mind on it. I won't bring another hybrid child into the world."

"Can't you see?" he said, voice trembling. He tangled his fist into her hair and pulled her closer. "Can't you? I'd love the child if he was hybrid or not, just like I love his mother." He rested his forehead on hers and closed his eyes. "Please, Soren. At least think about it before you throw me away."

Gripping his arm and untangling it from her hair, she kissed his knuckles as a warm tear slid down her cheek. "I'm not throwing you away, Kaegan. I'm setting you free."

"Please don't do this," he said thickly.

"If you care for me, you'll be my friend, my teammate, and nothing more. It hurts to talk like this, and it doesn't change anything."

"Friends." The word sounded like a curse on his lips.

Eyes riveted on his shaking, clenched fists, she nodded.

He rocked back on his heels like she'd dealt him a blow and sat heavily on an upended crate. "Jesus," he whispered. His throat moved as he swallowed, and he ran his hands through his hair. "Okay." The word was choked, like it made him sick to say it. "We'll do it your way."

The click of the clasp on Soren's worn satchel barely sounded over the noise of the tracks passing beneath them. The others slept on the blankets in the corner, but sleep had abandoned her the moment her soul had separated from Kaegan's. She pulled the sketch pad from her bag, turned her back on the snoozing team, and flipped to the third page. A rough sketch of a Dead man staring at the trunk of a sycamore tree. Each stroke was hurried in the picture, but she'd taken the time to draw the exact details of the watch that had frozen at three twenty-two on his wrist.

Page six showed a close up of a Dead child's face, the innocence washed away by the blood on her chin and lips. The pages shuffled, a comforting sound that brought back memories of hours spent outside of Dead Run River gates on good weather days. Splaying her hand against the spine, the journal fell open to the drawing of the red headed Dead, alone in the woods. This one was the last of her Dead series. From here, the pages were inked with the subtle curve of Kaegan's lips when he smiled, the cock of his eyebrow when something didn't settle with him. The way he looked covered in the blood of battle, the way she'd first seen him. The shadow of his stubble. His eyes. There were pages and pages where she'd practiced capturing the hungry look he saved for only her. The last was a scenic view of the cabin pond, the moonlight bright over the still water.

"Those are really good," Colten murmured behind her.

So lost in the memories scribbled on these pages, she'd missed his approach.

"Can't sleep?" he asked.

"No." She'd probably never sleep again.

Leaning back until her spine pressed into the unforgiving floor of the train car, she didn't even resist when he plucked the notepad from her hands. The moon was almost full and sat low in the sky, and it thrust its light through the holes in the walls, speckling the car with a mirror ball effect.

The pages turned slowly above her as Colten squatted to his haunches, studying the work she'd always worried about someone seeing.

What did it matter now? What did anything matter?

"You really love him, don't you?" he breathed.

She crossed her fingers over her stomach and inhaled deeply. His boots shuffled near her head as he turned and lay down beside her.

"What are we going to do with you?" he muttered, crossing his hands like her and staring at the spotted train car canopy.

"I assume stabbing me is off the table?"

He snorted. "Been there, done that." The sound of his breathing was the only noise for a long time. The silence wasn't uneasy like it had so often been with him. "We're going into a war we know nothing about, for a cause that is more instinct than logic, and to top it off, you and I have fallen for people we can't have. Won't have."

"Adrianna?" she asked.

He nodded and stared grimly on.

"Our timing isn't awesome," she said with a sad smile.

"Depends on how you look at it. We probably won't survive this, you know? It wasn't fair of us to get attached to someone so close to the end."

The train blasted a whistle and pulled as it slowed down. Propped up on his elbows, Colten frowned at the scene outside. Deads clawed lazily at a tall fence with barbed wire looping the top. The people inside didn't attempt to be quiet. It was some kind of market, complete with trash can fires and food smells.

"We must be in Albuquerque," he said, pushing up. "Lauren, Kaegan."

Adrianna was already sitting up.

Three fences and they were enclosed within a colony that rivaled the size of the Denver colony.

A station worker threw open the sliding car door. "Papers."

Adrianna handed him a folded sheet, and he read it under the beam of a flashlight.

"You'll want to get out here," he said.

"Why? We have leave to go all the way through to Mexico."

"Yeah, but trust me when I say, this is the last stop you'll want to stretch your legs at. From here on, there's no fences where the train stops to refuel. Just lots and lots of Deads."

"How long until we have to be back on board?" Kaegan asked.

"Uh," he said, squinting at the moon. "Two hours, give or take."

"Soren needs food," he said with a significant look at Adrianna.

No crap. She was standing right there in plain sight, and her growling stomach could probably be heard over the train whistle at this point. "I'll go and be right back. I smell meat in the market. I'll barter a knife."

Colten drummed his fingers on his hips. "Nah. Soren, you look like a Dead and we don't have time to beg acceptance. Kaegan and I will go. You guys wait for us on the loading platform. Anything else we need?"

Adrianna's canteen sailed through the air and landed in Kaegan's outstretched hand. "Fresh water," she said.

Uneasiness spider-webbed from Soren's stomach outward. "I don't like this. We should stay together."

"If we all go, we're bound to be noticed," Adrianna said. "Albuquerque isn't the place you want to get noticed, Soren. The boys have a better chance of getting in and out without trouble."

The next hour and a half was the longest of her life. She paced the loading area, careful to dodge workers unloading supplies. Deny it all she wanted, but even Adrianna was nervous. She couldn't keep her eyes from the direction of the market. Even Lauren looked spooked from her perch on the ramp.

"You need to load up," the man from earlier said. "The Crow's about to shove off."

"But you said two hours," Adrianna argued.

Shrugging, he hurried off.

"I'm not leaving without them," Soren breathed.

Adrianna swiveled her head from the train to the market and back again. "The papers are only good for the Gory-Anna. If we don't leave on this one, we'll be stranded here."

The whistle blew and the train lurched forward.

Come on, come on, come on!

"Soren, what's the call?" Adrianna gritted out. "Stay or go?"

"I can't leave him," she said, shifting her weight.

Another whistle and the train jerked forward again, this time holding its motion.

Two figures barreled toward them, down the loading ramp. Even in the dark, she knew it just had to be them. "Let's go."

Running, Lauren jumped the train first, then Adrianna. Soren hung off the side of the open door. "Hurry!"

Faster, Kaegan and Colten pumped their legs but the train was picking up speed.

"They aren't going to make it," Adrianna said beside her.

"They'll make it."

She ducked out of the way as Kaegan launched a canvas bag through the opening and then grabbed onto his outstretched arm as he flung himself upward. Grunting, she pulled as hard as she could, and he tripped into the car. Colten had latched onto the holes in the back of the car and was slowly climbing toward the opening.

"That was too close," she said when Colten was safe inside. "What the hell took so long?" And that's when she saw their faces in the scant light.

Cuts covered them, and Colten's eye was swollen and red.

"What the hell, McTavish?" Adrianna yelled, yanking his eye open with none too gentle fingers.

"Geez, woman," he said, hissing air through his front teeth.

"Who did this to you?"

Jaw clenched, Colten looked at Kaegan, then away.

"You idiot boys," Ade growled. "We almost missed the Crow!" Shoving Kaegan in the shoulder, she screeched, "Why?"

Kaegan's glare hadn't left Colten, and he tapped the squawking bag he'd thrown in with the toe of his boot. "All we could find was chicken." He lifted his shirt in the back and threw her journal at her.

Shocked, she barely caught it, and burning heat engulfed her cheeks like a wildfire.

Gruffly, he explained, "Colten stole this from you."

Colten collapsed into the pile of blankets and sighed. "Borrowed."

She fingered the worn cover and withered under the crack of hostility that filled the space, thickening the air until it was hard to breathe.

She didn't know what Colten said to cause Kaegan to go all silverback gorilla on his face, but from the way the two best friends glared each other down, she was sorely convinced she'd never in her life understand men or their relationship management decisions.

Chapter Twenty-Three

Soren's breath shallowed as the team crested the hill. A fence had been constructed around makeshift barracks, but that wasn't what had their eyes wide.

"They dug a moat," Adrianna breathed. "It's genius."

Indeed, a deep trench had been dug, and a thin layer of Deads meandered beyond the water, staring at the moving humans on the other side with bottomless eyes.

"This way," Kaegan said, edging through the trees.

Clouds, dark and fat with rain, sat low in the sky, blocking out any chance of sunlight. The smell of sea and brine filled the air, and the trees had morphed into palms and sea grasses typical of the coast, a stark reminder they weren't in Denver anymore.

Maybe Empalme had been a bustling city before, but not now. The jungle had ridden the waves of Dead victory and taken it back.

Ruin lay behind them and death before them.

Large billows of black smoke filled the sky a mile off, lacing the scent of ocean with the sickly sweet, rotten smell of carnage.

A small, crude ramp joined the sides of the moat, only large enough to put one foot directly in front of the other. Too thin for a clumsy Dead to cross.

Kaegan broke out into a run across the clearing, and she followed the others. He slowed only enough to catch his balance on the ramp. It was made of iron and looked like framework she'd seen dangling from a rusted crane on one trip into Denver when she was young. Holding her hands out, she followed the others and was midway over the water before the Deads reached the makeshift bridge. One fell into the moat with a giant, thrashing splash and she wobbled at the distraction. Catching herself, she shuffled the rest of the way until she found the steady ground of the base.

"You here to enlist?" a guard asked when they reached the gate.

"Yes, sir," Kaegan said. "We heard you could use some more bodies."

The man looked exhausted, haggard even, and deep lines of fatigue etched deeply into his skin. "That we could. Follow me."

Two more guards rolled the gate back, and she followed the team inside.

"Watch the front for me," the man told them. "My name is Alexander, and this is where you'll be staying nights. We only fight during the day. Up every morning before dawn, and we hit it hard from first light until dusk. Fighting's already started today so you'll be assigned something else until we can figure out your skill set." He walked with a confident gate, despite the bruised circles under his eyes, and turned. The smile dripped from his lips when he saw her.

"Dead in the gates," he shouted, and in one swift motion, a knife came down at her face.

Reacting, she grabbed his wrist and twisted, kicked his legs from underneath him and turned as another assailant barreled down upon them. Shoving her hand upward, she cracked his chin with the palm of her hand and elbowed him in the gut. Guards fell upon them in droves.

The others fought like wild animals, graceful and lethal, but she could see the fear in Lauren's gaze as one of them overpowered her and yanked her arm behind her back.

Furious, she spun, taking the guard in her grip with her and landed straddled on top of him.

"Soren," Kaegan clipped out, tossing a pistol through the air.

Time slowed.

Other men were running to join in the fight, but they wouldn't get to her soon enough. Out of the air, she snatched the weapon and cocked it in one motion, rested the barrel against the guard's temple.

"Stop," she called. "I'm not a Dead."

The oncoming brawlers skidded to a stop, and the man under her held his hands up in surrender, sweat pouring from his face.

Kaegan held a man by his shirt front. "She sure looks like a Dead to me," the pinned guard said around a swelling lip.

A slow clap echoed across a quiet barracks. The sound became louder as a man stepped forward. He was only a few inches taller than her, honey colored hair cropped short against his scalp, with eyes as dark as tar and a grim set to his mouth. A threadbare cotton shirt clung to the toned musculature of his chest, rippling with the movement of his hands. He was handsome, but didn't have any smile lines.

"I think it's safe to say your skills have been tested. Let them go," the man ordered.

She stood, released the man under her, and slipped Kaegan's borrowed pistol into the palm of his wide hand.

"I'm General Moore. I'm in charge here, and if you want to stay in this colony, you'll come with me."

Kaegan's hand fit the small of her back as they stepped over a guard, holding his stomach on the ground. "Whatever happens, we stay together," he whispered.

It was impossible to resist him when he talked against her ear like that. Warmth seeped through her shirt, caressing the skin beneath it until she wanted to close her eyes against everything and just enjoy this last touch from him. Her traitorous heart stuttered to life, beating against her chest like it needed an escape from the pain she'd put it through.

Barracks was a much nicer word than the colony deserved. Camp was more like it with its rows of worn, white canvas tents. Flaps whipped in the wind, and smoke rose from embers of hastily doused fires. Cookware hung from cut poles and clanked in the breeze. It looked like a ghost town.

"Most of our fighters are down at the beach," Moore explained. "By nightfall, God willing, we will have enough survivors to fill this place. We have enough coming in daily right now that they replace the soldiers we lose to battle. Your team will stay here." He pointed to a small tent.

Soren tugged the tie that bound the opening and pushed inside.

"One of our squadron leaders lived here with his team." Moore rubbed his thumbnail absently over his bottom lip. "We lost them two days ago."

Two blankets had been folded into a corner. A water bucket sat on top of it, waiting to be filled, and a handheld mirror dangled from a frayed rope. The back wall was filled top to bottom with tally marks.

"Marking kills?" she asked.

Moore twitched his head, an invitation to follow. "Some of them do it for motivation. Every kill counts."

He led them to a large tent in the center of the camp. The flaps had been tied back, and a sand smattered rug blanketed the floor. A large table with a topographical map decorated a large table, and a ladder backed chair sat in its shadow. A cot filled a corner, a thick blanket folded neatly on top. Two long strides, and he was opposite them at the table. Locking his elbows, his arms flexed as he frowned at the map.

"We're losing this war," he said low. He lifted dark eyes to her. "What are you?"

"I'm a traitor."

His lip twitched, eyes raking over her body. "Good. The rest of you stay here. I need to talk to the Dead alone."

"She has a name," Kaegan growled. "And she doesn't go anywhere without me."

Moore drew his bottom lip between his teeth, calculating. "What is she to you?"

"He's my handler," she said in a rush.

Kaegan's gaze stabbed her, striking the air from her lungs.

"And what do people call you?" Moore asked, intense dark eyes devouring her.

"Z."

His lips curled up, approval pulling a short laugh from him. "Of course they do. Fine, both of you come with me. The rest of you, wait here."

A crude building had been constructed in the back of the camp, where no tents were scattered. Supplies peppered the ground. Boxes of ammunition and explosives. Plastic storage containers of dried beans and corn. Blankets, cots, trunks, stacks of canvas, giant jugs of water, bug nets, and wood piles stretched down the fence line.

"This war is financed by the people who came out on top in this apocalypse," Moore said. Bitterness tinged his voice. "If we don't progress in the fight, they pull our supplies. It isn't for the good of the people they do this. They allow this war for the good of themselves. Some people are very powerful—hold most of the cards. When this is all over, they will rule the world." He turned and leveled her with a look both serious and sad. "Do you understand, Z?"

She nodded. "But it will be safer for those of us at the bottom too, General Moore." Less monsters, less death.

He cocked his head and rested his hand on the door handle to the building. "I hope so." He turned and yanked a heavy lock and chain from the door. "I hope so enough that I'm here, still trying."

The smell of Deads was overpowering, and she covered her nose with the back of her hand. Stifling a gag, she stepped behind Moore and waited for him to light a torch on the wall.

The flame ignited, wavering shadows crept across the floorboards and settled on the metal bars of a prison. Two Deads stood behind them, groaning and stretching their hands toward them.

Both had been stripped bare of clothing. Newly turned, they hadn't even rotted fully yet. Most of their flesh was intact, and their eyes lacked the milky film that came with decay.

"What's this about?" Kaegan demanded, his voice muffled behind a handkerchief he held over his face.

"Their backs," Moore said.

She looked from Moore to Kaegan, and then back again. He had Deads inside the gates. She'd known of entire colonies that fell in situations just like this. Anger boiled inside of her, burned up her arms and neck, and an inhuman snarl ripped from her throat. There better be the best damned reason on the planet for them to be here.

Fueled by a black fury, she rushed to the bars. The smallest Dead stretched his neck, like she was blocking his view of the real food, and she pushed him back, turned him, and pinned his spine to the bars.

Small, skinless growths twitched from his shoulder blades, and she gasped and threw him away from her. Face first on the wooden floor boards, the monstrosity stretched the appendages.

"Oh my God," Kaegan breathed behind her. "Are those wings?"

"The virus is mutating," Moore said. "Some of the new turns are growing them in the first few days of transition."

"Do they get bigger?" she asked, unable to take her eyes from the Dead trying to scrabble off the floor.

"These are the biggest we've seen so far. We're keeping them here to see if they grow over time, or if the mutation is stunted."

"If it's stunted now, it won't be forever," she said. "I worked with Dr. Mackey at Dead Run River. We've been trying to come up with a cure, but the mutations keep us guessing. So far we've been able to adjust the vaccine, but finding a cure has been impossible. This is bad."

"This," Moore said, gesturing to the Dead, "is a game changer. If their wings become viable, they'll be able to fly over our fences, land in trees, attack from the air. It will make our gates null and void, and no one will be safe. That right there," he said, jabbing a finger, "that's why I'm here. Politics don't matter — not right now. We are the last line of defense against hell on earth. The big move to save ourselves has to be right now."

"The migration," she breathed, fear seeping into her marrow and making it hard to move, "it's a trap."

From the unsurprised expression on Moore's face, she was right.

"Dead's aren't driven here by some inane instinct that sets them up to die easily." Her voice trembled like the torch flames. "The disease is smarter than we gave it credit for being. It's driving them here so this war can happen. Food is getting scarce for them. It has been for the better part of twenty years, and the disease is adjusting. It's drawing out humans. Giving the Deads a chance at sustenance. The chance at finding more hosts. This war wasn't our idea at all. It was the contagion's."

Nervous flutters erupted in her stomach as the old eighteen wheeler roared to life. The rusted clunker was covered with iron bars, caging in the soldiers it transported to the beach. Her team was crammed in there with about thirty other fighters. Faces blurred and blended until only one stood out.

Kaegan had been watching her somberly all morning. Probably because she was pissed.

Moore had offered him a sniper position once he'd blown everyone out of the water on his weapons test. He would've been out of the battle, out of the fray, picking off Deads from a tower, but here he was, shoved in the cannon fodder cage with the rest of them.

He was probably the only one in the entire group who hadn't been vaccinated. Another vision of Kaegan, turned and winged, assaulted the backs of her eyelids, and she gritted her teeth against the urge to make a scene.

"I can't go into this with you mad," he murmured from right beside her.

"Then you shouldn't be here."

"No, you shouldn't be here. You said you wouldn't fight."

"That was when I was yours to protect, Kaegan. You saw those Deads. We can't just wait for the next migration to end this. The virus will evolve in a year, and it'll be too late. Picking them off one by one is no longer an option. Our mission is more important than ever now, and I can't just twiddle my thumbs back at camp while the rest of you charge the battlefield. If you knew me at all, you'd see that."

Wrapping his hand slowly around the back of her neck, he growled, "I do know you. And if I have to sit back and be all right with your decisions to fight, you owe me the same respect. I fight with the team."

Shrugging off his hand, she pressed her face to the bar. He was right, double damn him.

Turning to her team, all gathered around and staring at the passing palm tree scenery, she said, "No matter what, we have to all stay together. Fight as a team like we've done all along. If we get split up, fall back, regroup, and we'll charge again."

"It won't be simple like that," a man said beside her, swaying in rhythm with the bumpy road. His blue eyes were probably handsome once, but now they'd dimmed and housed ghosts. "We said the same thing, my team. Now I'm the only one left."

"I'm sorry for your loss," she said, unable to hold his gaze. His sorrow was too much. How he was still standing, still going to battle, she didn't know.

The man's lip trembled, and his eyes looked like they should be rimmed with tears, but none came, like he didn't make them anymore. "Fight the ones on the edges. If you get too deep in, pull back, but never, ever lose track of where you are."

Clenching her shaking hands against the nerves that threatened to lock her body, she nodded. "Okay. Thanks."

The scent of burning flesh was faint at first, but grew stronger as they meandered on a washed out, sandy road. The truck slowed.

Outside, dozens of people hauled Dead carcasses, pulled them into piles. One was already burning, the flames licking the clouds, and plumes of shadow-colored smoke blotted out the sky.

The back door to the truck screeched open, and one by one, the soldiers trickled down the metal step to the dune covered earth beneath.

The sound of guns cocking, clips being checked, blades sliding from their sheaths overshadowed the faraway sound of Deads groaning and ocean waves cresting the shore. The body haulers didn't even look up as they passed. Maybe it was too hard for them, knowing they wouldn't see all of them return that evening.

Soldiers filed down a trail into jungle, but at a trio of carcasses, she paused. Bile curdled in her throat, threatened to come up as she considered, but she'd do anything to give her team an advantage at survival.

The knife in her hand made a slick sound as she sliced open the arm of a Dead woman who stared vacantly at the sky, face maimed.

"What are you doing?" Kaegan asked.

"The smell will confuse them. It'll hide your human scent." She pulled the dark pungent liquid from the arm and slathered it across his arm.

Lauren gagged when she did the same to her, but Adrianna stood stoically, awaiting her turn.

A couple of the soldiers from the truck stopped to watch, and one even followed suit, spreading the fetid blood across his neck. He nodded once and walked off behind his companion.

At last, Kaegan knelt and brushed his hand across the woman. Standing, he feathered two thumbs across her cheeks.

"I don't smell human," she said.

"No." He ran a light finger down her jawline and offered her the saddest smile. "But you look battle ready this way."

Turning to hide how much he still affected her, she asked, "Ready?"

Whatever she'd expected to see on that beach as they walked out of the coastal grasses and trees, it wasn't this.

Deads surged the sand, covering every inch of it as far as the eye could see. The ocean had been blocked out completely by the stumbling monsters. Crudely built towers leaned against towering palm trees, and the crack of sniper shot was almost constant. Up the beach, humans stormed from forest trails similar to the one where they stood. And the noise—she'd never forget the cries of the damned as long as she lived. It rattled her bones.

Kaegan turned away when she caught him watching. Colten and Lauren stared with horrified expressions. And Adrianna—her fearless friend, who'd been there since the moment of her birth—her lips were pressed into a grim line like her fate had already been decided. Soren pulled both battle swords from their places on her back. Her hair whipped her face, and she flung it back. If they died today, they'd do it together.

Three quick breaths, and she was off, the others trailing her. Her feet sank deeper into the sand with each step. The fighting below was chaotic. Screams and gunfire penetrated the steady hum of hungry Deads, and farther down the beach, large shells blasted, from a tank or maybe a cannon.

There was no training, no preparation. The other fighters fought and fell, scattered amongst the horde like the seashells on the beach. This was no way to fight. It certainly wasn't the way to die. A man cried out as he disappeared under a mass of rotting bodies, and enraged at the pointless loss, she screamed a battle cry as she ran into the first line of defense.

The Deads were loosest here, and Soren plunged her smallest sword into the first. *One.* Pressing forward, she pushed toward a couple of fighters cut off from escape. They brawled, fought for their lives, but they couldn't hold. Not forever.

Kaegan appeared beside her, slashing and maiming, his face closed down, focused. There was no organization, no commanding officers to give orders and rally the troops. The war was a free for all, and the survivors of this would only be alive out of sheer dumb luck.

Grabbing a Dead's throat to slow it down, she kicked another in the chest and ducked beneath the grasp of a Dead more bone than meat. He fell over her, and she thrust up until her sword caught the Dead woman through the jaw. *Two.* Stepping over the bodies, she pressed farther, but Kaegan must've seen what she wanted, because he was already adjusting his position toward the stranded fighters too. Colten and Adrianna fought, spun, sliced, graceful and deadly, while Lauren held her right side.

The Deads were never ending. Kicking the kneecap of one and bringing her blade down upon his skull, she shoved his body against the onslaught. *Three*. Now she could see why the warriors back at camp kept count. It eased the lonely feeling of just being one in a thousand. It motivated her to ratchet her number up as high as she could before she went. At least then, her life would've meant something.

"Soren," Adrianna called as one fell forward against her.

She jerked her head to the side just as one of Adrianna's knifes thunked into the side of its face.

They were almost there. She could hear the exhausted whimpers from the woman as she slashed with heavy looking arms. The look of desperation was written all over her face.

She tossed her small sword up and caught it by the hilt and rammed it into a Dead. *Four*.

"Hey," she called out. "This way!"

The woman jerked her gaze for just a moment, but it was enough. The Dead she'd been holding back lurched forward, mouth open, intent on her exposed throat.

"No!" Soren screamed, bolting for her. Rocketing off the couples' pile of carnage, she brought the hilt of her sword through the Dead's thin bones just before his teeth grazed the woman.

The impact of her body knocked them both over.

Kaegan yelled something from the crowd, but she couldn't understand him. All she heard was the snarls of the undead as they piled atop her. She moved to cover the woman's body with her own, but the weight disappeared from her back, and the pepper of gunfire shattered the humming death chant.

She yanked the woman upright and implored, "Stay with us," before turning to pull a shorter blade. She couldn't afford the big swinging arcs her battle sword would need when the team fought in such a tight grouping. Hell, she could feel Adrianna against her back, moving with her like she was glued.

Endless Deads stumbled toward them, inhibited by the deep sand, but steady on their path of destruction. She spun the hilt of her blade and gripped the familiar handle, just as much a part of her as her own arm.

She wouldn't do it. She wouldn't die today, and neither would her team. Her blood sang with revenge.

Revenge for all the lives taken.

Revenge for making her Other.

Revenge for ending the world.

Five, six, seven, eight, nine, ten, eleven, twelve…

Chapter Twenty-Four

They'd survived, but for how long?

Soren hovered above her sleeping team. After a day of brutal, bloody fighting, not a single word had been uttered on the ride back to camp. Silence had hung between them as they dragged themselves through camp. Lauren and Colten had nodded off before the chili had even begun to simmer over the fire just outside the tent.

Lauren had already taken a nip on the shoulder. Her saving grace was the vaccine she'd taken when she was a child, so still human, she only slept like the dead.

How long could they fight like this? How long could Kaegan without losing his soul to the disease?

She could vaccinate him in his sleep.

He was so exhausted he probably wouldn't even feel the needle. But then he'd notice the pain later. The pockmark that would rot away where the vaccine was injected. He'd know what she'd done.

Still. She glared at her satchel, lying limp in the corner. Guist had included a single vaccine in her go-bag, and he had to have meant it for this. He'd known Kaegan was at risk of turning. She cracked her knuckles. He'd know though, and he'd despise her forever. Would it be worth it?

"Soren," Moore said from the open tent flap.

She jumped like she'd been scalded. Maybe she should've been for her traitorous thoughts.

Standing, she shot one last look at her team and followed him out. The eyelash moon hung high in the sky, surrounded by a dusting of stars that lit up the silent camp in muted hues. The hour was late, and the fighters were sleeping, resting their bodies for another day of death come morning.

"What happened today?" he asked, linking his hands behind his back as he walked.

"We fought, joined up with a couple of other groups, and got lucky."

"Got lucky?"

"Yes. We caught the attention of the snipers. Without them, we wouldn't be having this conversation."

"Lucky." He mulled the word around in his mouth like it was unfamiliar to his vocabulary. "You said you gathered a few groups?"

"Joined up with," she corrected. "And yes."

"I hear that by the end of the day, you led a group fifty strong."

She shrugged. There hadn't exactly been time to do a head count, but that guess was as good as any. "You're unorganized on the battlefield, General Moore. Your troops are scared and disheartened, and there isn't a single person out there leading. You have teams that are thrown out there with no warning of what is coming."

"Where did you train?" he asked.

"Who says I trained?"

"What was your number?"

The question caught her off guard, and she hesitated. That number was supposed to belong only to her. "One hundred fourteen."

"Where did you train?" he asked again.

"The Denver colony, under Laney and Derek Mitchell, Sean and Vanessa Daniels, Finn Geer, and Aaron Guist."

His dark eyes were hard, like an eagle on prey. "Soren Mitchell?"

"The one and only." Her voice sounded sad, even to her.

"I have something for you." He held open the canvas to his tent, and she stepped into his office.

A leg of beef sat atop a large, metal plate. "Kaegan informed me of your dietary needs."

Of course he did. That man hadn't stopped trying to take care of her since she'd met him. Ending their relationship hadn't stifled his protective instincts one bit.

"Thank you."

"Don't thank me yet, because I have a favor to ask." He sat, gripped his hands in front of his mouth. "I want you to head a battalion."

She scoffed. "You want me to lead a bunch of humans into battle against creatures who look like me. You know they won't do it."

"Fifty did today."

"Part of that number was my own team, who've had a chance to figure out who I am. The others were in desperate trouble and needed the safety of numbers. No one was leading that, sir. It was a mess."

"Then tell me who qualifies more than you do. Hmmm? Who? Who has your training? Who has your skill with a weapon and your calm head in battle? Oh, I heard all about you from several witnesses, Ms. Mitchell. Deny it all you want, but you were made for this."

"I'll give you some pointers, assist whoever you choose to lead them, but this isn't me, General. I haven't been accepted by humans my whole life. It's not going to magically happen in my final days."

"Z," he said, standing. "Their lives depend on you."

Wrapping her hands around the leg of beef, she hoisted it away from the table, and then turned at the door. "I'm sorry."

Her? The leader in this war of the damned? That couldn't get any more laughable. He'd lost his mind. Lost it! Too many men lost under him, too many days on the battlefield, something. Whatever his game was, she wasn't going to be any part of it. She was peon cannon fodder, just like the rest.

Who qualifies more than you do, his voice caressed her mind.

Probably lots of people. A damned human to start with. She thought of all the scared and weary fighters she'd fought alongside today. All down for the cause but none of them held a candle to anyone on her team.

Their lives depend on you.

She hovered at the door to her tent, watched her team, the people she loved, sleep. Colten's arm was thrown over Adrianna's hip in a protective embrace. Lauren had pulled her knees to her chest and twitched in her sleep. And Kaegan. Her Kaegan—so long, his calves hung off the blanket and rested in the sand. His arms were crossed over his heart, like doing so would keep it from breaking. She mirrored him and sighed.

No, General Moore had it wrong.

Her life depended on them.

Everywhere Kaegan looked, rotting faces moaned for his flesh. Just a taste that would turn him into one of them. They were so thick, he couldn't see the sky, couldn't see the earth, couldn't see…

Hush now, Soren whispered.

He'd frozen in fear, machete clutched in his sweating palm, useless against his fears. The monsters, dark and foreboding, parted. Soren weaved through them, an angelic smile on her face.

His beautiful Soren.

You're scared, she said, though her lips didn't move. *Of what?*

His chest constricted, choking him with words he was desperate to hide. Words that clawed their way out of him, gutting him in the process.

"I'm scared of losing you," he rasped.

The smile fell from her face and sadness swelled in her eyes like the churning sea. "You can't lose something you never had."

Decaying hands stretched from the sand, ensnaring his feet until he couldn't move. He reached for her, but she fell back, overtaken by the Deads.

They devoured her, and he couldn't move to stop them.

"Aaah!" he yelled, sitting straight up. It was dark, and in his panic, he couldn't see, couldn't move, couldn't remember where he was. Panting, his chest heaved until it hurt, and his hand landed on something warm.

"Paws to yourself, you handsy giant," Adrianna muttered sleepily, and reality slammed back into him like a tidal wave, harsh and suffocating.

It was still too early for dawn to bestow her subtle light, but Mother Moon was helping as best she could. The corner of Adrianna's blanket had draped over him in the night, and he flung it off. He wouldn't get any more sleep tonight.

"Bad dream?" Soren asked from her seat beside the long-extinguished fire. She washed blood from her hands with the lip of her full canteen.

"Yeah." He sat beside her and ran his hands through his hair, preening away the remnants of the unsettled feeling the nightmare left him with.

"About?"

"You," he admitted.

Eyes on the embers, she said, "I have to talk to you about something."

Uh oh. "Shoot." A fitting word because sometimes, her words felt like wounds.

"I'm leading a battalion today. Probably will until…well, until my end."

Her voice stayed as passive as her eyes. A bone, free of its meat, lay on the ground, and he stared at his untied laces. She'd been to see Moore. Okay, maybe her leading wasn't a bad thing. She'd have more protection than he and the team could provide. But then again, what if she felt the need to protect all of the people under her? A battalion — that could be hundreds of soldiers. It could exhaust her, spread her too thin.

Hell, he didn't know what the right move was. But looking at her here in the dark, something clicked. He'd known all along she was special. Gifted. Damn it, she was the gift, to him and to this war. Watching her in battle proved that. She saved human lives. She slaughtered Deads with such grace and skill, sometimes it was hard not to stop and watch her. Anyone with eyes in their head could see she was the weapon that could turn the tide of this failing war.

"I always knew you were destined for more," he said.

"You think I should?"

He swallowed the urge to say no. To ask her, beg her, to walk out of camp with him and leave all notions of this fight behind. If they weren't in it up to their eyeballs already, then those winged Dead gargoyles yesterday drowned them in duty. "Yes," he said before he could chicken out.

She fidgeted with a string that had come loose from the hem of her shirt. "I don't dream." She looked up, eyes daring him to think her strange.

She wasn't though. Everything about her was perfect.

Memories of her face disappearing as Deads clawed and bit into her flesh made him repress a chill that had been hiding in his spine. "You aren't missing anything."

"When I was growing up, I used to ask Ade and Seamus to tell me all the details of their dreams. Eventually I didn't have to ask. They'd just tell me first thing in the morning before school. I wanted one so bad. A good one, I mean, but I don't think good dreams are given to…you know."

"You don't sleep, Soren. You don't dream because you don't sleep enough to. There's nothing wrong with you. Dreams aren't being withheld because you don't deserve them—it's just your makeup." Couldn't she see how amazing she was? She was better than everyone but felt like less. It was a damned tragedy.

"I slept when we were together. More than I ever have. I almost had a soul." She stood abruptly as he tried to keep his heart from breaking into a million pathetic pieces. "I have to talk to General Moore. Tell him I'll lead his troops."

"He should be leading them himself," Kaegan said, pushing off the ground to follow her.

"I think he has. But there's no one to help him organize here. Feeding everyone, placing new recruits, protecting and dispersing supplies. I haven't seen a single guard he seems to trust. He's overwhelmed, just too stubborn to say it."

He plucked a long stem of grass and rolled it between his fingers. "When Colten and I were younger, we'd play war. Mr. McTavish, Colten's dad, told us when he was a boy, they played cowboys and Indians. But we'd play fighters and Deads. We had wooden knives and sticks shaped like guns, and we spent hours imagining how each fight would go down. This…" he said, sneaking a look at her thoughtful expression. "This isn't what I expected it to be like."

"It shouldn't be like this at all. It feels thrown together, like everyone decided at the last moment, *this migration we'll fight*. Maybe it's because we came near the beginning, I don't know. What I do know is that every fighter here will die if they remain separated, without leadership. I don't want to do it, but I don't want to fight every battle like we did today. The disease is winning."

Crickets and frogs and the first morning birds chirped away outside the gates. If he wasn't drawn to her face, he would've missed the precious smile that flitted across her lips for just a moment. "Adrianna and I used to play fighters and Deads too. I was obviously…"

"The Dead," he finished, chuckling. He could just imagine her when she was ten. A beautiful little hellion, he bet.

"When I was seven, I remember I'd started noticing the little girls in the colony carrying around dolls. Adrianna didn't. She carried around a pocket knife, but the other girls had dolls their mothers had found or made for them. So when I talked to my mom about wanting one, she made this little doll that looked like a Dead because she thought it would help me to accept myself. And I didn't want to be rude because, geez, the woman spent three weeks making this ugly little thing."

"What did it look like?"

"Um—" she crinkled her nose "—it was sewn together with obvious black stitches over gray cloth, had scraggly yarn hair, and it had an X for one of the eyes. I named it Pickles. And when we'd go to the playground, she'd always make sure I had the doll so I wouldn't feel left out when the other girls brought theirs. Except it freaked the other kids out." She laughed, a tinkling sound that froze the air in his chest just so he could hear it better. "Adrianna gave a kid named Zane a bloody nose one time because he said Pickles was ugly."

"Of course she did." As much as Adrianna could be a pain in the ass, she was probably the only other person on earth who understood his devotion to Soren. She knew her, really knew her, too. "Whatever happened to Pickles?"

"I saw her in a box in the gun storage at the Denver colony when we were there. My mom is sentimental. She wouldn't ever get rid of something like that."

"I can't remember if my mom was sentimental or not. Sometimes I think I've just made up things about her because I'm afraid of admitting I've forgotten."

"Do you remember what she looked like?"

"I try to think about her face, but it's blurred with time. She had dark hair and a great smile. I dream about her from time to time, but when I wake up, I can't remember her face. It guts me. See?" he said, shrugging off his vulnerability. "Dreams aren't always puppies and kittens."

"Do you think Max is all right?"

"Who's Max?"

"The dog that was following us before we boarded the train."

"I don't know. Hopefully so. He was the one that led us to your trail the day you were taken."

"I like this," she whispered in a rush. "I was afraid we'd never be able to talk again after—" She halted, tilted her chin up until she searched his eyes. A rim of moisture spilled over, and a single tear slipped down her alabaster cheek.

He stilled his hand. If he touched the moisture there, she'd pull away again, and he couldn't take it. "No matter what we are, Soren, I'm still here. I always will be. I've never been on a team like this. Whatever you want to call me, you're family to me." So much more, even. "The battles are going to be hard, and you'll have more pressure on your shoulders. You'll carry a bigger burden than the rest of us, so when you need something, ask. I'll make sure it gets done."

The oath slipped from his lips so easily because he knew, if she ever had cause to ask something of him, it was because she still trusted him. He'd withheld information from her, hurt her with the way she'd found out, and he'd earn back her trust if it was the last thing he did on this earth. Consequences be damned, he'd go to hell and back for her.

Deep oranges and grays stabbed the horizon by the time Soren went to General Moore outside his tent. He beckoned them in and lit a candle, the light illuminating the deep lines of fatigue on his face.

Simply, she said, "I'll lead them."

Relief flitted across his features before he stilled and replaced his stoic mask. "What do you need from me?"

"I want to talk to my troops before we leave the gates this morning. They should have a choice about this."

"Done."

"She needs the snipers there too," Kaegan said. "Hold them back with the rest so we can talk to them before they make their way to the towers."

A quick nod of his head, and an "anything else?" later, and they jogged back to the tent to make breakfast.

"What happened to your arm?" he asked, pointing to the long cut down her bicep.

"Colten nicked me yesterday when I got too close. It was my own fault. I've never fought in close quarter combat before."

He grunted and washed the cut with fresh water while she scrambled the eggs Moore had offered her. At least they were getting something out of her new job title. It wouldn't benefit her, but the team could use the protein, and from the way she hummed under her breath as she stirred the yolks across the bottom of a cast iron skillet, that was more important to her.

He woke the others, and they ate hastily before setting to the task of preparing weapons. Cleaning, rechecking, loading, filling clips, sharpening blades. Day two and the routine already seemed an integral part of the day. Or perhaps they were all a little superstitious. Yesterday they'd survived by the skin of their teeth. Do everything just the same, and maybe they'd make it to dinner tonight.

Soren was quiet, her gaze faraway. The others didn't know what had transpired in the night, but it was her place to tell them she was leading this Dead slaying party. Did she know how important she was? He didn't want to reinforce it and remind her of the pressure. Something stirred within him though, watching this quiet woman serve her team breakfast, knowing what was to come. Something fiercely protective. She'd put on her warrior's face, the one she wore yesterday, but he knew her heart. She was good to her very core.

A bugle sounded near the back ramp gate. Soren shot him a look and kicked dirt over the fire. Lauren, Colten, and Adrianna followed behind, talking quietly, and he walked so close to Soren, he could feel the warmth from her arm. There was nothing in the world he wanted to do more right now than hold her hand, just for a moment. Just to squeeze it and let her know everything would be all right somehow.

She didn't seem to need the comfort though, her face a mask of detachment. She was already with her troops.

Men and woman filed from their tents and doused campfires, joined them in their path toward the row of trucks that would take them to battle. General Moore sat on the step of one of the eighteen wheelers and gave a two fingered wave when he saw Soren.

Minutes ticked by as the troops gathered, some restless to fight, others battle hardened and weary. Faces blurred as the numbers grew. Moore talked to a group of seven men holding long range weapons and gestured for them to stand beside the ground soldiers.

Adrianna and Lauren fist bumped over something she'd whispered into the girl's ear, and Colten looked at the sky with a shit-eating grin. Kaegan didn't even want to know. They stood with the others, Soren with her arms crossed and legs splayed.

"Quiet," Moore yelled.

The noise of conversation died to a murmur, then to silence.

"I know this is an unusual start to the day, and believe me, you will be at the Boneyard slaying Deads shortly. But things are going to be different around here. We've started losing more fighters, more life to those monsters, and we can't keep going the way we are without losing this war completely. You are all here because you know what's at stake. Because you know your sacrifices, the Dead lives you take, will make a difference in the future of the human race. Yesterday was the first day in weeks we brought home good numbers with minimal losses. Many of you saw her fight. Many fought beside her or heard rumors about Z."

"What's going on?" Adrianna hissed.

"I've chosen her to lead you into battle today," Moore called over the growing noise.

The troops erupted. Shouts echoed across the manmade island. Some agreed, most did not.

Moore gestured Soren over, and she walked, chin up, to step onto the truck. Holding the metal railing, she leaned forward.

Kaegan let out an ear-splitting whistle and moved to stand beside her. She was fierce, frightening almost in the way she watched the troops like a predator perched for the kill. Her hair was braided tightly on one side, the rest of her tresses flowing long and free and wild. Feathers and beads adorned her pale locks, and the tank top she'd changed into was dark and tight, exposing nothing but hard edges. Blades covered her, clanked with her movement. Her Uncle Jarren's pistol sat her hip, a charm he'd seen her rest her hand on for comfort often.

"You don't know me," she called in a voice steady and strong. "But if you choose to let me lead you, you will. It won't be easy, and some of the things I'll ask of you might seem strange, but trust me, I'll keep us alive as long as I can."

"Why should we trust you?" a man called from the back. "You look like a Dead!"

Without missing a beat, she called, "Which has given me an advantage. They don't react to me like they want to hurt you. I'm human, with human parents, and the same drive to bring an end to the apocalypse as you. I'm not a Dead. I value human life, just the same as you. You're free to fight on your own. I won't force you to fight under me. You can go back to fighting and dying in twos and threes. But that won't win this war. There's safety in numbers just like between colonies. If we're going to make a difference—if we're going to demolish these numbers, we have to be intelligent about it. Thoughtful and mindful of the fighters next to us because they will keep us alive. Doing it on your own doesn't work here. Not with this many."

A man in the front stepped forward. His eyes flashed as he turned to the crowd. "She's right. I fought with her yesterday. I was surrounded, and she and her team came for me. What she says is true. The ones of you lucky enough to have survived the pandemonium of the last two weeks know. You've lost people, and it's been a numbers problem. I'll fight under her again."

"What do you need from us?" one of the snipers called.

"I need your guns on the action around the main attack. Picking off Deads by the water isn't going to help us. We need aerial support from you guys. Not too close to put us in danger, but we need every weapon we can get for protection. The longer each of us lives, the more of those Dead bastards we take down."

A couple of men clapped in the crowd. "Yes," one called out.

"You're here because you know we're making history."

More cheers.

"You're here because you're honorable. Because you want to keep your families, your children safe from the monsters beating on the colony gates. Fight with me," she said, neck straining with the truth of her words. "And let's take this world back from those undead mother fuckers together!"

The noise was deafening as troops raised weapons over their heads. How could they not believe in her? Kaegan couldn't take his eyes from the honest set to her lips. She didn't fit into the human world, but here she looked deadly, like she'd been forged to lead them. Jumping from the back of the truck, she opened the steel cages and clapped the passing soldiers on the back. Some stared on with empty looks, but more shook her hand, gripped her shoulders, smiled as if relieved they would no longer be alone in the fray.

Her eyes locked on his, and she nodded. A small gesture, not meant for anyone else to see, but it brought warm relief where he'd felt cold after they'd imploded. They were in this together, and whether she wanted to admit it or not, it meant something.

His blood hummed with battle readiness and adrenaline as he climbed into one of the trucks behind her. He gripped her waist and bent until his lips brushed her ear. "You did good."

The truck engines roared to life, fueled by God knew what, and jerked beneath them. Her hair lifted in the cool morning breeze, and he wanted to catch the silken threads.

Her knuckles turned white as she gripped the bar to steady herself. "Tell me that after we make it through today."

Chapter Twenty-Five

"You did good," Kaegan said, jumping the last rung of the tower ladder.

Soren had secretly lived for those words every day for the past two weeks. He was showing signs of superstition, a quality she found quite endearing from a man who didn't seem afraid of anything. Eyes on the marsh grass beneath her feet to hide her blush, she waited for him to shoulder the rifle he'd been sniping with.

Joey Vedder, that dimwit, shot one of her soldiers right beside her. He'd been missing like crazy the last few days. Nerves or vision, she didn't know which one was getting to him, but he had to go. She'd asked Kaegan to give him the boot and take over as soon as the miss had happened. Fatality was a part of the game, but not from the hands of their own team.

Tomorrow, Joey Vedder was going to get a quick lesson on the finer points of being a ground soldier on the front lines.

"How many did we lose today?" he asked.

"Seven." She wished he didn't ask every day. Every life lost was a strike against her soul, and now, after losing so many, her heart was open, weeping blood she couldn't staunch.

"It would've been more without you."

She climbed the dune and stooped to tie the laces of her boot. Deads groaned behind them, but Moore had ordered a fence be erected to keep the Deads away from the body haulers per her request. They could escape down the beach at any time, but at least this way, they were encouraged to stay put at nights when the fighters were asleep in their tents. The migration would come to an end soon, and the monsters would move on. Before that happened, they had to off as many as possible.

"We're making headway, I can tell from the tower," he said as he leaned against a scraggly tree brave enough to grow this close to the shore.

The migration was coming to an end. They hadn't made enough. "Rumor is we're getting a shipment of shields in tomorrow." Might be too late, but maybe not.

"Seriously?"

"Yeah, that's what Moore said. And more beef rations came over on the Crow as a reward for the numbers he gave the higher ups."

Her fingers wouldn't work on the shoestrings, she was so exhausted, and Kaegan folded into the sand. "You need to take a day off," he said, looping the strings tight. "You can't keep going like this."

"It's just from gripping the swords."

"That's not it and you know it. Your muscles are sore, but you don't feel it. You can't take care of your body like the others can. Everyone gets a day off a week, but you haven't taken a single one."

"Neither have you, or the team."

"Because we'll keep going as long as you do." He stood and brushed sand from his knee. "At least think about it."

The Deads would only hang around a few more days at most if the other migrations were anything to go by. Taking a day off wasn't an option so close to the end. Not wanting to miss the last truck, she dragged her numb legs through the deep sand onto the trail. Adrianna lay under a palm tree while Lauren and Colten looked on beside her. They'd aged a hundred years in two weeks. Gaunt and tired looking, every day wore on their hearts. She could see the battles on the Boneyard killing them. They were killing her too.

At the base, a medical tent had been erected in the unloading zone. As soon as the trucks had all crossed over a large, lowered ramp, the Deads that made it across were killed and the gates opened for the weary fighters. The line for the medical tent stretched on and on. Adrianna had a cut that needed stitches, but Soren would do it when they got to their tent so she wouldn't have to wait in the sun.

"Z," soldiers said respectfully as she edged around them to beg some sutures from the busy nurses. She smiled — or she thought it was a smile, it might have been an exhausted grimace — and nodded her head. Some she clapped on the shoulder and asked about friends or loved ones she didn't see beside them. Others wanted to talk about the day's skirmishes, but she was tired and escaped the conversations as soon as was polite.

Med pack in hand, she shuffled back to her tent. She must really look like a Dead now.

The supply area was filling up with gifts from colonies all over. Whatever they'd heard about the Boneyard, they were coming together to lend their support. The Crow had become the main mode of warfare supply transportation, and shipments were made almost daily. Weapons, ammunition, clothes, medical supplies, food. Gone were the days they went hungry after a long day of fighting. And Moore always made sure she was fed on fresh meat when she returned. Had to keep his favorite weapon oiled and ready.

She wanted to go home.

In her weakest moments, she thought of life outside of the Boneyard. Yearned for it even. Some peaceful spot where she didn't have to wash the blood of lives she'd taken from her skin when she came home every day. She could feel herself changing, could see it in her team. Adrianna had stopped joking by the fourth day. Lauren didn't pick up her chalkboard anymore, and even the bright love for life had dimmed in Colten's eyes. Kaegan tried to keep up appearances, but he had nightmares. She'd never tell him in a million years, but every night, his body went so rigid, she was afraid he would stop breathing, so she kept near constant vigil over his body until morning when he was conscious again.

She still couldn't sleep.

Beans simmered over the fire, and Kaegan sat slumped over, watching a lazy fly hover over the food. When she approached, his gray gaze lifted to her, and he attempted to smile. "I'll go get your dinner from Moore. Be right back."

"No. You need rest and food. I'll get it."

"Please." His expression was so raw, like he was too tired to keep up the façade covering the damage battle did to him. The damage she did to him.

It ripped her guts out.

"Okay," she said, then he walked away.

"You're torturing each other, you know." Adrianna sat beside her and offered the injured hand. It looked awful, but at least the bleeding had mostly stopped. "You two could die in any fight, at any time, and you're spending your last days hurting each other. It's not right."

"And it's right what you're doing to Colten?" she snapped. Hissing through her teeth, she said, "Sorry. I know you're just trying to help." Lowering her head, she pulled the thread through Adrianna's gash. "I don't know what I'm doing with him. I'm confused half the time, and the other half, I'm so busy worrying about staying alive and keeping everyone safe, I can't tell my head from my ass."

Ade gestured to the base. "You're doing what you have to here, Soren. A man like Kaegan needs more, and you know it. You'd be a good mom."

"Ade," she warned.

She snatched the needle from her hand and stood. "You would. And any kid you had would be fuckin' awesome, just like his mom."

The tent flap fell as she whooshed inside, leaving Soren with the simmering beans. She was too tired to have a row with Adrianna, too exhausted to even think about putting together all the fractured pieces that used to be her and Kaegan.

A hulking shadow fell over the toes of her boots, and she looked up to thank Kaegan for retrieving her daily ration. Only it wasn't Kaegan but another familiar face.

"Finn?"

"Funny story," he said. "We had messengers telling us about a mysterious zombie-woman leading a war against the Deads. Now, I've never seen any other zombie-people, so your parents and I put our heads together and started thinking, maybe, just maybe, it was our Soren spearheading this little shindig. They say hi, by the way."

Rocketing to her feet, she threw her arms around his thick neck and buried her face in his shoulder. It was so good to be reminded of home she could cry.

"Hush now, girl. You got an audience."

She thought he was talking about her soldiers, but when she looked up, Kaegan stood with a look so intense, his eyes should've sparked.

"You remember Finn," she said.

"Good to see you again," he said dryly and dropped a blood stained sack at her feet, then disappeared into the tent.

"What's going on?" Finn said, eyes on the dirty canvas.

"A war." More than one, apparently.

Cocking an eyebrow like he knew exactly what kind of war she was talking about, he shook his head. "I didn't come alone. I brought troops from Denver with me. They're settling into their tents right now. Also, Sean's been pulling every favor he has in his back pocket, and we've brought his dealings with us."

"Like what?" she asked, afraid to get too excited.

Finn's entire face was taken by a wicked smile. "Like tanks. Two of them, fuel, ammunition for them. We parked them across the moat. And these." He tossed her one of Guist's arm guards he'd created and perfected years ago. Black, nylon, bite-proof lifesavers that her soldiers could strap on their forearms and hold Deads back.

"How many?"

"Two hundred pair. Brought the gun locker too, and that's not all. I saved the best for last." Pulling her to her feet, he dragged her by the hand until they were near the front gate. Trails of people filed across the tiny metal ramp, the line stretching to the woods. Deads attacked but were outnumbered and were dropping like flies. "Your parents, Guist, Sean and Vanessa, they've been traveling far and wide with a call to arms. Every able body."

"Finn," she breathed, tears stinging the backs of her eyes. "This gives us a chance. The migration is almost done. The Deads will go in the night, and we'll be left with just a few to pick off." She inhaled a shaky breath and tipped her face to his. "This gives us a shot at making a big run."

He gripped onto the fence and watched the new recruits file into base. "I knew the migration was coming to an end. We were racing time trying to get here. I was afraid we'd miss it."

"Tomorrow," she murmured. "We'll have to take our shot tomorrow if we want to take the most numbers."

"You been sleeping, zombie-girl?" He frowned down at her.

She hadn't looked in a mirror in weeks, but she could imagine she didn't look like the girl who'd left Denver a few weeks ago. She didn't feel like the same girl either. Maybe she'd never get back the parts of her she used to like, she didn't know. "No. Sleep doesn't find me anymore, Finn."

"Battle scars?"

"Heart scars."

Such sadness swam in his eyes, crinkled with age. "Your parents would be proud of the woman standing in front of me. Rumors of the good you've been doing here have united entire colonies. We knew you were meant for big things, Soren. Stupid us, we just thought you'd find the cure." He dragged his eyes to the Dead bodies piling up as the new recruits downed them. "But maybe you have."

Two tanks ran over the hastily erected fence, destroying it so troops could storm the beach from more drop points. Snipers raced up tower ladders, and ammunition runners darted back and forth with boxes of bullets. Body haulers and burners had been prepped only to retrieve Deads closest to the trails to be safe.

They were about to piss off the freaking beehive.

People would die. Soren looked to her left. Colten whispered something into Adrianna's ear and brought a faint smile to her lips. Lauren watched her, nodded, and squeezed her hand once. To her right, Kaegan and Finn stood like giants of old. Scarred and focused. Ready.

Behind her, more than two thousand brave men and woman walked with weapons at the ready. They weren't here because they were drafted or forced. They were here, offering their lives to make a difference in the apocalypse. She was so damned proud of the humans around her, her heart filled to bursting. Honor like that wasn't found among the Deads. She'd picked a side before arriving in Empalme, but sometime in the last weeks of bloodshed and bonding, it had been cemented in her makeup. She didn't pity the creatures anymore. They weren't the people they were in life. Just husks and hosts for a disease that lay destruction to an entire planet — threats to her friends and family, to her soldiers.

Her speech had been made, brave good-byes spoken on tentative lips just in case. Now her body hummed with the desire to end this.

Today would go down in human history either way. Either they would annihilate the majority of the Dead population in one epic onslaught, or they'd die trying in the biggest human loss of life in two decades.

"Go big or go home, right?" Kaegan asked, looking down at her with a sad smile.

Dread had been her constant companion through the night. The feeling like this was the end wouldn't be stifled, and when she looked at him, she didn't feel the numb exhaustion from battle weariness anymore. She felt afraid. "If something happens today—"

"It won't." His fingers found hers, and the fog of fear evaporated.

His touch was everything, and after this was over, she'd find a way to make it right with him. Their fickle fates would just have to piss off. She'd compromise if it meant keeping him.

"Light 'em up!" she screamed, and the battle cry of two thousand men and women filled the dawn.

She ran alongside them, these humans who'd put their lives in her hands. The men and women who chose to let her lead, let her make plans, let her choose the course of their destinies.

Wind whipped through her hair as she screamed along with them, lifting her battle sword in the air. She'd give everything for them.

She hit the front line with the force of a storm, brought her arm guard up, and bashed a Dead in the skull with the hilt of her blade before scissoring her swords against the face of the next. She found her rhythm, thrusting, spinning, ducking, elbowing, pushing back—always pushing back.

Soldiers fell and died beside her, and she saved who she could. The screams on their lips spurred her on.

Water. She was water, and Deads were helpless against her movement against them. *Traitor.* No, not a traitor. She wasn't one of them. They were incapable of love, and she loved people to oblivion. Adrianna, Colten, Lauren, her family. And Kaegan had pushed her over the edge, filling her with adoration so bright it was blinding. Slashing, smashing, pushing, her clothes were red. The sand turned black and lapped at her boots.

Maybe it had been hours, or perhaps minutes, she didn't know. On they pushed, held the line. Screams and groans mixed together. The sound of waves and the dull thuds of bodies fighting and falling haunted the beach. The second wave of soldiers attacked the fray, fresh and ready, and she paused in a pile of bodies. Panting, she took in the moment. Colten and Adrianna fought side by side, working together. Lauren backhanded a Dead with her arm guard beside Finn, and Kaegan…where was Kaegan?

Frantically she searched the faces in the crowd, but none were her Kaegan. Her horrified gaze dropped to the mass of bodies around her, scanning, terrified.

"Soren," came Kaegan's whisper on the breeze. "I'm here."

She knew before she even turned around that doing so would destroy her. Kaegan sagged to his knees in the spattered sand. Mud and filth caked his body, streaked with the perspiration of his battle efforts. His face was pale, shocked, and fresh red streamed down his shoulder, gathered in his curled palm, and dripped from his middle finger.

The wound wasn't from a blade. The muscle connecting his shoulder and neck had been torn, the edges jagged. She'd seen a hundred Dead bites before.

"Soren," he gasped, swaying.

"No," she said shaking her head in denial. Tears streamed her face, and her throat constricted until nothing came out but whispers softer than the breeze. "No, Kaegan."

He had a few minutes before he would turn. Before he became the thing they fought. It wasn't enough. Her hand fell from the gun at her hip. The one she hadn't ever used. Jarren's pistol that she would finally pull the trigger on to free the man she loved.

She ran and fell to her knees in front of him, and his hand slid up her neck. He caressed her tearstained cheek and looked at her with such ceaseless pride, she broke.

"I can't," she sobbed.

"You won't have to," he said, eyes filling with tears that matched her own.

Of course she would. She couldn't let him walk the earth a Dead. It was cowardly for her to ask someone else to do it. No, the burden was hers.

Gripping her hair, he bent down and pressed his lips to hers. He eased back and rested his forehead against hers. "I've waited a lifetime to do that."

Swallowing a sob, she tilted her chin, kissed him, and dragged him closer. His mouth moved against hers, and he shifted the angle of his head, cradled hers in his hand, and lapped the seam of her mouth until she opened for him.

How had she lived so long without this?

Parting her lips, he brushed his tongue against hers, tasting. Every second that ticked by brought the joy of finally touching him. Every second brought agony with its loss.

"Soren," he whispered against her lips.

"I can't lose you," she said, breaking apart. "I know what I can do, and this is too much. I love you."

Cupping her cheek, he smiled. His dark hair fell forward, and she brushed it out of his face. Every plane of it was precious, consuming... mortal.

"You won't."

She frowned. Maybe he'd forgotten what a Dead bite did. Right now, the virus was surging through his unprotected system, over-whelming his organs.

He lifted the sleeve of his T-shirt to reveal a raw, circular wound. "I took the vaccine this morning. I took the one in your satchel because I couldn't live without you anymore. I compromised. Having a family doesn't mean anything if it isn't with you."

"You took the vaccine?"

He cupped her face in both wide palms. "For you."

"Why didn't you tell me?"

"You would've run from me if I told you. I was scared you'd blame yourself, and you already have so much on your shoulders. I wanted to wait until tonight, after this last fight. You're mine, Soren. You have been since the moment I saw you. It was my decision, one I'll never regret, and one you'll never be able to change with your good intentions. I. Choose. *You.*"

Her shoulders shook with the sobs that wracked her body, and she fell into him, so relieved she could die of it.

Kaegan was alive.

He was still human, and he was hers.

Nothing else mattered.

Epilogue

Soren walked through the woods with Max at her side. He'd found them again after the Battle of the Boneyard. He'd waited in the woods outside La Junta, and had followed them all the way back through the gates of the Denver colony.

Her fingers rested in his coarse fur as they walked a deer trail, and a low growl rumbled in his throat. A Dead pulled against the snare that had wound around its ankle, and she pulled her knife.

She didn't commune with the Deads anymore. Those days had been demolished with her time served in the war. Now her goal was the same as the rest of the human race: snuff out every Dead, and let none escape. Only then would they be rid of the disease.

It had taken two-and-a-half decades, but the humans had fought back and won. Life wouldn't ever be the same as it was before the end of the world. Colonies stood while the cities of old still crumbled. There wasn't a rush to rebuild after the war. What was the point? The colonies served their purpose, and people could finally enjoy safety.

The Dead dropped like a stone, and she wiped the dark blade on her pants, dragged him away, and then reset the snare. A tiny tree jutted from the earth inside the wire loop, its fragile green pine needles stretching toward the light that filtered through the canopy.

Searching the large trunk in front of her, stretching her neck until she looked into the matching needles of a towering spruce, she smiled. Pulling her canteen, she poured water over the infant tree and stood.

When she turned, Kaegan was there, leaning against a giant pine. His smile was sexy, his eyes hungry as she'd never been able to quite catch in her drawings. He was beautiful.

"Dinner is on," he said, stretching his hand out to her.

It had been two years since the Boneyard, and still he took her breath away. Slipping her palm into his, she gave a sharp whistle to Max, who fell into step under the fingertips of her other hand.

"I've been thinking," she said.

His voice was laced with a smile when he said, "Uh oh."

"Maybe someday it wouldn't be so terrible to try for a child."

He was quiet for a long time, and the first of the forest frogs croaked its evening song.

"Why?" he asked, so quiet he didn't disturb the peace of the woods.

"Because you'd make an amazing father, Kaegan. And I used to be so scared that our child would be like me, but she'd be raised in Denver, surrounded by people who love her. And it would be a shame if my mom and dad never got to be grandparents. I see the way they look at Lauren's baby."

"I like watching you hold little Connor," he admitted. "You'd be a great mother, but I don't know if we can. Lauren was lucky to get pregnant after being vaccinated."

"Well, that'll be the fun of it then, won't it? We won't expect it, but if you give me a baby, it'll be special. She'll be one of the first warrior women of the beginning of the world." She grinned and turned, walking backward in front of him. "Plus it'll be fun to practice."

"You keep saying *she*," he said, cocking his head. "How do you know we won't have a son?"

She shrugged and looped her arms around his taut waist. Pressing her head against his chest, she closed her eyes against the precious sound of his beating heart, the only music that meant anything to her.

Smiling, she whispered, "I had a dream."

Acknowledgments

There is a heap of people who deserve a giant thank you — people who believed in this series and in me as an author. This series has been such an emotional journey and one of the coolest experiences of my life. I gave a piece of myself to each of these books, something I don't have the ability to share with anyone outside of these words on a page, and as scary as it was, I met the most incredible people through this little zombie adventure. Thank you to Robin Lonscak, for working tirelessly to polish these books and for bringing these characters to life with me. To Sean Riley for streamlining this story and getting as excited for Soren and her story as I have been. To the awesome line editors and cover artists who worked on this project. I'll be honest, when I received the line-up for the team on these last two books, it looked like a freaking dream team, and every single one of them came through for this finale.

Thank you to Elizabeth Harper, for her vision for Omnific and for giving my zombies the perfect home. She's our fairy godmother — no really, ask any author at Omnific, and they will say the same — and it's been a privilege releasing books with someone so willing to take risks for her authors to give them a shot at something great.

Thank you always to my wonderful husband, Anthony, and my two children, Liv and Will. They have been my rocks through all of this. To my fellow Omnizombie boo, T. A. Brock, for keeping me sane behind the scenes. To my parents, Paul and Paula, who have been a huge support through my career.

I don't even know where these zombies would be right now if it weren't for Traci Olsen, who I am convinced is a wizard or at the very least, magical. When *Love in the Time of the Dead* went under contract, I was wide-eyed, nervous as hell, and had no idea about the adventure I was about to go on with this woman. T, we've had some fun with these zombies, haven't we?

And last but not least...readers, if you're reading this, it means you've gone through all three books of the Dead Rapture series, and been affected by these characters who have made me feel so much.

You have given these characters life inside of your imaginations.

You are the reason I write.

From the bottom of my heart, thank you.

About the Author

Tera Shanley writes in sub-genres that stretch from Paranormal Romance, to Historic Western Romance, to Apocalyptic (zombie) Romance. The common theme? She loves love. A self-proclaimed bookworm, she was raised in small town Texas and could often be found decorating a table at the local library. She currently lives in Dallas with her husband and two young children, and when she isn't busy running around after her family, she's writing a new story or devouring a good book. Any spare time is dedicated to chocolate licking, rifle slinging, zombie slaying, friend hugging, and the great outdoors. For more information about Tera and her work, visit:

www.terashanley.com

New Adult Romance

Three Daves by Nicki Elson

Streamline by Jennifer Lane

The Shades series: *Shades of Atlantis* & *Shades of Avalon* by Carol Oates

The Heart series: *Beside Your Heart, Disclosure of the Heart* & *Forever Your Heart*
by Mary Whitney

Romancing the Bookworm by Kate Evangelista

Flirting with Chaos by Kenya Wright

The Vice, Virtue & Video series: *Revealed, Captured, Desired* & *Devoted*
by Bianca Giovanni

Granton University series: *Loving Lies* by Linda Kage

Paranormal Romance

The Light series: *Seers of Light, Whisper of Light* & *Circle of Light* by Jennifer DeLucy

The Hanaford Park series: *Eve of Samhain* & *Pleasures Untold* by Lisa Sanchez

Immortal Awakening by KC Randall

The Seraphim series: *Crushed Seraphim* & *Bittersweet Seraphim* by Debra Anastasia

The Guardian's Wild Child by Feather Stone

Grave Refrain by Sarah M. Glover

The Divinity series: *Divinity* & *Entity* by Patricia Leever

The Blood Vine series: *Blood Vine, Blood Entangled* & *Blood Reunited*
by Amber Belldene

Divine Temptation by Nicki Elson

The Dead Rapture series: *Love in the Time of the Dead, Love at the End of Days* &
Love Starts with Z by Tera Shanley

The Hidden Races series: *Incandescent* (book 1) by M.V. Freeman

Something Wicked by Carol Oates

Romantic Suspense

Whirlwind by Robin DeJarnett

The CONduct series: *With Good Behavior, Bad Behavior* & *On Best Behavior*
by Jennifer Lane

Indivisible by Jessica McQuinn

Between the Lies by Alison Oburia

Blind Man's Bargain by Tracy Winegar

Erotic Romance

The Keyhole series: *Becoming sage* (book 1) by Kasi Alexander

The Keyhole series: *Saving sunni* (book 2) by Kasi & Reggie Alexander

The Winemaker's Dinner: *Appetizers* & *Entrée* by Dr. Ivan Rusilko & Everly Drummond

The Winemaker's Dinner: *Dessert* by Dr. Ivan Rusilko

Client N° 5 by Joy Fulcher

The Enclave series: *Closer and Closer* (book 1) by Jenna Barton

Historical Romance

Cat O' Nine Tails by Patricia Leever
Burning Embers by Hannah Fielding
Seven for a Secret by Rumer Haven

Anthologies

A Valentine Anthology including short stories by
Alice Clayton ("With a Double Oven"),
Jennifer DeLucy ("Magnus of Pfelt, Conquering Viking Lord"),
Nicki Elson ("I Don't Do Valentine's Day"),
Jessica McQuinn ("Better Than One Dead Rose and a Monkey Card"),
Victoria Michaels ("Home to Jackson"), and
Alison Oburia ("The Bridge")

Taking Liberties including an introduction by Tiffany Reisz and short stories by
Mina Vaughn ("John Hancock-Blocked"),
Linda Cunningham ("A Boston Marriage"),
Joy Fulcher ("Tea for Two"),
KC Holly ("The British Are Coming!"),
Kimberly Jensen & Scott Stark ("E. Pluribus Threesome"), and
Vivian Rider ("M'Lady's Secret Service")

Sets

The Heart Series Box Set (*Beside Your Heart, Disclosure of the Heart* &
Forever Your Heart) by Mary Whitney
The CONduct Series Box Set (*With Good Behavior, Bad Behavior* &
On Best Behavior) by Jennifer Lane
The Light Series Box Set (*Seers of Light, Whisper of Light, Circle of Light* &
Glimpse of Light) by Jennifer DeLucy
The Blood Vine Series Box Set (*Blood Vine, Blood Entangled, Blood Reunited* &
Blood Eternal) by Amber Belldene

Singles, Novellas & Special Editions

It's Only Kinky the First Time (A Keyhole series single) by Kasi Alexander
Learning the Ropes (A Keyhole series single) by Kasi & Reggie Alexander
The Winemaker's Dinner: RSVP by Dr. Ivan Rusilko
The Winemaker's Dinner: No Reservations by Everly Drummond
Big Guns by Jessica McQuinn
Concessions by Robin DeJarnett
Starstruck by Lisa Sanchez
New Flame by BJ Thornton

Shackled by Debra Anastasia
Swim Recruit by Jennifer Lane
Sway by Nicki Elson
Full Speed Ahead by Susan Kaye Quinn
The Second Sunrise by Hannah Downing
The Summer Prince by Carol Oates
Whatever it Takes by Sarah M. Glover
Clarity (A *Divinity* prequel single) by Patricia Leever
A Christmas Wish (A *Cocktails & Dreams* single) by Autumn Markus
Late Night with Andres by Debra Anastasia
Poughkeepsie (enhanced iPad app collector's edition) by Debra Anastasia
Poughkeepsie (audio book edition) by Debra Anastasia
Blood Eternal (A Blood Vine series single, epilogue to series) by Amber Belldene
Carnaval de Amor (*The Winemaker's Dinner*, Spanish edition)
by Dr. Ivan Rusilko & Everly Drummond

coming soon from
OMNIFIC PUBLISHING

Missing Pieces by Meredith Tate
The Way to Go series: *Way to Go* (book 1) by Mandy Colton
Command the Tides by Wren Handman
The Hidden Races series: *Illumination* (book 2) by M.V. Freeman
The Record of My Heart by Georgina Guthrie
The Counterfeit by Tracy Winegar
The Embrace series: *Entwined* (book 3) by Cherie Colyer